Kelpies Don't Fly

Book 5 of the Valkyrie Bestiary Series

by Kim McDougall

About This Book

Critter wrangler rule #15: Always look a gift horse in the mouth. And if it has sharp teeth, never, never get on its back.

For ten years, Kyra Greene thought she was the only Valkyrie this side of the rainbow bridge. Until she gets a stunning message from her cousin, Gunora, asking for bail money.

Facing the ghosts of her past isn't on Kyra's to-do list. All she wants is to settle into her new home with Mason and her menagerie of furred, feathered and scaled rescues. But the many gods of Terra have other plans.

Gunora's plea for help sets a new Inbetween adventure in motion. Kyra and her crew will find themselves on the wrong side of the law and going to war with a herd of murderous kelpies. But this time, Kyra might finally set past wrongs to right.

Kelpies Don't Fly is book 5 of the Valkyrie Bestiary Series.

BOOKS BY KIM MCDOUGALL

The Hidden Coven Series:
Inborn Magic
Soothed by Magic
Trigger Magic
Bellwether Magic
Gone Magic

Valkyrie Bestiary Series
Dragons Don't Eat Meat
Dervishes Don't Dance
Hell Hounds Don't Heel
Grimalkins Don't Purr
Kelpies Don't Fly
The Last Door to Underhill (Novella)
The Girl Who Cried Banshee (Novella)
Three Half Goats Gruff (Novelette)

Writing as Eliza Crowe

The Shifted Dreams Series:
Pick Your Monster
Lost Rogues

For Griffin.

July 3, 2081, Montreal Ward

Gita stood in the middle of our empty living room with tears streaking down her leathery cheeks. Her plants and plant stands were gone. The cages and terrariums, all emptied and cleaned, were sitting in the back of my truck, ready for the transfer to the newly renovated barn on Mason's property. Most of my critter family were already there, waiting in travel carriers until I could move them into their new digs.

My apartment echoed with emptiness. And memories. The tile floor was slightly puckered from water damage around the spot where Hunter's aquarium had been. The little kraken could never keep his suckers inside the tank. The bracket for the curtain rod (now bereft of curtains) was bent downward from years of supporting my perching gray cat, Willow, as she surveyed her unruly roommates.

The 1950's era kitchen table and chairs looked even more wretched in the emptiness as if they had lost the support of our usual mayhem and disarray to validate their shabbiness.

Gita sniffled. Her watery eyes held all the uncertainty that was curdling in my gut.

"Maybe this isn't such a good idea." My voice echoed hollowly in the empty room.

Gita wiped her eyes with one ragged sleeve and stood taller.

"Nonsense. We can't stay here and you know it. Not enough room. There never was."

"I know." If we stayed, I'd have to find homes for some of my critters. And who would I give up? Princess? My faithful hell hound who'd crossed through worlds to have my back? Sweet Pea and Niblet who'd found me when a witch kidnapped me? Or Kur, my ice-sprite who liked to snuggle his cold butt against my leg in the mornings? Moving in with Mason meant I could keep them all. And more than that, it meant I would wake up every morning beside the man I loved, and at the end of a hard day, I'd have him to come home to.

"You love him, don't you?" Gita asked with that uncanny way she had of reading my thoughts.

I nodded.

"Then you're doing the right thing." She patted my hand. Her skin was papery and brittle, as if a stiff wind could reduce her to a pile of bones. But simmering under that skin, I keened a force of nature—the banshee who could bring down an apartment complex with the potency of her wail.

I had some really cool friends.

One of those now stepped through the door from the office. Emil would be taking over my apartment. He was an opji vampire who'd helped me out a few times in the field and in the office. My apartment was convenient for him since he'd be managing the day-to-day affairs of Valkyrie Pest Control. And convenient for me. Leaving the apartment empty would be an open invitation for burglary, vandalism and squatters. And considering the weapons I kept stored in the old garage, having a live-in office manager was ideal.

Emil's trim form and boyish good looks masked a strong will. He didn't take crap from anyone, but his good humor also made him a customer favorite, especially with the ladies.

He wore his bronze-colored hair in a curly mess that partly covered enormous brown eyes—eyes that were currently glossy, like a blush had just washed over his face and was already gone. The corner of his mouth twitched too, vacillating between a grin and a frown. That could mean only one thing.

Yep.

Gabe strode through the door behind him.

"Hi Kyra."

I crashed into him even as he raised his hand in a wave. My nose didn't reach his shoulder, but I hugged him tight, squishing my face into his black and silver collarless shirt that could have come straight off a runway model. He patted me awkwardly on the back, not used to this sudden rush of affection. I took pity on him and stood back to study his face.

"You've lost weight," I accused. I hadn't seen him in weeks. The adorable dimples on his cheeks had turned into deep creases. Dark circles under his eyes marred his usual golden glow.

"It's good to see you too." He grinned.

"It *is* good." I squeezed his arm again and let my hands drop. "I was sorry to hear about your brother."

Gabe stuck his hands deep into the pockets of his jeans and nodded. His older brother, the one being groomed to take over the family business, had been in a coma after a car accident in May. He'd finally succumbed to his injuries.

"I called when I heard." I thumped his elbow with my fist. "You didn't answer." In fact, I'd left a dozen messages and would have stormed his apartment if Emil hadn't warned me away.

"He just needs time to sort things out with his family," he'd said. So I'd given Gabe time, though his continued silence chafed like nettles.

Gabe looked down at his big hands now clasped in front of him. "It wasn't personal. I didn't want to talk to anyone."

"The only reason I could drag him out of the house today was because I told him you desperately needed help with the move."

"Which I see was a lie." Gabe glanced around the empty room.

"Maybe." Emil didn't look contrite. "But I do need to pick out living room furniture. A man of your style-sense could really help with that." He picked an invisible piece of lint off Gabe's shirt, not looking him in the eye. Gabe stepped back and Emil grinned to hide his disappointment.

"I'm glad you're here anyway," I said. "You can come help us unload at Mason's. I'm sure Jacoby and Hunter would love to see you."

"So it's true, then." Gabe smiled, his first sign of real happiness since he arrived. "You really went to another world to find that little brat?"

"I did."

"And she didn't even bring back souvenirs," Emil said.

"We weren't exactly sight-seeing."

"Still, an alien rock or shell would have looked great on the mantle."

"You don't have a mantle," I pointed out. "And it doesn't work that way." Traveling to the Nether hadn't been like hopping on a train. We'd crossed over the veil that separated this realm from the others. While my body had been anchored by my father's life-tree in an oak grove in Pennsylvania, my spirit— or my ki, as I'd come to understand it—had done the traveling. We hadn't been able to bring back any material objects. But that didn't mean we hadn't brought back our share of psychological and emotional keepsakes, some of which we still didn't fully understand.

That thought made me check my widget. It was nearly noon. Mason should be home by now.

I glanced around the space that had been my home for over ten years, waiting for…what? A sense of foreboding to hit me? Premature homesickness?

Gita took my hand and gently pulled me toward the door.

"Home is where your family is," she said. "Let's go find them."

The drive to Mason's house—now my house—was silent. It had rained all morning, but the sun was finally peeking through the clouds. The road steamed as puddles evaporated in the summer heat. We headed over the Gallop Bridge. To our left, the St. Lawrence River was lit up like a jeweled carpet, while Lake of Two Mountains glistened on our right.

In the middle of the bridge, we slowed to a stop at the ward gate. My fingers gripped the steering wheel hard. The ward's magic hummed over my skin like a swarm of gnats. I glanced at Gita.

"You're taking this move surprisingly well," I said.

She sat rigidly in the passenger seat with tears tracing the path of least resistance down her craggy face. She didn't like cars or sunshine. Or bridges, rivers and traffic. Or a hundred other things she might encounter outside of her closet nest. But she was here with me because I'd asked.

She sniffed. "I've lived in more places than there are dreams in a young girl's heart. Change is the only constant. You would do well to embrace it."

Huh. The hermit banshee was giving me a lesson in change? I thought I was a go-with-the-flow kind of girl.

"Arriz has set up a nice nest for you in the barn's old tack room," I said. "It's bigger than you're used to."

"It'll do fine." She sniffed again and closed her eyes.

The traffic began to move and the lane split in two. I took the right side reserved for those with official Hub passes. As we approached the guard at the gate, my teeth buzzed from the immense power of the ward hanging overhead.

I couldn't imagine how those guards worked here everyday without it affecting them.

I flashed my Hub ID with an official transit pass stamped on it, and the guard waved me through. I'd applied for the pass only last week. It let me come and go through the ward with greater ease. Now that I would be living off the island but working from the office in Sayntanne, I would need it.

Emil and Gabe, following in Gabe's little silver-bullet, got stuck in the general line and would be several minutes behind us.

When we arrived at Mason's, the goblin kids were playing soccer in the grassy lot beside the barn. Princess added a new level to the game as she tried to get the ball away from both teams. Jacoby was riding piggy-back on one of the bigger kids, and they were all whooping and hollering.

Gita stared out the windshield at the hoopla in the yard. Despite her brave words about change, she clutched the seat belt across her chest like a lifeline and refused to get out of the truck.

Now it was my turn to pat her hand. "Take your time. I'll see if your room is ready."

She nodded and a drip of snot bobbed at the end of her nose.

Before I even stepped from the truck, Princess bounded over to plaster my face with wet hound kisses. I gave her a few scratches behind the ear before gently pushing her off.

"Kyra-lady! Come plays!" Behind Princess, Jacoby bounced like a toddler needing the potty.

"Not until I get the truck unloaded." I shooed them away and went to find Arriz, Mason's goblin estate manager. He was standing between the barn and a thick cedar hedge. An arched gateway let us peek through the bushes into the old graveyard with headstones from the original estate's family. Tall maples kept it shaded even on a bright day like today.

Arriz was watching the gate like he expected someone—or something— to step through. He'd been finishing the new roof on the barn with his son, Dekar. The younger goblin still held a hammer, but his stance made it seem more like a weapon than a tool.

"Something wrong?" I asked.

"Maybe. Maybe not." Arriz took off his cap and rubbed his balding head. "Keep feeling eyes on my back. Seems that we have a hidebehind lurking in the woods."

"A hidebehind? Are you sure? I've never seen one."

"Few people have. Like finding a stick bug in a pile of kindling." He wiped his face and pulled his cap back over the tufts of graying hair. "I'll leave out some milk for it tonight and hopefully it'll soon be on its way. You need help unpacking?"

"Sure. If it's not too much trouble."

By the time I opened the rear hatch, the entire goblin family was waiting to help me unload.

Arriz seemed elderly, but it was hard to tell with goblins. His gray-brown skin had a weathered look and what was left of his dark hair was flecked with white. Dark eyes were sunken into his face and made his long, hooked nose seem even more prominent. He could be called thin, but whenever I saw him, I thought "tough" like well-worn rawhide. He'd lost his wife to the Inbetween, leaving him alone to raise his brood of goblits. Mason and I found them trying to gain a permit to enter the city. Mason offered Arriz a job as estate manager, and here they were.

The kids ranged in age from rambunctious to nearly adult. Dekar was the oldest and helped his father with jobs around the property. He was a taller, brawnier version of his father with curling black hair that made a nest for his long goblin ears. Suzt, the only girl, spent her time caring for her siblings. Next in line was Muzzy, who looked just old enough to want to hang around with his father and older brother, then Tak, Gibus and finally the twins, Tums and Tad, who never sat still for long.

"If you show me what's breakable, I'll keep those boxes away from the little ones." Dekar said.

"Sure," I said. "If everyone grabs a cage or a crate, we'll be unpacked in no time."

Dekar jumped into the truck bed and started handing out boxes to his siblings along with orders to be careful. He had that no-nonsense way of an oldest child who'd grown up too fast with too many responsibilities. Once the others were loaded up, he jumped down, holding the largest crate. He followed his siblings inside, shouting, "Don't just dump everything in the doorway!"

Princess, not to be left out, dashed back and forth between the barn and the truck, while Arriz and I unloaded more boxes.

"You've got great kids," I said. "You must be proud of them."

"Yes. Mostly. The young ones get restless." The sharp ridge of his brow and heavy, slanting eyebrows gave him a stern look, even when he smiled.

"I was wondering if the older two, Muzzy and Tak would like jobs. I'd pay them. And it would only be part time, so they could continue with their studies."

The goblits had returned for another load and overheard us.

Arriz rubbed his chin under the pointed beard.

"Maybe. What would you have them do?"

"Just feed the critters and clean cages. With me working on the island, I'll need the help and I don't like to leave it all up to Gita."

Tak's face lit up. "Oh, can we Papa?"

Arriz nodded solemnly. "As long as it don't interfere with your studies." Suzt was teaching them their numbers and letters and she was a strict tutor.

"No sir! I promise!"

Jacoby squeezed himself into the group and declared proudly, "I has a job. I 'prentice to Kyra-lady!"

"I want a job too!" Gibus whined.

"Us too!" Tums shouted for both twins.

Thank you, Jacoby.

Tak smirked. "You're too little to have jobs."

Gibus, who didn't look much younger than his brother, frowned.

Muzzy squeezed his shoulder. "You can be my assistant. How's that?" The younger goblin grinned shyly. The twins pouted only for a moment. Then Gabe's sleek new car pulled up and the goblits were soon caught up in the wonder of mechanics that seems to infect young boys of all species.

I left Gabe and Emil with their flock of new admirers to look for Gita and found her still sitting in the passenger seat of my truck, hands pressed on the console in front of her as she stared at the barn that would be her new home.

I rapped on the window. "You okay in there?"

Gita didn't startle. I think it's physically impossible to surprise a banshee. But she did turn her head to look at me with wide black eyes.

The passenger door opened and one bony leg reached for the ground, followed by another. Gita stood blinking in the morning light. She made a faint attempt to smile that only added creases to her already crinkled eyes.

"Is my room ready?" She took a halting step forward, and stopped when Arriz came around the side of the truck.

"Gita, this is Arriz." I waved my hand toward the goblin. His expression had gone oddly blank, except for wide eyes that were fixed on the banshee. Was that astonishment or fear? Then he bowed deeply as if addressing the queen at a fae court.

"Milady, please let me show you to your room. I hope we can make you as comfortable as you need." He took her elbow in a delicate grip. Gita batted her eyelashes and patted his hand as he led her away. When they were halfway to the barn door, he leaned in and whispered in Gita's ear. The banshee giggled.

"That's not something you see every day," Gabe said.

"It's really not." I shook my head. Who would have thought the old bird still had a bit of the flirt in her?

For the first time that day, my worry about moving eased. I knew this was the best thing for my family. We'd have more room and more freedom, but I couldn't help feeling a little selfish about it too. It was no secret that I wanted to be closer to Mason. Part of me worried that this desire would blind me to other problems. But seeing Arriz take to Gita like that made me realize that I wasn't the only one ready for a change.

The goblits had finished unloading my truck and coaxed Emil into another game of soccer, using an old tangle of rags for the ball. Despite being the smallest, Tums and Tad ran circles around the others. Princess thought they were playing just for her benefit and ran off with the rag ball in her mouth, but she dropped it at the opening in the hedge that led to the old graveyard. Her stance went rigid. The hair on her back bristled, and she lowered her head, letting out a long, warning growl.

"Something's in the hedge." Gabe was already moving to his car where he stored enough weapons to arm a small country, but I stopped him.

"It's okay. Arriz says there's a hidebehind lurking about."

"A what?"

"Hidebehind. They're mostly harmless."

Gabe paused with his hand on the trunk of his car. "Good to know. Did that hell beast of yours get the memo?"

"Princess! Leave it!" I called. The hound let out one woof in protest, then turned back to the game.

Tums had the ball and danced around Emil with some fancy footwork, until Emil roared and lunged at him. He grabbed the goblit and flipped him upside down to dangle him by the ankles. Tums squealed in delight. Jacoby and Tad tackled Emil and the game dissolved into a melee, with goblits shrieking (in fun, I hoped) and Princess barking at the whole pile of bodies, not sure which one to bite.

Gabe watched the mock battle with a sad smile.

"Look, I have to get back." He shook his head. "Tell Emil I said goodbye."

"Nuh-uh. You're not getting away with that." I grabbed his hand as if my hundred-and-thirty pounds could force his two-hundred-plus pounds to stay. He looked at his hand clasped in mine and raised an eyebrow.

"I'm not trying to get away with anything."

"Yes you are. Emil's been worried sick about you. Me too. Now you want to sneak away again without even saying goodbye?"

"I don't know what to say." His lips thinned to a rigid line. He ran a hand through his glossy hair, leaving it mussed.

"How about the truth. If you love him, tell him. If you don't, tell him that too. He deserves to know."

"It's complicated."

"Love is always complicated. That's just an excuse."

"Is it?" He turned on me, his eyes flashing. "Is it really? How's this for an excuse then? My parents are pushing me to marry my sister-in-law, when the dust hasn't even settled on my brother's grave."

"They what? Why?"

Gabe sighed, but it was a tight surge of air, that didn't seem to relieve any tension.

"Her clan and mine have always been rivals for the top seat in the Saivites. Her marriage to my brother settled the conflict for a time. But now that he's gone…"

The Saivites were the Hindu godlings in Montreal. After the Olympians, they were the loudest voice lobbying for a new political party in the ward. Gabe's father was the leader of the Saivites and had been trying to lure Gabe back into politics for years.

"Now that he's gone, what?"

"She's threatening to move back in with her father. And she wants to take Sai with her."

Oh, gods. Sai might be the Devi clan heir, but he was also Gabe's son. When his brother, Aadeshi, hadn't been able to produce, his wife had slipped into sixteen-year-old Gabe's bed. Sai was the result.

"Can she do that?"

His expression darkened. "She can try." Then a little smile softened his mouth. "He's a really good kid, you know? Smart and funny. And kind. I don't know where he gets that from. There's very little kindness in our house."

"And that's why you're going to leave Emil hanging?"

"Yes."

We watched Emil stumble to his feet with two goblits on his back. He roared like an ogre and spread his arms so the little ones ended up hanging off his shoulders amid squeals of laughter.

A shutter fell over Gabe's eyes. "Things will get messy before they get better. I don't want him involved."

"You still shouldn't leave without saying goodbye."

He nodded again, a curt gesture that showed off the rigid line of his shoulders. Gabe was as tense as a nocked arrow.

Then he turned, kissed my cheek and said, "I'm glad you're home."

I nodded, not trusting my voice.

He stepped onto the field of play and scooped up the soccer ball with the toe of one foot. He made a fancy move, tossing the ball high in the air, head-butted it toward the makeshift goal and scored. The goblits ran after the ball and Gabe pulled Emil away.

Their heads were bowed, foreheads nearly touching as Gabe spoke low and fast. I watched the color drain from Emil's already pale face. He sucked in his cheeks and pursed his lips but only nodded. Gabe hugged him. Emil's arms hung at his sides. Then Gabe turned and stalked off to his car. In moments, the only sign of his presence was the dust hanging in the air from his spinning tires.

Emil stood in the middle of the yard, goblits racing around him in play. He looked lost. But before I could go to him, Princess froze in that pointing stance that told me she'd seen something again. Then she dashed toward the hedge with tail wagging, and a figure stepped through the arched gate. Princess dropped to her belly and whined.

It was Mason.

He stopped when he saw all the activity in the yard. A three-day beard made him look scruffy and dangerous. His shirt was wrinkled and wet blotches stained his knees as if he'd been kneeling in the mud. His eyes hid in deep shadows made worse by the dark rings around them. There were leaves in his hair.

He hadn't been sleeping or if he did sleep, it was on the forest floor. He thought I didn't know, but I woke every night to find him gone from our bed. It was well past noon, and he was just coming home from whatever it was he did in the forest for hours on end.

Princess snapped up the ball and thrust it at Mason. He smiled, but it did little to lighten his expression. Princess nudged him again. He grabbed the ball and tossed it back into the yard. The hound dashed after it with her tongue lolling. The soccer match resumed and the happy squeals of children filled the awkward silence.

Mason limped toward the house.

I stepped into his path. "You okay?"

"Fine." He brushed off my concern without even looking at me, then stalked to the door, opened it with a jerk and slammed it behind him. Worry gnawed through my gut like the very hungry caterpillar my mother used to read about.

Emil came over. I could see the worry in his eyes. I didn't want to talk about it. Instead, I handed him my keys. "Take the truck home. I'll get a lift into work in the morning."

Emil took the keys. But he wasn't going to let it go. "What's wrong with him?" He nodded toward the house.

"It's nothing. Mason's adjusting to…" I didn't know how to explain any of it—that we had nearly been lost in an alternate dimension while trying to recover Jacoby. Or that Mason had been blessed by a demon in the Nether and was waiting for his demonic attributes to manifest. Or maybe they already had. Maybe that's why he kept slipping away to be alone. He was already affected and didn't want me to know.

"He's fine." I clamped my jaw down hard.

"He doesn't seem fine. You either."

"We will be. Things are a little edgy around here right now, but it'll be better once we're all settled into a routine."

I headed into my new home, hoping that I'd spoken the truth.

Is That a Hidebehind Behind That Tree?

July 7, 2081

This is one for the entomology and cryptozoology enthusiasts. Has anyone come into contact with a hidebehind? We might have one lurking near the house. Our property manager seems concerned.

I've never actually seen a hidebehind before. I'm not even sure what they look like. They are notoriously shy. But I've heard tales. A hub official I worked with said his cat was attacked by one last year. Should I be worried? We have children in the area, not to mention my menagerie of critters. Should I keep them inside? Is there a way to encourage the hidebehind to move on? Any advice would be appreciated.

Comments (8)

I have had extensive contact with hidebehinds in my fourth incarnation. I was a Sumerian high-priestess at the time. Enlil, the many blessed, saw fit to send us many *sukkals*, servant deities to aid us in our work of honoring the gods. He sent these in the form of hidebehinds. Most were quite docile and made excellent servants.
metempsychosist14289 (July 7, 2081)

> So I shouldn't worry about them attacking my critters?
> *Valkyrie367 (July 7, 2081)*

>> Only during mating season. They can get aggressive and a bit mindless when the rut is upon them.
>> *metempsychosist14289 (July 7, 2081)*

>>> Thank you. Is it presumptuous to ask—what incarnation are you on now?
>>> *Valkyrie367 (July 7, 2081)*

> Not presumptuous at all! I love to talk about my past
> lives. This body is my 14,289th incarnation.
> *metempsychosist14289 (July 7, 2081)*

Best way to solve any fae creature problem is with a 12-gauge slug. Right between the eyes.
BigGameHunter (July 9, 2081)

> Yes, you're very manly and your gun is longer than anyone else's.
> *NotBuyingYourSh*t (July 9, 2081)*

> > You got that right!
> > *BigGameHunter (July 9, 2081)*

Early the following morning, Mason tried to sneak in the front door without waking anyone. It didn't work. I'd been awake for hours, sitting at the table in the little breakfast nook, wondering where he was—again—and watching the sun slowly reanimate the world. I knew it was Mason because two days ago Nori had moved to her new apartment in the city, and Dutch hadn't come home the night before.

And only someone with a guilty conscience would try so hard to be quiet.

The door opened and closed with deliberate care, then I heard a bit of shuffling and something drop—a shoe?—with a loud thud. Mason swore in a whisper.

"You can stop sneaking around," I called out. "I'm awake."

A moment later, he appeared in the kitchen. He looked like he hadn't slept a wink. Normally he tamed the curls that spoiled his otherwise proper hair. But this morning the curls had taken over, a sure sign that he'd spent the night running his hands obsessively through his hair. His clothes were rumpled, and something dark and wet stained his t-shirt. I smelled alcohol.

He still had that whole dark hair, dark eyes and a build that seemed cleaved from stone going for him, but his real allure normally came from the deep calmness that usually emanated from him. It was confidence rather than arrogance. Serenity in the face of adversity. When the magic got real, when weapons were drawn and teeth bared, there was no one I'd rather have at my back.

I'd thought that confidence was unflappable, but I was wrong. First our battle with Polina had stripped him of his gargoyleness and his immortality. Next, during our trip to the Nether he'd nearly died trying to be my champion. Then, to top off the festivities, Mason had been blessed by a demon masquerading as a god. We still weren't sure what kind of party favors that little celebration would bring.

I watched him pour the last half-cup of cold coffee into his mug. He sipped it and watched me watching him. The silence between us seemed like a solid mass, like a lump in my throat I couldn't swallow past, but I forced myself to ask, "Where were you?"

I left out the accusatory "all night." We weren't some old married couple, and he wasn't out cheating on me. Of that I was certain. But I was worried. Really worried. Every night this week, I'd woken up to find him gone.

"Out walking."

"At night?"

He shrugged. "Old habits."

There was more to it than that. I could feel it. But before I could articulate the worry burning a hole in my stomach lining, he slammed the mug on the counter, closed his eyes and clenched his fists at his sides, like he was counting to ten and asking the gods for patience.

I rose and went to him. It was instinctual. He was hurting. His pain pinged off my keening like ice pellets. My hand went to his arm, seeking comfort even as I tried to give it.

"Tell me what's wrong."

I let out the tendrils of my keening and tasted his magic. It was acrid like burned sugar.

"Don't do that!" He flung off my hand. I reeled in my keening like I'd been stung.

"Sorry. I'm worried about you," I mumbled. He usually couldn't sense my magic probes.

"Stop!" Color rose up his cheeks. His eyes flashed with manic fire.

"Stop what?"

"Just stop!"

What could I say to that? My stomach churned with that combination of fear, worry and guilt that always came with confrontation.

His lip curled, then he turned on his heel and stalked off.

I stood by the edge of the breakfast nook with my offending hand still raised and watched the tense muscles of his shoulders as he walked away.

Grim had been sleeping on his favorite table by the window. He opened one eye at the disturbance, but didn't comment.

A moment later I flinched when our bedroom door slammed.

I could do nothing about Mason until he decided to confide in me. I just had to have faith that he eventually would.

We'd met while battling a rock troll only two years ago. Then we'd spent a full year pretending the attraction between us didn't exist and another several months finding the courage to act on it. Our relationship was still new. It didn't have the deep roots of a decades-old romance. But we'd been through a lot together. We'd faced death side-by-side more than once. We'd both watched the other get hurt, and swore to never let that happen again. We'd traveled through the Inbetween and even across dimensions. So while our relationship might be young, it wasn't untested.

That's what gave me the courage to wait for him.

While I was waiting, I puttered around the house, tidying and exploring. The decor was elegant and manly. Too manly. A round fire pit dominated the living room with couches and chairs, all in dark leather, arranged around it. Willow, my very ordinary gray cat, slept curled up on a folded throw blanket on the couch.

At the far end of the room, heavy cherry wood bookshelves lined the wall, and these were filled with real paper books, many of them leather-bound first editions. Behind that wall ran the short hallway that led to our bedroom, guest bedroom and the stairs to the upper level where Dutch slept. A desk and office chair took up the space in front of the bookcase, and a vid-screen could be pulled down to cover the shelves when needed. Mason and Dutch often used the desk for business, but right now, Jacoby lay across it like a discarded dish rag. One scrawny arm was flung over his face and the other hung off the desk. He was snoring.

The only other distinguishing feature in the living room was the wall of glass that looked out over an immense stone patio. A long narrow table sat in front of this window. It held statuettes of several different styles. Some were soapstone carvings that looked Inuit in design. There was also an African mask, a Tibetan singing bowl and other wood, stone and metal knickknacks, all mementos of Mason's long life and many travels.

Grim—our decidedly *not* normal cat—had decided this was the best spot in the house to take in the sun. He was as big as a Maine Coon, steel gray with black points on his ears and tail, and he seemed to flow around the pieces of art like liquid fur. I ruffled his thick mane and his tail thumped in warning.

Yes, the decor might reflect Mason, but at least I'd put my stamp on it with my critters, and little by little, it was starting to feel like home.

After lunch, I put on my work shorts (these were distinguishable from my regular shorts because they had more stains) and went down to the barn.

Arriz and his boys had finished setting up my new critter central. The old horse stalls had been pulled down to make room for more cages and terrariums. Hunter and my abaia eel, Buddy, had a new aquarium, twice the size of their old one. There was even a fridge humming in the corner for fresh fruit and bait fish for Hunter. And I still had room for more cages. That meant I could bring home more critters. Looking at my new setup, I wanted to rub my hands with glee. I felt like a kid who'd been given a free pass at the toy store.

Muzzy and Tak were busy with the morning feeding. They were bright kids and had taken to their new job with enthusiasm. I had outlined their chores that morning, and they'd made a feeding schedule that they tacked to the barn wall. Gibus, the middle child, and the one who often felt left out, tagged along behind them as they swept the floors and made sure the hay and feed bins were restocked.

With all these chores taken care of, I suddenly found myself with spare time. It was an odd feeling. I'd been running for months with no time off. What could I possibly do with a whole day to myself?

I found a pair of garden gloves and some tools and spent the rest of the afternoon tilling a small space between the barn and the goblin cottage. We needed a vegetable garden.

Dekar stopped on his way to the goblin cottage to see what I was up to.

"I can turn the soil and prepare the bed for seeding," he said.

"That's okay." I smiled. "I like to play in the dirt."

He shrugged and left me to it.

I really did like the manual labor. It put my mind into a kind of stasis where I didn't have to worry about Mason or Gabe or anything else. As I hoed a particularly nasty snarl of crabgrass, I plotted out the different plants I could get going this late in the season. Of course, Gita would have the final say on the selection, but I hoped to add a few of my favorites—basil for salads, chamomile for tea, and pansies, just because I liked their tiny faces. I turned another clod of soil, happy to find it squirming with fat earthworms.

Errol arrived with Niblet. Since getting around the barn and property was taxing when your legs were only an inch long, Errol had harnessed one of the two lizard-mouse creatures I'd nicknamed the squamice. Niblet and Sweet Pea turned out to be pretty easy going about having things strapped to their backs. Gabe found that out when he attached cameras to them for scouting small spaces. Errol took that trait to a new level and had turned the squamice into his personal taxi service. He hopped off Niblet next to the garden and the squamus began digging in the soft ground.

"Gjgth?" Errol asked. *Practicing your magic?*

"No. Sometimes gardening is just gardening."

"Hthgbt!" Even if his words hadn't popped into my head, his tone was clear. I was wasting a good opportunity. Errol had been teaching me to commune with the magic of green growing things and the natural force that simmered just below the surface of Terra's crust.

"Fine." I centered myself, feeling the connection through my feet. Now, instead of dreaming of pansies, I explored that energy with every swipe of my hoe. I sent my keening deep into the earth and followed the channels of power, feeling them branch off into thousands of roots—trees, flowers, fungi. They were all one. And I was part of it.

The light began to fade and so did my strength. I leaned on my hoe and wiped sweat from my brow.

"Bhthgth." *Enough.* Errol nodded with satisfaction. He nudged the now sleeping Niblet with his walking twig and climbed onto his squamus taxi. I watched them leave feeling a double satisfaction. I'd not only finished tilling the garden, but I'd given my green magic a good workout.

I stretched the kinks from my lower back.

Arriz came out of his cottage carrying a bowl and a glass.

"Need a break?" He held up the glass.

"Thank you." I put the hoe aside, climbed the few steps to the porch and accepted the glass of cold water. I drank it down in one breath.

"I needed that."

Arriz grunted and frowned. I'd come to learn that was his sincerest form of appreciation. He bent to place the bowl on the ground next to the porch. It was full of milk.

"Everything all right in there?" He nodded toward the barn. "The boys aren't causing trouble, are they?"

"No, they've been very helpful. I want to thank you again for all your hard work getting things set up."

He shrugged. "Mr. Mason pays me to do a job, I do it."

"Yes, but your attention to detail is appreciated." Arriz had gone above and beyond by completely renovating the old barn. It had a new roof, windows, and staircase. He'd filled all the cracks in the ancient mortar so the wind wouldn't whistle through it this winter. My critters had a solid home, space to roam and a family to care for them. I couldn't ask for more.

Arriz quirked an eyebrow. It was his only concession to my praise.

I pointed to the milk-filled bowl on the ground.

"You feeding strays?"

"The hidebehind," he said. "It's best to keep on his good side. Can be fearsome creatures. And they take offense easily. Milk shows that we respect him."

"This hidebehind, what does it look like?"

"Like a stick bug, only bigger. Much bigger."

"Exactly how big?"

Arriz held his hand above his head to indicate a creature that would be at least six feet tall. I was about to question that description when a black car pulled up in the driveway and parked beside the gatehouse that doubled as barracks for any Guardians in residence. Berto, the duck-billed gargoyle who often acted as Mason's captain, came out of the gatehouse to confront the new arrival.

Oscar Lewis stepped from the car. Berto nodded as soon as he recognized him and retreated back inside.

"Kyra!" Oscar waved. As far as I knew, Oscar was purely human, but he looked like a gnome had slipped into his gene pool at some point. He was short and stout, with tufts of wispy white hair around his ears. He was also the interim Alchemist Prime Minister and our friend with the really cool gadgets.

I waved back and started down the hill to the driveway.

Oscar took one look at my dirt-stained shorts, sweaty shirt and messed up braids, and frowned.

"You forgot about dinner, didn't you?" He was dressed in a neat suit but had left off a tie.

"Of course not. I just lost track of time." Yes, I'd completely forgotten that Mason had invited him for dinner. They were supposed to go over plans for the next few weeks when Mason would be making his bid for Prime Minister official. But Dutch, who never forgot an appointment, would certainly have prepared something.

"Come and have a drink while I clean up."

Oscar mumbled something about the damned heat and followed me inside.

I was right about Dutch, and the smell of coq au vin welcomed us. It filtered out the patio doors that were open to let in the last of the day's light and a small breeze. Inside, Grim slept by the cold fireplace, but other than him, the living room was empty.

"So where's Mason?" Oscar demanded. "He's been avoiding me for a week, but he promised we'd hammer out our schedule of appearances. We need to announce his candidacy in less than two weeks."

"I'll just check the kitchen," I said. "Pour yourself a drink, and I'll be right back."

The All-father only knew where Mason was. I hadn't seen him since he'd stormed off that morning.

I found Dutch preparing a salad in the kitchen.

"Have you seen Mason?" I asked.

"He's around. I told him dinner would be at seven."

Around. Great. That could mean his office, the bedroom, or he'd run off into the woods again. I went through the kitchen door and across the patio to the French doors that led to our bedroom—a shortcut that let me avoid the living room and Oscar's impatient glare.

Mason wasn't in the bedroom.

Damn. He'd better remember that Oscar was coming or I'd have a long awkward night making excuses.

I undressed and splashed cold water on my face and chest, then found a clean pair of jeans and a blouse that was only slightly wrinkled. I really needed a shower but didn't want to keep our guest waiting. I brushed out my hair and re-braided it before heading back to the living room where I found Oscar pouring a glass of whisky.

"I'll take one of those," I said. It felt like a whisky night.

"He's not here, is he?" Oscar's bushy brows lowered over his eyes.

"He is. Somewhere. It's just that since returning from the Nether, he's been a little…preoccupied."

Oscar made a low noise in his throat, a sort of "hmmmm," that was very gnomish in origin.

"You two having some trouble?" He handed me a glass.

"No. Maybe." I sighed. "Something's going on, but he won't talk to me." My fingers gripped the glass hard enough to hurt.

Oscar put a hand on my shoulder. "You okay?"

I rubbed my tired eyes.

"No." I couldn't say more. Not without releasing the dam of emotions I'd been holding in. I wasn't fine. In all truth, I was pissed. And hurt. And just damned-well fed up.

Mason had been secretive and aloof. And now he'd blown off dinner when he knew how important this was to Oscar. At least I wasn't the only one being disappointed these days.

Before I could say anything more, the front door opened and Mason strode in. He looked like crap with dirty pants and messy hair. His eyes were haunted.

"Oscar." He said by way of greeting.

"You seem surprised to see me. We had a dinner date or did you forget?" When Oscar frowned, he went at it whole hog. His bushy eyebrows lowered to nearly eclipse his eyes. A deep line creased his forehead and his chin scrunched up to meet his pursed lips.

"No, of course not." Mason ran a hand over his face. "Let me get changed." He headed down the hall toward our bedroom. His footsteps were quiet and measured like he was still walking through the forest, trying not to leave a mark of his passage.

Oscar and I sat on the couch and pretended everything was fine. He made polite conversation while we waited.

"That is a most beautiful creature." He pointed with his glass at Grim, who was asleep by the fireplace. The grimalkin opened one eye to inspect Oscar. Then he rose and sauntered over and jumped, landing lightly on the couch. He put two paws on Oscar's thigh and proceeded to make biscuits. He tipped his silver nose in the air and watched Oscar through hooded eyes. His happy toes left pinprick holes in the fabric of Oscar's pants, and he was purring like the rumble of an earthquake.

Oscar's eyes widened and he raised a hand. "Should I pet him?"

"I wouldn't."

He lowered his hand and Grim curled up beside him, tucking his tail under his nose and leaning on Oscar's leg.

"Is he a new rescue?"

"Yes, he sort of followed us home from our last adventure."

"From another world, you mean. You do live an exciting life." His sharp gaze roamed over Grim again, then he turned it on me. "Maybe you could dial down the excitement just a bit? Hmm? At least until Mason is elected."

I smiled sweetly and made a crossing motion over my heart. "I promise, I am excitement-free for the foreseeable future."

Critter wrangler rule number fourteen: never make promises you can't keep. That one's just a good life lesson in general.

Mason returned, clean and freshly dressed. He poured himself a large glass of whisky before joining us in the seating area. He didn't sit beside me, but perched on the arm of the sofa.

Oscar rose, politely ignoring the dirty look tossed at him by Grim and fetched his briefcase by the door.

"We've got less than two weeks before the gala, and over twenty events to fit in before then." Oscar pulled a large-screen widget from his briefcase and started flipping through a calendar. Mason watched over his shoulder with a frown. He looked worn out. And if I wasn't so annoyed, I would have felt sorry for him. But when Oscar started outlining the many media appearances he'd set up for Mason's official entry on the political stage, I lost some of my annoyance and really did pity him.

Mason wasn't one to enjoy the spotlight, and his frown deepened with every new interview or event that Oscar laid out. I wanted to reach out and squeeze his arm or at least keen his magic to get a sense of his mental state.

But Mason had made it clear that neither of those options were welcome.

I rose to check on dinner.

"Don't go too far, missy." Oscar stabbed a finger at the calendar on his widget. "You'll be expected to make some appearances too."

I gave him a feeble smile. "Of course. Looking forward to it." *Not.*

I helped Dutch set the table. He was taking the evening off, so he showed me what he'd prepared for dinner, then squeezed my arm and said, "It'll be okay."

I didn't know whether he meant dinner or life in general, so I thanked him with a wan smile.

All through the meal, Oscar chatted on about the upcoming elections and Mason's competition in the race for Prime Minister of the Alchemists. Mason spoke little and ate less. Finally, Oscar took the hint and turned his attention to me.

"I don't expect you to be at every event," he said. "But I need you most evenings. It wouldn't do for Mason to show up to the ballet alone. We want him to appear stable."

"And I make him stable?"

"Family makes him stable. You're his family. You'll be there?"

I nodded. I'd have to tell Emil to reduce my schedule for the next few weeks.

"And you'll need a new wardrobe." He eyed my blouse like it might grow fangs and attack him.

"Okay." I fiddled with the napkin on my lap. I hated shopping.

"And you need to tell me right now if there are things in your past that might become an issue during the campaign.

I let out a small laugh. "You're kidding right?"

"I'm not." His gaze was fierce.

I'd known this was coming, even encouraged Mason to enter the race, but it was just starting to hit home. This election was going to shine a light into places I'd rather keep in the shadows. What would the media make of our involvement in Polina's attempted coup, for instance. And Leighna's death? Those in the know, such as Hub directors and upper level ministers knew that we'd been on the winning end of that battle. But when Merrow stepped in as interim Prime Minister of the Fae, she'd successfully kept most of the story out of the news.

And then there was the whole sordid tale of my flight from Asgard after I burned down the only bridge between our two worlds. But since I was the only Aesir left on Terra, I guessed that secret was safe.

"You already know all our 'issues'," I said. "If the whole debacle with Polina becomes a problem…well, then it's your problem."

I crossed my arms over my chest. I wasn't going to take the blame for that mess, even if me finding the baby dragon had started the whole thing.

I glanced at Mason. He was slumped in his chair, staring into his whisky glass.

Oscar made that gnomish sound in his throat again. He laid his wrinkled hand over mine. It was warm and solid and the touch brought a tightness to my chest. I hadn't realized how much I needed comforting.

Mason suddenly pushed away from the table, stalked through the living room and out the glass door to the patio. He disturbed Grim on his way. The grimalkin stretched and rose. He looked at me pointedly before following Mason outside.

Good. Maybe Grim would be able to discover where he was going.

Oscar watched Mason's abrupt departure with a frown puckering his lips.

I crossed my fork and knife on my plate. I hadn't done justice to Dutch's amazing meal, but the food seemed to stick in my throat.

Oscar turned his accusing glare on me. "What in the hell is going on?"

"He's just a little tired. That last trip took a lot out of him."

"He'd better get his game face on before the gala. We can't postpone his announcement."

"I'm sure he'll be fine."

I ushered Oscar out the door, ignoring his grumbled protests.

I really wasn't sure about Mason's state of mind, but I also wasn't his keeper. He'd keep his promise to Oscar or he wouldn't. I could do nothing to sway the outcome.

4

With Dutch gone, I washed the dishes from our dinner with Oscar. Some chores are odious, like vacuuming or putting away laundry, but I always found washing dishes cathartic. Something about it soothed my frazzled nerves—the warm water and suds caressing my hands, and the gentle chimes of clean, dry dishes as I stacked them in the cabinet.

The window above the kitchen sink looked out over the small side patio and walled garden. The house and barn were built into the hill. A fieldstone retaining wall held the land back to create this little cozy garden right outside the kitchen. Someone had planted herbs in boxes and flowering plants in pots around the patio. A small fountain burbled in the center of the flagstones. It was a pleasant place to read in the afternoons, but usually it was empty.

Tonight, there was activity in the garden. The fountain was a stone basin with a griffin sitting in the middle of it. His wings were spread in an arc over his head. Water was drawn up through the griffin and cascaded from his wings in a gentle splash. A little red blob frolicked in the fountain. Hunter gripped the statue with his tentacles and climbed up it to bat at the water coursing down.

Gita sat in a garden chair using her widget to illuminate the paperback she was reading. My heart warmed at the sight. I'd pulled my family out of their home, but they were already making a new one.

It was a rare-enough sight to see the banshee outside that I boiled a pot of water for tea and took two mugs out to join her.

Hunter flicked water at me as I passed him with the tea tray.

"Yes, I brought something for you too." I put down the tray and tossed him a shortbread cookie. He caught it with one tentacle and sank into the fountain to devour his treat.

"Part of me will miss finding him in my kitchen cabinets," I said.

"And your laundry and shower." Gita snorted.

"And don't forget the coffee machine."

I poured tea and we drank in silence for a moment. The night was full of music—the murmur of the fountain, crickets in the grass, and somewhere, I thought I heard a soft, sweet violin. Could that be one of the goblins? I listened harder, but it seemed to be coming from the other direction. Maybe one of the Guardians in the gatehouse.

The music faded and I slumped back in my chair.

"I can't help feeling like this is the calm before a storm."

Gita watched me with pursed lips. "Remember the first time we met? You came to me with that boy. What was his name?"

"Liam."

"Yessss, Liam. The curls on that boy could make even an old crone's juices flow."

"Gita!"

She cackled. "Metaphorical juices, dear. But I knew you weren't destined to be together. Liam was a ball of sunlight and you," she poked a finger at me, "you wore darkness like a cloak against the rain. It was all around you." She swirled her hands about my head like she was fluffing my hair. "But now?" A smile creased her wrinkled cheek. "Now the darkness is gone. Don't let it back in." She jabbed my thigh with her bony finger to make her point.

"And how do I do that?"

"Stupid girl! With love, of course. Don't let this one get away."

"I might not have a choice in that."

"Of course you do. You always have a choice. You chose to come out here and talk to me instead of finding Mason and talking to him."

I swished the last of the tea in my cup. She was right, of course. But what if I did go after Mason? He blew hot and cold these days, and I never knew which Mason I'd get.

"Oh, excuse me, I thought you were alone."

I turned to find Arriz standing in the light by the kitchen door. He held a small bouquet of wildflowers in one hand. He thrust them at Gita and turned to go.

"No, you stay. I was just leaving. It's way past my bedtime, anyway." I rose from my chair and collected the tea tray.

The goblin and banshee ignored me. They had eyes only for each other. I sighed and let myself back into the kitchen. At least one man remembered how to do romance right.

I FELL ASLEEP listening to that sweetly sad violin music, and woke when another sound invaded my dreams. It was a long, low howl. As sleep evaporated like mist, I lay in the dark, listening. The wolf's call rippled over me again. A pack mate answered from a distance. Something hooted near the house, and another raucous call like a cat readying for a fight drowned that out.

The Inbetween was a hopping place tonight.

I opened my eyes and rolled, dropping my arm onto Mason's side of the bed.

It was empty.

The night was hot and my hair clung to my neck. In my sleep, I had clutched the sheet under my chin and now my shirt was damp with sweat.

I stretched for my widget on the nightstand and tapped it to light the screen. It was after midnight.

The creatures outside settled down, but that made me realize I'd been listening to another whine.

My sword.

Since it had tasted demon blood when I'd fought Dodona, it had been more vocal than usual. Cranky and whiny. I'd put it in a time-out in my closet, but it wanted attention now.

I got out of bed, threw open the closet door, and pushed aside a box of my unpacked knickknacks. Not that I had a lot of knickknacks, but it didn't feel right to inflict my velociraptor bobble-head and plush vampire-Elvis doll on Mason's many works of art.

Behind the box, I found my sword. It vibrated in my hands.

"Okay. Settle down."

I unsheathed the blade and drew it across the top of my forearm, just deep enough to draw a thin line of blood. The sword instantly calmed. I swiped up the drops of blood with one finger and smeared them down the dull metal. I could almost hear it sigh. That would sate it for a while but I would need to perform Leighna's calming spell soon.

Now I was wide awake. No point in trying to sleep again, especially with Mason gone.

The hallway leading from the bedroom was dark, but the wall of windows in the living room let in a faint light from the sickle moon.

Grim sat on the table by the window, neatly perched between a bronze griffin statue and a primitive sandstone sculpture of two entwined bodies. His tail swished over several smaller pieces of sandstone. He turned his luminescent eyes on me and slow-blinked before returning to his vigil, staring out the window at the dark forest about a hundred paces beyond the stone patio.

"Something out there?" I asked.

"Yes." His voice rumbled, low and deep.

The day after we returned from the Nether, Grim had shown up with a little white cat in tow. Since then, he'd come and gone as he pleased, sometimes bringing his girlfriends home, sometimes not. Tonight he was alone, which was the only reason he responded to my question. Except with Mason or Jacoby, he refused to speak when others were around.

"Is it Mason?" I asked.

The tail twitched. "Yes, but someone else too." His paw batted at one of the small figurines. It fell to the carpet with a dull thud.

"Someone bad?"

"Maybe." He pushed another figurine off the table. Thud.

"Stop that!" I rescued a third figurine as his paw reached for it. Grim jumped down and swished past me, tickling my bare legs with his tail. He sat by the French doors and waited with that cat expression that said, "Let me out."

I opened the doors as another howl echoed from somewhere in the forest. Grim seemed unperturbed by it and strutted into the darkness. Of all my creature house guests, I worried about Grim the least. There wasn't much in the forest that would take on a jaguar of the night sun.

I hugged my arms over my stomach and stared into the darkness. The open window let in a breeze, but it was warm and sticky like the rest of the air.

Mason's car was parked beside the garage. He was somewhere on the property.

Again the howl, this time closer to the house. Then it faded to that mournful music I'd heard earlier. Who was our resident violinist?

The sound tugged at my keening, not exactly magic, but compelling. I took a step outside. My foot hit the cool patio stones and I stopped.

I should go back to bed. I should leave the night creatures to their business, Mason included.

Even as that thought flitted through my head, I was heading back to the bedroom, but not to bed. I put on shorts and shoes and grabbed my sword. Then I followed the music into the night.

The goblin cottage was quiet as I slipped past it. My feet skidded on dewy grass, and I slid down the slope toward the hedge that bordered the cemetery. Grim waited for me by the lower end of the barn. Without a word, he turned and trotted through the arch in the hedge.

"This way," he said.

The grip of my blade tingled in my fingers as if the sword knew we were on an adventure. The music had faded and the howling wolf-creature had moved off, hunting farther into the Inbetween. Other inhabitants of the forest breathed easier. An owl hooted. Crickets chirped. I wasn't too concerned with the calls of the woodland creatures. Most would leave me alone.

I was more concerned with finding Mason. Every day this week, I'd woken to find him gone. Tonight I wasn't even sure he'd come to bed at all.

I ducked through the arch in the hedge. Moonlight polished the alabaster headstones. Leaves hung like wet rags from still branches. I crept through the cemetery, feeling exposed in the large open space.

A year ago, dragons had disturbed most of the bodies in the yard. Since then Mason and the Guardians had reburied them and straightened the headstones. I stepped over the spot where Ollie had dug up the bloodstone and started me on a path that would put me right in the middle of a fae civil war.

I still missed that little blundering, blue dragon.

At the other end of the yard, I hopped over the low, fieldstone wall. Now I was in the forest proper. I held my unsheathed sword before me as if it could light my way, but my blood had quieted the blade and it remained dark and still.

My eyes adjusted to the lower light under the trees. Even though I could see the faint path between trunks, I had no idea where to look for Mason. What was I even doing out here in the middle of the night? He could be anywhere.

"Stop dawdling," Grim said. "It's this way." He slipped into the shadows. I followed him onto a narrow path, not much more than a deer trail, and we headed deeper into the woods. I let my keening taste the magic of the night. So many tiny lives all around me, busy with the importance of staying alive. But no big-bads were nearby. I crept onward.

Grim didn't look back to see if I followed. I could just barely make out the fluff of his pantaloons in the dark. Twice, he disappeared altogether, and I stumbled along blindly until I spied the swish of his tail again.

And then I didn't need his guidance. The familiar scent-taste-feel-sound of Mason's magic washed over me.

Grim stopped on the trail and sat, tucking his tail around his toes. He stuck his nose in the air, pointing it into the trees.

"There."

A flickering glow came from ahead. I crept forward. Grim stayed where he was.

"Aren't you coming?" I asked.

"This is your problem now." He twitched his whiskers, then turned and melted back into the shadows.

Fine. It was probably better this way. Whatever Mason was into, we didn't need an audience. I crept through the trees toward the light. Finally, I made it to the edge of a small clearing and hid behind the trunk of a fat maple tree.

In the middle of the clearing, Mason sat brooding in an easy chair with his feet propped on a coffee table. Beside him stretched an empty and dilapidated couch in front of the stone remains of a hearth and chimney. A fire burned in the hearth.

It was a bulla.

After the Flood Wars, magic rampaged over the land, swallowing entire towns and taking back cities with lush greenery. Once in a while, for reasons that only a god could understand, Terra spat out bits of the old world—usually entire buildings or even towns. They emerged nearly unscathed like time capsules from the twentieth century. Scavengers called them bullas—from the Latin word for blister—and stripped them of every resource including copper wiring, diesel fuel, glass, and metal.

I'd never heard of just one room being regurgitated, but…more things in heaven and earth and all that.

I hid behind the tree and felt a little ashamed for it. Why should I hide from Mason? Except that he was clearly hiding from me, and I needed to find out why.

His eyes were shadowed. A deep frown creased his cheeks. An open beer bottle was propped between his knees, but he didn't drink from it. He leaned forward, placing elbows on knees and head in hands. The way it stuck up, I could tell he'd been pulling on his hair all night. He tossed the beer bottle into the hearth. It settled against others with a clang and sent sparks zig-zagging into the sky. From the shadows beside his chair, Mason pulled out another bottle, cracked it open and took a long sip.

I turned away from the surreal scene and pressed my back against the maple's trunk.

Okay, even I knew this was weird. We had beer back at the house. And chairs. And even a fireplace. Why did Mason feel the need to sneak off into the Inbetween to drink?

Something was wrong—the insomnia, the erratic moods, the impatient scowls. Something had changed in him since we left the Nether, and I had a sinking feeling I knew what it was.

When Mason had championed me in a trial set by a bunch of wannabe gods and led by Dodona, a self-declared oracle, the pain and fear that he'd faced would have been enough to drive anyone into a drooling, mewling madness.

But he endured.

For me.

In the end, he won the oracle's blessing, but she turned out to be a demon. So blessing was a relative term.

Was that what was bothering him? Was he experiencing his blessing of the demon, some monstrous new trait that he felt the need to hide? Was he fighting a new dark power like Kester's ability to call shadows as a weapon. But then, why wouldn't he confide in me?

Because it was bad. Really, really bad.

Mason would protect me, if he could. But if he'd discovered his aspect of the demon, we would all need protecting—the goblins, my critters, the Guardians. All of Montreal.

Demons were nasty and unpredictable. Death and darkness fueled their magic. They consumed the life-force of lesser beings, in a relentless pursuit to fill the emptiness that grew inside them.

Or so the stories said.

During the Flood Wars, in a time when humans had already done a darn good job of massacring their world, the demons swooped in to off the survivors. Only with the help of the fae were the humans able to send the last demon back through the veil to whatever hellish dimension he came from.

Again, so the stories said.

Apparently, not all the demons left Terra. I'd met one other—Kester Owens. He didn't conform to what I thought I knew about demons in general. He seemed to have mastered his need to consume human or fae magic. He survived and thrived in Manhattan Ward. So maybe Mason could too. But he wouldn't be able to do it alone.

Suddenly, I was exhausted. The sleepless nights and anxious days had finally caught up with me. I needed to sit. I leaned against a tree and slid down the trunk. My hip snagged a branch and it cracked.

"Shhhh!" A harsh whisper came out of the darkness.

I froze.

A creature stepped from the shadows of another big maple, only ten paces from my hiding spot. It held a long bony finger to its lips. In the dim light, I only got an impression of a tall lean figure with stick-like limbs and a long tail. The hidebehind?

"Who's there?" Mason called out. The creature's thin legs jerked and he scuttled into the forest. I caught sight of long wings glistening down his back before the darkness swallowed him.

"Kyra, I know you're out there. Go away!"

I rose, brushed dirt and twigs off my pants, and stepped into the clearing.

"Don't come any closer." Mason was standing now. A beer bottle dangled from one hand. He'd put the chair between us like a shield.

"Why not?" I stepped forward.

"I mean it!" He backed up a pace.

"Mason, I don't know what's going on with you, but I know you won't hurt me."

"You don't know!" He threw the bottle and it sprayed beer over the underbrush. "There's so much noise!" He clutched his head in both hands and doubled over.

I rushed forward. My only thought was concern for him.

He shouted. "Stop!"

I skidded to a stop and held out my hands like he was a wild animal in need of taming.

"Stop what? Mason talk to me!"

"Stop thinking so loud! I can hear it! All of it! You love me. I get it. But you're also afraid of me. Everyone is. I feel their eyeballs on me like their stares are acid, burning away my skin, just like…just like…*she* did."

He was panting now. His words had come out in a jumble and I took a moment to understand them. When I did, my heart hurt for him.

But I also felt a glimmer of hope.

I reached down and plucked a weed from the ground. It was clover. Good. I could work with that. I pushed a bit of magic into it, just like Errol had taught me. The clover sprouted and bloomed in my hand. It was a test.

Mason screamed and passed out.

C H A P T E R

5

lugged Mason onto the chair. He was out cold. I sat on the couch, trying not to imagine the things that might be nesting in the cushions. My blade was quiet and I leaned it against the sofa within easy reach. I opened a beer and sipped it until Mason moaned and rolled his head.

He saw me and recoiled in his chair. Not exactly the reaction a gal wants to see in her guy. But after a moment, he relaxed.

"You're quiet," he said.

I nodded. "I can be quiet."

I'd wrapped my magic in a tight coil and tucked it away, a trick I'd developed so I could sneak up on the more magically sensitive creatures.

Mason ran his hand through his hair again. "You've been a bit…noisy lately. Everyone has. That damned demon did something to me, and now I can hear the worms crawling through the earth."

I leaned forward and squeezed his knee. He flinched like I'd scalded him. My magic shifted. It circled him in a protective halo while I kept the vast force of my power locked away so I didn't overwhelm him. His eyes widened and the fist gripping the arm of the chair relaxed. I'd extended my personal ward to protect him.

"How did you do that? It's gone! Everything is so…still." He pushed out of the chair, but I held him back.

"Don't go anywhere. I can only ward you if you stay close."

"Ward me?"

"Yes. Dodona didn't affect you." I took a deep breath and spit it out. "I did."

"You what?"

When Mason had stood up against the Stewards and offered himself as my champion, I'd given him part of my ki—my very essence. He would fight for me, no matter what, and I wanted to do the same. Inside Dodona's labyrinth, I couldn't help him, but with my ki, he could feel me beside him.

Jacoby, not to be left out, had offered part of his ki too, and we'd seen the effect of that when Dodona tried to burn Mason alive. The essence of fire dervish protected him.

Now it seemed obvious that my ki had given him the keening.

"I had my first seizure when I was fourteen," I said. "It was like a sluice gate opened, and I was suddenly flooded with the sound of every heartbeat in my class, every thought, every desire. All at once. Thankfully, we had a fae janitor at school, and he recognized the signs of the keening. That night my mother gave me my sword." I patted the pommel of my blade. "She told me about my Valkyrie heritage, and I began my training. It's not easy, but you'll master it. And one day, you'll recognize the keening as a strength, not this debilitating weakness."

"The keening." He huffed out a breath and sat beside me.

I nodded. "You didn't get your aspect of the demon. You got your aspect of…well, me."

He stared at me for a long minute. I tried not to fidget. I couldn't read minds, but the keening was sensitive to emotions. Under that glare, I could feel that his were in turmoil—fear mixed with relief, resentment with gratitude and just a hint of awe.

Finally, his hand snaked out and covered mine. It was warm and solid. "Sometimes I wake in the night, and I can still feel it," he said. "Like I'm still lying on that field in front of the labyrinth, naked and burned…"

I shuddered. The memory of him so vulnerable—red and raw like a baby bird—hadn't left me either.

"I guess what happens in the Nether doesn't stay in the Nether," I said.

"I guess not. You were really just a kid when this happened to you? How did you deal?"

"My mom took me out of school for several weeks. Told them I had mono. So when I returned, I wasn't just the freak who had seizures in class, I was also the one with the kissing disease. Fun times."

He pulled me toward him, and I climbed into his lap. My psychic ward circled us in a protective bubble.

"But then I learned to control it. And you will too. Errol can help. He's a whiz at magic manipulation." I leaned back against him and he hugged me closer.

"I just want to stay here where it's quiet. With you. I've missed you," he whispered against my ear. "I stayed away because I was afraid of hurting you, but it nearly killed me. And it hurt you. I could feel your pain like it was my own. I'm so sorry." He laid his forehead on my shoulder and emotion shuddered through him like silent sobs.

"It'll be okay now. We'll figure it out together."

His lips found that spot on my neck that made me lose all reason. He kissed down the edge of my jaw. I turned into it and met his lips with mine. He tasted me like it was a first kiss, then went deeper, reclaiming me after a long absence. My fingers twined in his hair, pulling him even closer. One of his hands lifted me as he tugged off my shorts. He was leaking magic at an enormous rate. I bolstered the ward around us before he attracted every curious predator in the forest.

"You know," I gasped in his ear as his hands skimmed between my thighs. "If you let it, the keening can be really intimate."

"How?"

"Like this." I uncoiled just a finger of my magic and let it touch his. He flinched like I'd jolted him with two-hundred milliamps of electricity.

"It's okay," I soothed. "Let it happen. You're safe here. Let me touch you. All of you."

He nodded, his eyes never leaving mine. I draped him in my magic, let it run down his back in an intimate caress. A rough animal sound rumbled up from his chest. His next kiss was fierce. We tumbled off the couch. The ground was warm underneath me. Terra cradled us. Mason shucked off his shirt and pants and straddled me. I stared up at him. The moon glinted behind his head, wreathing him in a silver halo. My fingers trailed over the hard line of his chest and down…and down some more, pushing just an iota of magic with the touch.

"Do that again," he said gruffly.

And so I gave Mason his first lesson in mastering the keening.

The next morning I woke to the delicious heat of Mason's bare chest pressed against my bare back.

He was home. Everything would be all right now. I lingered in the embrace for a few minutes, then squirmed out from under his arm. He didn't wake.

I'd kept my ward around him all night, giving him the rest he needed. It would wear off when I left the room, but hopefully he'd sleep a little longer. I'd find Errol right away and have him start Mason's training. The sooner he could protect himself from the onslaught of everyday magic, the sooner things would get back to normal.

I dressed quietly and let myself out the patio doors. Errol was already awake and cruising around the barn on his squamus.

"I need your help." I explained the situation and Errol promised to start magic survival skills with Mason immediately.

Muzzy and Tak had the morning feeding well in hand, so I didn't linger in the barn. I came back through the living room and nearly stepped on Grim who'd found a patch of sunlight. He opened one eye, but didn't offer to move. I stepped over him, then leaned down to run my hand over his back. The fur was hot as embers from the sun.

Grim tensed.

"What are you doing?" He nearly spun his head off his shoulders, goggling at the fingers sunk into his fur.

"I'm petting you. See?" I ran my hand down his back.

"Why? Why are you doing that?" He arched into my touch, as if he couldn't resist the new and exciting sensations rippling through him. But his tail had other ideas. It swished like a viper attacking prey.

"It's what people do. Relax."

His toes kneaded the carpet, displaying inch-long claws sharpened to wicked points. It was amusing to see the contrary emotions warring within him. I stroked from the crown of his head to the base of his tail. I was pushing my luck and I knew it. Willow normally let me get in 3.2 pets exactly before she'd turn on me.

I got in one more stroke before he hissed and sunk teeth into my hand. He didn't break the skin. It was a warning shot.

He stalked outside to wash my scent off his fur in peace.

"Why do you taunt him?" Mason asked.

I turned to find him watching me from the kitchen.

"Because it's so much fun."

He looked like he had just woken after a two-day bender, but the hardness had gone from his eyes. He wore only boxer shorts and a scruffy beard. I hesitated near the door. He opened his arms and a small smile played at the corner of his mouth.

I crossed the empty space between us and he folded his arms around me. He was warm and he smelled like Mason. It was an earthy scent, like pine cones and autumn leaves with just a hint of rock dust, and it was uniquely Mason. As unique as his magic.

"I've missed you." His voice was a soft tickle in my ear. He kissed my cheek then leaned his head on my shoulder.

"I'm still worried about you." My words were muffled against his shirt.

"Don't be. I'm fine. Or I will be. Call it inter-dimensional jet lag." He straightened and tipped my chin up so he could kiss me.

"You do look fine." I ran a hand down his rippled stomach, stopping only to tweak the elastic on his shorts.

He laughed. It was throaty and full of genuine humor.

"Sit. I'm making breakfast."

He hummed while he took out eggs, cracked them in a bowl and whisked them with a fork. Next he soaked four pieces of bread in the egg for French toast.

While the frying pan heated, he brought me coffee.

I took the mug and eyed him skeptically.

"Why are you so happy?" I asked. "You can't possibly have mastered your keening already."

"No, but now that I'm know I'm not going insane, or worse that some demon hasn't infected me, I can deal with a little psychic noise." His hand strayed under my chin and his thumb caressed the edge of my jaw. It was like he couldn't stop himself from touching me, after days of being apart. My heart ached with relief.

He returned to the stove, still humming his odd little song which sounded a lot like the violin music I'd been hearing.

I set out plates, cutlery and syrup, while he served up our meal. Along with the French toast, he'd made little hearts out of strawberries to decorate the plates. Aww.

"What are your plans for the day?" he asked while we ate.

The breakfast nook faced the back of the house, where the ground began to slope. From this vantage point, we could see the door to the garage on the upper level of the barn. Dekar and his brothers were cleaning out the garage, getting it ready to store feed for the winter.

"I've been organizing the barn, getting everyone settled in. I still can't believe it's all mine, and already I'm plotting out how I can fit more cages inside."

"You just tell me and I'll build you another barn." He smiled. "Two barns."

Then we forgot all about food. He pulled me into his arms and lifted me. I wrapped my legs around him and he pushed the plates away to sit me on the edge of the table.

His kiss was sticky with syrup. His tongue tasted my lips and I opened to him. He groaned and pulled me against him. My fingers curled into the hair on his chest, and I felt the deep thrum of his heart under them.

He pulled away just enough to look me in the eye. "I want to start every morning just like this." His voice was ragged but full of power, like a prophecy. A shiver ran through me. Just the feel of him wrapped around me still sent a thrill through me.

"Every day," I said. My hands traced his skin down his stomach. He made a small noise of surrender and his lips blazed a trail along my jaw. I turned to meet them with a full kiss. His hands twined in my hair like he might never let go.

A gentle cough told us that Dutch had entered the kitchen.

"Excuse me."

We both turned like deer caught in headlights.

Dutch was the impeccable serving man. He would never make the situation more uncomfortable by addressing the fact that he'd caught us about to baptize the kitchen table.

I smothered a laugh with my hand and tugged on my shirt that had ridden halfway up my belly. Mason stood straighter. Dressed only in boxers as he was, he couldn't hide the signs of our near miss.

"Oscar called this morning," Dutch said, keeping his gaze straight. "He asked to speak with you as soon as you woke. He indicated that it was of the utmost importance."

A sigh rumbled through Mason. He ran a hand through his hair. "Fine. I'll call him now. I need more coffee first."

"I'll make some," I said.

Mason, not caring if Dutch watched, snuck in one last kiss. "This isn't over," he said in a fake menacing whisper.

"Go get dressed," I whispered back.

Mason headed to the bedroom, and I turned to the sink to rinse and refill the coffee pot.

Dutch gently but firmly took it from my hands. "Please, miss. Let me."

I stood back feeling suddenly like an intruder as he filled the pot with water.

Still feeling awkward about being caught like a couple of teenagers at the drive-in, I said, "I didn't mean to get in your way."

"Not in my way." Dutch smiled. It turned his usually rigid face kinder. "It's my job."

I'd taken care of myself since I was a child and my mother first got sick. I was having a hard time letting Dutch fuss over me.

I smiled back and tried to put some assurance into it.

Since Dutch insisted on doing the breakfast dishes too, I decided to check in with Emil before I went back out to the barn.

Emil had sent my schedule for the next day. It was light, only one job in the afternoon, and that was a coney infestation at the golf course on Cartier Street, an easy enough job, if the nest wasn't too big.

There were several other messages, all about upcoming job bookings and one marked urgent. I clicked on that one first.

Emil wrote:

> *Kyra,*
>
> *This message came through your business mail, but I thought you'd want to see it asap. I hope everything is ok. Call me if you need anything.*
>
> *Emil*

Another message was attached.

> *Hey cuz,*
>
> *It's been a few years, hasn't it? Hub has got me locked up on bogus charges. I'll tell you all about it when I see you. But I need 1500 credits for bail. Can you help a girl out? I figure you sort of owe me anyway.*
>
> *Gunora*

Minutes passed while I stared at the screen. The words were all there in the proper order. Verbs, adjectives, nouns. Everything standard sentences needed to make sense. And yet they made no sense.

Mason returned to refill his coffee.

"Everything all right?"

"Yes. No." My mind churned with possibilities and implications.

"It's a message from my cousin Gunora."

"A dryad cousin?"

"An Aesir cousin. Aaric's sister."

"How's that possible? I thought you were the only Aesir in Montreal."

"So did I."

Gunora couldn't be in Montreal. When I left Asgard, fleeing from my guilt and pain over Aaric's death, I'd burned down Bifrost, the rainbow bridge that joined Asgard with Terra. No other Aesir could follow.

"Kyra, what does she want?"

"What? Oh." I turned to Mason and realized he'd asked that question already. "She's in jail. She wants me to make bail for her."

"We'd better get to Hub Station then. I'll get the car."

I stopped him with one hand on his arm. "You don't have to get involved."

He plucked my hand off his arm and kissed my fingers. "She's your family. You're my family. I'm already involved."

C H A P T E R

7

The ride into the city was painful. Going through the ward gate set Mason's keening into a spiral. After that he clenched the steering wheel in a vise-grip and drove like a teenager with his first muscle car. Twice, he swerved violently around slower vehicles, eliciting a symphony of honking horns. I braced my foot against the console as he took a bend in the road at a hundred clicks.

"Maybe I should drive." My heart thudded against my ribs.

He glanced at me but said nothing. The lines around his mouth tightened like he was holding back a curse.

Bringing him into the city was a bad idea. His keening was already in overload, and it would only get worse once we were on the crowded downtown streets.

I let out a relieved breath when he whipped into a tiny parking spot on a side street a block from Hub headquarters. He killed the engine and leaned on the steering wheel. The car's air-conditioning couldn't compete with July heat, and sweat trickled down the side of his neck. He pulled at his collar like it choked him. I refrained from touching him, as if he were made of spun glass.

"You should wait here."

The muscles on his jaw bunched. "I just need a minute."

"It'll get easier. I promise."

He gave me a weak smile and leaned his forehead against his fists which were still wrapped around the wheel.

"Go on ahead. I'll catch up."

I really didn't want to leave him alone in this condition, but pushing the issue would only make him more agitated. I opened the door and stepped into the heat.

Montreal summers could be brutal. Surrounded by water, the city didn't bake—it steamed. The sun reflected off the asphalt, cooking me from above and below. By the time I walked a half block, I was sticky with sweat and drained of energy.

Hub Station was busy with officers and civilians coming and going through the double glass doors of the main entrance. I walked around the side of the building to dispatch. This was Hub's real core, the spot from which officers and contractors like me got their marching orders, and the entrance for detainees.

No cool blast of air welcomed me when I opened the door. The air-conditioning had to be on the fritz. The office was stuffy and morbidly hot. The blades of one pitiful fan limped around in circles, but they barely disturbed the tepid air. The dispatch reception area had recently been painted a bilious green. The color assaulted my eyes. It somehow managed to be too vivid and too monotonous at the same time. I couldn't imagine the thought process that led someone to choose it, except that maybe it was a tint-error freebie from the paint store.

Bruce Gagnon was on duty. I liked Bruce. He tried to project an old curmudgeon persona, but he was really a softy. Sometimes, when I finished a job after hours, he even let me file paperwork the next day, though that was probably as much to his benefit as mine.

"What you got for us today?" he asked. "Venomous lizard? Spitting troll bats?"

"Nothing like that. I'm here on a personal matter."

"Oh?" His eyebrows rose an inch. Bruce loved gossip. His loose lips usually worked in my favor, helping me to keep tabs on the inner workings of Hub. But now I would be the center of interest for the gossip mill. I chewed on that for a minute. There was no way around it. I couldn't leave without at least trying to help Gunora.

"A…uh…friend of mine was brought in. I'm not sure on what charge. But I want to post her bail."

"Name?"

"Gunora…Odinsdottir." I couldn't be sure what name she was going with these days, but that one was a good bet.

Bruce's fingers tapped as he searched the database. "Here she is. Whoa! She was brought in as part of the Knacker raid."

Oh, damn. I rubbed my forehead as if that could wipe this day from my memory.

The Knackers were a gang involved in just about every criminal activity in the city—drugs, sex trafficking, illegal gambling. But their most notorious source of income was cage fighting. They pitted humans against shape-shifters and the nastier sort of fae. People were often picked off the street—homeless or run-aways—and the Knackers regularly raided the shanty towns outside the ward gates for fresh blood. Humans never lasted long in the ring. That was the attraction for spectators. The more blood, the better the draw. The fights moved around a lot, popping up in abandoned warehouses or old underground metro stations. Hub was always trying to infiltrate the gang in hopes of heading off the next fight before it began.

"Says here, there's a restriction for her bail. I gotta call this up the chain."

"What do you mean 'a restriction'?"

But Bruce was already dialing. "Captain Lowe," he said into his widget, then waited.

"What kind of restriction?" I repeated. He held up a finger to stall me.

Mason walked in the door and headed over to the desk. Bruce was arguing with someone on the other end of the line. Captain Lowe wasn't available.

"Well, get someone else down here!" He hung up and tossed the widget on the desk.

"What's the problem?" Mason asked.

"Captain Lowe is in a meeting. They're trying to find someone else to approve the prisoner's release. It might be a while. Have a seat." Bruce pointed to the molded plastic chairs along the wall.

"Thanks." I'd learned it was never a good idea to badger the dispatch officer. He could make your life hell if he chose to.

I sank into one of the chairs. The fact that they were the same shade of green as the wall suggested someone had actually planned the color.

Mason headed back outside with his widget pressed to his ear. I leaned forward, arms braced on my knees.

What was Gunora doing in Montreal? And how had she become caught up with the Knackers?

My toes tapped the linoleum in an erratic beat.

Minutes passed. Sweat tickled a line down my lower back.

Mason returned and sat beside me. His bulk barely fit into the sickly green seat frame.

"It's all good," he said. "I pulled a few strings. Glenda should be here soon."

Captain Glenda Lowe was a high-ranking officer at Hub. I'd met her last fall when she headed up the task force that secured a runaway snooker at the new train station. Since then, she'd been promoted to the special crimes unit and was deep in the investigation against the Knackers.

Mason looked calmer now, but I wondered how much of that was an act. He seemed as tightly wound as a spring holding in its potential to explode.

I didn't need this complication with Gunora right now. I needed to focus on Mason and my family. But Gunora had once been my family too. My Valkyrie family. And like all families, we hadn't always gotten along.

When I'd first arrived in Asgard, I'd known little about my heritage. My mother had given me my sword when my keening power kicked in at age fourteen, but that didn't mean I knew how to use it. The other Valkyries had been training to fight since their toddler fingers could grip a blade.

My skills were lacking in every arena—fighting, magic and socializing. Gunora was at the head of our class. In the training ring, she rarely lost. Her magic out-classed all other students, and she was top of the food-chain when it came to popularity.

Any time you put a bunch of young women together, cliques inevitably form. The Valkyries-in-training were no different. If they'd been high school students, Gunora would have been the home-coming queen. She always had a gaggle of girls following her around, agreeing with every caustic comment that came out of her mouth.

They weren't always kind to me. I was different. My magic was bizarre. My keening overloads made me a freak. But my greatest sin was that I caught Aaric's attention.

Tall, ginger-haired and blue-eyed, Aaric was the subject of much female gossip and speculation. A smile from him could set the girls chattering all afternoon. And if he chose to dance with you at one of the many formal affairs arranged by the older aunts and cousins, then your reputation was made.

Aaric danced with me. A lot. The other girls were tight-lipped with jealousy. Not Gunora, of course. She was Aaric's sister. She simply thought her brother could do better than some human-dryad half-breed. And she made sure everyone knew it.

But all in all, she hadn't been as cruel as most of the others. She even took my side once in a while, when Aunt Dana pushed me too hard.

A memory came to me, made vivid by old pain and anger.

"Come on, Auntie," Gunora said after Dana beat me to the ground during a training exercise. "She's only human. You can't expect her to survive that kind of fight." Her eyes filled with concern, though a smile played around her lips. Dana threw up her hands and stalked off the field as if there was no hope for me. I wiped blood off my lip with my unwounded hand before pushing up from the sand.

"You should really get that looked at." Gunora pointed to the tear in my shirt and the score of blood across my chest. I had another contusion on my right forearm where I'd blocked the flat of Dana's blade in a particularly vicious assault meant to teach me to never let my guard down. Later, I'd find out that the arm was broken. Just another little gift from my giving auntie.

Gunora helped me stand. "I'm sure the med-mage can fix you up." She solicitously wiped sand from my face and shirt. "That is if he knows what to do with human physiology. Your heart is on the left side, isn't it?" She frowned as if she truly didn't know the answer.

The other girls watched, taking cues from Gunora. They were all tall and ice-eyed, with tight braids that didn't come loose in the training ring. Some laughed. A few were embarrassed enough to do it behind a hand. Others looked bored. The frail human was hurt again. It was just another Tuesday.

"What are you thinking?" Mason's words jarred me from my memories. He watched me with the fierce look. My anxiety-laced magic must have been leaking off me. I reeled it in.

I shook my head to shuck off the cobwebs of memory. "About one of the last times I saw Gunora. It seems like a lifetime ago."

"You two will have a lot of catching up to do."

"Maybe." In truth, I didn't know what to expect. In the later years,

Gunora and I had formed some kind of grudging friendship, if only because we were forced into close proximity by our families and the Valkyries. But so much had happened since then.

Mason watched me with one eyebrow quirked up. I turned away to study my hands gripped between my knees. He knew my worst secrets—it had been my hand holding the blade that took Aaric's life, and before his body had cooled, I'd run away and burned the only bridge between Asgard and Terra, trapping all my kin on that side of the veil.

But if Gunora was here, that meant she hadn't been in Asgard when I'd gone rogue. Did Gunora even know that her brother was dead? I'd have to tell her about Aaric. And about my part in his death.

My gut twisted in a knot of worry dipped in guilt and sprinkled with dread.

The door beside Bruce's desk opened and Captain Lowe marched in. She had the hard look of a military officer, but her hair had grown out since the snooker fiasco, and it curled around her ears in a soft bob.

"Mason, Ms. Greene." She nodded at us.

"Glenda. Thanks for taking time to see us." Mason didn't reach out a hand to her, but kept his fists clenched behind his back. I rose and gave Lowe an awkward nod.

"So I hear you want to post bail for one of the lot we brought in last night." She scrolled through a page on her widget. "A Gunora Odinsdottir. Is she some relation to you?"

"A cousin," I said.

"You understand that she is charged with a very serious crime?"

"Um, no. I don't really know."

"We haven't been given any details," Mason interjected smoothly.

Lowe read a bit further. "She was apprehended in the Knacker raid. We've been planning this take-down for months. We have good intel that the Knacker overlord was in attendance last night. We just don't know who he is." She made a point to look me right in the eye. "Or who *she* is."

"There has to be some mistake. I'm sure Gunora was just a spectator." I hoped I was right. "She couldn't be involved with the Knackers."

"These fight rings ignite divisiveness in the ward. Any kind of support for them is a crime. But your cousin was apprehended backstage, in the area where they keep their fighters caged before the big events. No one is allowed back there except Knackers, or so I'm told."

"Still, there could have been a mistake…"

"Are you saying you're willing to vouch for her?"

Was I? Knowing full well that if our positions were reversed, Gunora would let me rot in jail, I said, "Of course."

Captain Lowe frowned. It was a frown that could freeze mercury. Then she sighed. "Fine. I'm willing to let you take her, but only because I've got over a hundred people to question and your cousin already passed the thaumagraph."

Thaumagraphs were expensive alchemical lie detectors. Hub wasn't sparing any expense with this investigation.

"Thank you."

"Don't thank me yet. You will be responsible for her. She skips bail and it's on you." Glenda glared at me like I was an unruly kid in detention.

"I understand—"

"And," she raised a finger, "you will make sure she comes in for her arraignment. Betting on illegal fights is a serious charge."

"I will."

Lowe stared at me until I fidgeted.

By the one-eyed god, it's hot in here.

Glenda finally caved. "Fine. Pay the bond and I'll send her down." She turned and marched out of the room.

Twenty minutes later, the door from the inner offices opened and Gunora stepped out.

had spent over forty Terran years in Asgard and didn't age a day, thanks to the healing properties of Asgard's famous Golden Apples. I returned to my home world looking no older than nineteen. In the years since, I felt like I'd aged a century, but the mirror only showed a few fine lines gathering at the edges of my eyes. At seventy-nine, I could pass for a college senior—still fresh-faced, but with the sparkle of wonderment buffed off my gaze.

Gunora hadn't aged a day. And considering she was three years my senior, that was quite a feat.

"Cousin!" She swooped down to plant a kiss on each of my cheeks. I was shocked at this display of affection and jerked back. Gunora laughed.

She was the same Gunora I remembered, just as beautiful and just as hard-edged. Her braids were gone and she wore her ash-blond hair in a long curtain down her back. She topped me by four inches, but still managed to look thin and willowy. Her eyes were the same crystalline blue and they kept her secrets well. She was dressed for a night out on the town, with tight black pants and a gauzy blouse in a blue that accented her eyes. A black belt hung at her waist to hold her sword sheath. Like a good Valkyrie, she never went anywhere without her blade.

She also exuded magic. It massed around her like an aggressive aura. I slammed down my personal wards.

Beside me, Mason made a gurgling noise like he'd been punched in the gut. He turned and headed for the door. Gunora didn't spare him a glance. All her attention was on me. She pulled me in for a fierce hug, then pushed me backward.

My neck snapped with each gesture. I felt like a rag doll in her embrace.

She gazed down at me with a grin.

"I'm so glad you got my message! I didn't know who else to call. I've only been in the city a month or so. I know, I know. I should have called sooner. I did actually. Your assistant—is he as adorable as he sounds on the phone? Anyway, he said you'd been away from the office for a few weeks. Must be nice to have time off for vacation. I can't remember the last time I had one. I meant to call again, but you know…stuff got away from me. I've been busy. So have you, I guess—"

"Gunora! Stop!" Now it was my turn to shake her. Her mouth slammed shut on her manic ramble, but her eyes continued to dart around the room as if looking for exits, weapons or enemies.

"Are you okay?" I let her go and stood back. She wiped a sheen of sweat off her forehead and nodded.

"Just too much coffee on an empty stomach. Can we go now?"

"I think so." I glanced at Bruce, who watched the drama from behind his desk. He nodded that we were free to go.

I waved Gunora toward the door. "I have a car outside. You can stay with us tonight."

"Yeah, sure. Whatever you say."

Gunora blew a kiss to Bruce. I followed her outside.

It was coming—the moment when I'd have to tell her about Aaric, Bifrost and my part in destroying both.

Gunora paused on the sidewalk, blinking in the bright sun. We walked to the intersection and paused for the light to change. I had so many questions but decided to start with the most immediate one.

"What were you doing at a Knacker fight?"

She cocked her head and looked at me with a curious smile, like I was a puzzle she couldn't figure out.

"I heard there was a giant fighting in the ring. I wanted to see for myself. You know, a bit of nostalgia."

I nodded. I could understand that. The Aesir and the giants hadn't always been friends, but my grandfather had formed an alliance with King Gillingr of Jotenheim. For a lone Aesir in a city full of fae and humans, a giant would be the closest thing to kin.

"Did you speak to him?" I asked.

Gunora shook her head and jerked a thumb at Hub Station. "He's probably still in lockup."

The light changed, and she started across the street.

"The car's this way." I pointed in the other direction.

Gunora stood in the road and clamped one hand on her hip.

"Yeah, about that." She squinted into the sun. "I'm not going with you."

"But I'm responsible for you."

"Whatever. That's your problem. Thanks for the bail money. I'll buy you lunch sometime." She turned to stalk across the intersection, but I grabbed her hand.

"You can't go. Not until you at least tell me what's going on. Why are you even here?" I waved a hand at the street. "In Montreal, I mean. How did you even get here?"

Gunora's expression changed like she'd ripped off a mask. All the softness left her eyes. She curled her upper lip.

"You don't get to ask questions. And don't tell me what to do. Not you. Not after what you did." Instead of pulling her hand away, she leaned into me and snarled, "I know that you burned Bifrost. And I know that because of you I can't go home."

She shoved me.

I was so stunned I didn't even try to stop myself from falling. I crashed against a lamppost and crumpled to the ground.

A car honked and the driver slammed on his breaks as Gunora ran into traffic. She flipped him the bird and leaped across the road, dodging a couple walking arm in arm and a family with a stroller. In a moment, she was lost in the crowd of a hot July afternoon.

I sat up. Blood pounded in my ears.

She knew.

Mason was running up the sidewalk toward me.

He crouched, but kept a good distance between us. I was sweating emotion. That had to be hard for him to bear. "Did she hit you?"

"Just a shove. I lost my balance." I groaned and tried to stand. My back twinged. I'd have a nice bruise where I hit the post.

Mason gave me his hand and pulled me up.

"Are you all right?"

"I'll be okay." I brushed dirt and gravel off my shorts and legs.

"Wasn't she supposed to come home with us?" he asked.

"Yup." I scanned the crowd, but Gunora was gone.

"We should go after her."

"No. Leave it."

Mason frowned and scanned the crowded street. "If she does something stupid, Glenda will have your head."

"I know!" I snapped. He recoiled and his expression made me feel terrible. Being in the city among so many people gushing magic, he had to be struggling with his keening. I reeled in my magic and tucked away my emotions. It was the least I could do.

"I'm sorry. Let's just go home."

We walked like wounded soldiers the block and a half to the car. As I was opening the passenger door someone shouted, "Hey!" I turned to see Gunora standing at the corner. Mason just shook his head and got into the car. I waited until she caught up to us, but kept the open passenger door between us like a shield.

"Look. I'm sorry. I shouldn't have lashed out at you."

I narrowed my gaze. She looked sincere. Her expression even managed a smidgen of contriteness.

"Really, I am." She held out her hands as if she had nothing to give but her apology. "It's just been a really long night. There are a lot of crazies in that lockup. But I'm sorry. And if you'll still let me, I'd like to come stay with you. At least for a couple of days. If nothing else, I think we need to talk."

I stared at her for a minute longer, then sighed.

"The heat must be frying my brain," I said. "Get in."

9

s soon as we got home, Gunora pleaded exhaustion. I set her up in the spare bedroom right next to ours.

"You need something to wear?" I asked. We weren't the same size, but I could probably manage shorts and a t-shirt. Gunora nodded dully and I left. When I came back, she was already tucked in bed. The blinds were drawn, hiding the afternoon sun. I left the clean clothes on the dresser and quietly let myself out.

Mason stood by the living room window, gazing at the forest beyond the patio. When he heard me come in, he turned with a frown.

"Did you tell her about her brother?"

"Not yet. But I will. She already knows about Bifrost."

"So she hit you. Nice."

"It was, actually. By Valkyrie rights and traditions, she should have killed me."

"What will you do?"

I sighed. "I don't know. I've dreaded this for so long, but I started to think it would never happen. I started to believe I really was the only Aesir on Terra, and no one would ever come looking for me or make me accountable for what happened."

"It wasn't your fault." Mason took my hand and gently tugged me toward him. I leaned my head against his shoulder, happy for the small contact.

"Not all of it," I said. Aaric had taken his own life. It took me years to accept that, to put the blame where it belonged. "But I did burn down Bifrost."

"You were scared. And you'd just seen your lover die."

"It was impulsive and irrational."

He tipped my face towards his, forcing me to meet his gaze.

"It was a mistake. People make mistakes. She'll come around. And if she doesn't, she'll have to deal with me." He kissed me. It wasn't passionate, or an invitation for intimacy. It was just an affirmation. A kiss to seal the promise.

"Thank you." And though I knew he'd let me fight my own battle, it was good to know I had backup.

"I'm going to head down to the barn to help the boys get ready for the evening feeding," I said.

"I'll join you." Mason rubbed the back of his neck. "I need Errol's help. Today's trip to the city proved that I'll never get through Oscar's line up of events without some training."

We walked hand-in-hand across the patio and down the slope. The barn doors were open wide, and yet as soon as we stepped inside, the temperature dropped a few degrees. That was the amazing thing about bank barns. Built into a hillside, the earth acted as a natural air conditioner—cooler in the summer, warmer in the winter.

Muzzy and his younger brother, Tak, were preparing for the evening feeding. Gibus, not to be left out, trailed along behind them as they filled water bowls and cleaned cages.

"Have you seen Errol?" I asked the boys.

"He's gone to the river with the twins," Muzzy said. "Took one of those funny lizard mice thingies with him."

Mason nodded and left to find his new tutor.

I stood in the middle of the barn and turned in a circle to admire all my neatly arranged boarders. This was my favorite time of day. The nocturnal critters weren't yet awake. The diurnal critters were sleepy. Even Jacoby, who'd been bouncing around the barn all morning, had finally crashed in a patch of sunshine with Willow curled at his back. There was a hush over the room— not an expectant hush, but more of a lazy, satisfied calm.

I breathed in the sweet scent of the clean hay that filled the cages. Dust motes twinkled when they floated through the sunbeam from the open door. The tiny, sleepy magics of a dozen critters pinged off my keening. All these sensations soothed my nerves that had been so badly used in the last few days.

I filled a small pail with frozen crayfish from the freezer. Hunter preferred fresh, but I hadn't had the chance to catch any. Maybe I'd ask the twins to find some in the creek.

Gibus tugged on my sleeve. "Are those for the octopus? Can I feed him?"

I smiled and handed him the pail. "Only if you don't call him 'octopus.' Hunter is pretty touchy about that. He's a pygmy kraken."

Gibus scratched his head. He had thick black hair that stuck out like bristles on a broom.

"What's the difference?"

"It would be like someone calling you a brownie instead of a goblin."

"Humans do that. They're dumb."

"It's because they don't know any better. When you know better, you do better. Right?"

"Right!" A grin lit his face. "So can I feed the piggy kraken?"

That was close enough. "Sure."

Hunter didn't seem to mind when Gibus called out, "Here piggy, piggy!" and tossed crayfish into his tank. The kraken popped his head over the rim and snatched a crayfish out of the air with one tentacle. Buddy slowly rolled by beneath him.

"You always were a sucker for taking in strays," Gunora said.

I turned to find her standing in the open doorway. My cotton shorts and t-shirt made her look like a child who'd outgrown her clothes. The shorts were too short. The shirt hugged her across the shoulders and breasts. And oddly, she'd buckled her leather sword belt around her waist. The sheathed sword hung down against her bare legs. She should have looked ridiculous But true to form, Gunora didn't slouch or cross her arms to hide. Instead, she owned the look. And she did look good—tall, and strong, with a glow of youth on her cheeks.

"I thought you were resting," I said.

"Couldn't sleep." She walked around the barn, peering into cages. Kur swiped his tiny hand at her nose. She stopped at the terrarium with Bijou, my bedazzling snail, and gazed at him for a while. Then she turned to take in the whole set up.

Gita chose that moment to poke her head out of the old tack room. She looked Gunora up and down, summed her up with one disdainful sniff, and retreated back into her nest.

"Was that a banshee?"

I nodded.

"Wow. You've got quite a setup for yourself, don't you? The handsome guy, the goblin slaves, a captive banshee in a closet."

"They aren't slaves. And the banshee is free to leave any time she wants."

"Uh-huh."

She finished her circuit of the barn, and ended up in front of me.

"Seems like you did okay. We should all be so lucky."

"You said you wanted to talk." I wiped the fishy smell off my hands with a rag.

"I do. You owe me that much."

"Fine but not here." The goblits eyes were as big as meatballs, watching the strange woman. They were smart enough to feel the confrontation brewing between us.

"Let's take a walk," I said.

"Lead the way." Gunora stepped aside and I left the barn.

We strolled through the gate in the big cedar hedge to the old cemetery. Gunora wandered among the graves, reading inscriptions and running her fingers along the headstones. She didn't seem in any hurry. But despite her apparent air of calm, something felt off.

The energy coming off her now was less glowing and more scratchy. Her hands seemed to be in constant motion. She turned to me and I saw that her eyes were glazed and her shoulders seemed narrower, like they held a greater weight than she could handle.

I wondered if she was high, or maybe coming down after a rough night. The drugs found in some of the darker clubs of Montreal were spectacular for both their magical highs and cavernous lows. They would have been readily available at the Knacker fight.

I licked her magic with my keening. It didn't taste like drugs, but something was definitely wrong. I remembered the day I realized my mother had cancer. It was weeks before she admitted it to me, but I'd keened the bitterness of her tumor, a sour shadow that masked her magic. Gunora's magic didn't taste quite like that, but close.

"Captain Lowe said you'll have to appear for an arraignment."

She cocked her head and grinned. "I had nothing to do with that cage fight. Well, nothing they could prove anyway."

"Don't tell me about it. I don't want to know." I crossed my arms over my chest. If Gunora really was guilty, I wouldn't be drawn into her mess.

"Why not? It's your fault I was there in the first place."

"How is that?" Exasperation made my voice harsh. I'd put my relationship with Hub on the line for her. I'd vouched for her against my better judgment, but somehow it was my fault she got into trouble?

She leaned into me. Her eyes glinted like chips of ice.

"Because of you, I can't go home. You owe me." She poked her finger forward, stopping only a hair from jabbing my shoulder.

My first years back on Terra, I'd run from my past, hidden in the dryad forest under my grandmother's protection, always fearing that the Aesir gods would reach through the veil and find a way to punish me for my crimes. As the years went by, I stopped running, stopped looking over my shoulder. But I never forgot.

And now it was time to face my past.

"Where did you hear that?" I asked.

"Heimdall told me." Gunora smiled. She leaned in and spoke in a dramatic whisper. "He was pretty upset."

I closed my eyes and took a deep breath. Heimdall was the god who kept watch over the rainbow bridge, always on the lookout for signs of Ragnarök, the time when gods would fall and the world would end. He'd been deep into a cask of mead when I fled Asgard, and still he pursued me across the frozen fjords for days. Sometimes, in the quiet of the night, I could still hear his terrible cries as he watched his beloved Bifrost burn.

My secret was out. Everyone knew. I felt an unexpected calm.

"I did burn Bifrost." I looked Gunora in the eye. Her eyes narrowed. "I didn't mean to destroy it…No, that isn't true. I did mean to." I took a deep breath and started again. "I was scared." I closed my eyes and for a moment the Asgard warriors were galloping toward me again on their magnificent and terrifying mounts. The horns atop my grandfather's keep blared the call of the traitor and if the guard found me, they'd show no mercy. I'd killed one of Odin's beloved sons. And so, yes. I'd burned the bridge.

I opened my eyes to find Gunora watching me. She leaned back. Her nostrils flared and her bottom lip puckered. I couldn't decipher the expression. Was that rage? Concern? Amusement?

"Aren't you going to say anything?"

"I'm waiting for the truth. I know about Bifrost, but there's more, isn't there?"

I sucked it up.

There was so much more. There was Aaric, Gunora's big brother, the one who'd threatened her boyfriends with painful deaths if they broke her heart. The one who'd taught her to climb trees and fight dirty to win. Aaric had told me that as children, they'd been inseparable. He'd wanted me to love her the way he did, but that was never in our stars.

"Aaric is dead." The words fell like stones.

Gunora stared at me, her face flat. I hadn't expected her to wail and gnash her teeth. But I'd expected more than a cold, calm gaze.

"Did you hear me?" I grabbed her arm, prodding her the way you poke at a healing wound to see if it still hurts.

She jerked her arm away. "I'm right here. Of course I heard you. I'm still waiting for the truth."

I spun around and stomped into the shadow of an old oak at the edge of the yard. My teeth hurt from clenching. If she knew the damn truth, why was she making me say it aloud?

"Fine. I killed him. Or at least my sword did. He needed a Valkyrie blade to finally end his life." I spun around and flung the words at her as if I could fling the memory away. "Are you happy now? He used me and I let him."

Gunora leaned against a stone monument and smiled. "Was that so hard?"

"You knew already."

She nodded. "The giants still get news from Asgard. There aren't many of them on Terra, but I met one years ago down south. I know the whole sordid tale. I've known for years. To be honest, I wasn't surprised to hear it. Aaric asked me to do the deed years ago when his beloved Verna died."

I flinched. Aaric's first wife had always been a sore spot. Her ghost had lingered between us, a palpable presence in our lives. The only time Aaric was able to banish her was in the bedroom, and that had given me hope for our future. False hope, as it turned out.

Gunora leaned forward. Her top lip curled in distaste. "You always were such a dupe. Aaric never loved you. He loved Verna with his last breath. She was better than you in every way—smarter, more beautiful, a better fighter. And you're right. You were just a tool Aaric used so he could finally be with Verna again."

Her words slashed like tiny razor blades, cutting and cutting and cutting, making old scars bleed fresh.

I strode across the grass until I was right in her face. My fists clenched at my sides. I wanted to hit her. I wanted to mess up her pretty face. I must have looked like a lunatic—red faced and sweaty, breath coming in ragged gasps.

Gunora put two fingers on my chest and shoved me backward.

"Don't be a dupe *and* a drama queen."

Rage and hurt warred for space in my head. I hated her, and yet I had no right to. Gunora only spoke the truth, but she had a talent for forging it into a blade that could eviscerate.

"Look, Did I hate you when I heard what you'd done? Sure. But that was years ago. I'm over it. Still, I think we both can agree that you owe me."

Slowly, I backed down. I was so tired, I could have lain on the ground and slept for a week.

"What do you want, Gunora."

She unsheathed her sword and pointed it at my throat. "I want your blood."

good Valkyrie never leaves home without her sword. How many times had Aunt Dana quite literally pounded that message into my head? Gunora had learned the lesson. Her sword glinted in the soft afternoon rays.

And where was mine? Tucked away in my bedroom closet, of course. To be fair, the cemetery grounds were part of my home now. I shouldn't need to defend myself in my own backyard. But here we were.

I looked past the point of her sword and felt strangely calm.

"So that's what you want? Vengeance?"

She snarled and lunged. I jumped back, fell over a headstone and landed flat on my back.

My heart hammered in my chest. I keened a burst of pure rage and rolled as Gunora's blade hit the ground where my head had been. I scrambled to hands and knees, then dove for cover behind headstone. I might have left my sword behind, but I never went anywhere without my pocket knife. I scrambled backward, giving myself the seconds I needed to pull it open.

"Gunora, stop!"

Her shout of rage nearly drowned out my words. Her blade came down on the marble stone only inches from my head. I spun and grabbed her wrist, pinning it to the stone. My right hand pressed the small blade to her throat.

Her face, twisted in ugly rage, was inches from mine. My arms began to tremble. Her blade shifted under my grip..

"I don't want to hurt you!" I spoke through gritted teeth.

"That's always been your problem." She kicked my shin. Hard. My leg fell out from under me, but I used the momentum to plow into her.

Her sword went flying as we fell together, grappling, grunting, banging knees and elbows against the hard ground. I flipped her and dug my knee into her back. My fingers ached from gripping my knife. Gunora made a wheezing, gurgling sound.

She was choking and shaking violently. Was she having a seizure? No, she was laughing.

I stood back and kicked her sword away.

She rolled onto her back, sat up, then rose on wobbly legs, still grinning. Her face was red and sweaty, her eyes wild. She he wiped a drop off blood off her lip.

I looked into her eyes, trying to anticipate her next move, but they were blank and empty as if no one really looked back at me. I clenched the small blade in my fist.

"Sometimes you need to hurt someone to save them." Gunora's voice was low and throaty. "That's what Dana tried to teach you, but you wouldn't learn. A Valkyrie death blow hurts, but to the warrior bleeding out on the field, it's a mercy that lets him drink mead in the hall of the All-father."

What was she babbling about?

"How is your vengeance a mercy?" I asked.

"Not…vengeance…blood." She struggled to get the words out. Every muscle in her body seized. She threw back her head, and veins stood out on her neck.

An uncanny wind blew through the yard, tossing her hair around her face.

Then she began to glow. It started in her eyes. Her light blue irises became neon lights. Then her skin was suffused in a soft pink aura.

And she changed as easily as shedding a glamor.

Her cheeks grew plump and lines appeared at the edges of her eyes. Her shoulders rounded and broadened, bracing her now larger breasts. Her hips widened.

In seconds, she'd aged twenty years.

An older Gunora stood before me, still pretty, but plump and solid. Motherly.

The word came to me with a sinking feeling. This wasn't glamor. It was worse. So much worse.

Gunora screamed.

Her back arched so sharply I thought it might crack. That strange light effervesced around her again, and in an instant the matron was gone, replaced by an ancient crone.

The eyes that pleaded me for help, were almost lost in the folds of her wrinkled face. Her hair had gone white and sprang from a liver-spotted scalp like milkweed flax. She was stooped and frail. My cotton shorts hung on bony hips and revealed stick-thin legs. She sagged against a headstone, one hand on her chest as she gulped in air.

Tears streamed down the crone's face for only a moment. And then she was gone too. The maid returned with eyes like ice on fire. The wind whipped in a frenzy now. Gunora was engulfed in a ball of white light.

The next change took her almost immediately. Maid Gunora doubled over, panting. When she looked up, it was with the face of a forty-year-old woman.

"Help me!" She reached for me, but the matron was already shrinking again. The shifts accelerated. The crone morphed and glowed, replaced by the maid. And back to the stout mother again. Around and around. She was a blur of light, her three faces blending into one.

I keened the immense output of magic streaming off her. No one could sustain that amount of magic for long.

Gunora screamed. Then the light went out. The wind died. Gunora crumpled to the ground and lay still.

White hair covered her face. Frantically, I pushed it aside and found a pulse at her throat.

She was alive but looked as old as a crone. Her breathing was shallow and her face dangerously pale. I had to get her home.

Her eyes fluttered. "My blade." Her voice was weak, barely above a whisper.

A Valkyrie would never leave her blade behind on the field of battle, but I knew her request meant more than that. I grabbed the sword and thrust it into her hands, no longer worried that I'd have to fight her.

A tired smile curved Gunora's lips as she drew strength from the blade.

"I'm going for help," I said. "I'll be right back."

She nodded weakly and I took off at a run.

I burst into the house screaming for Mason. When I finally caught my breath and told him what happened, we both piled into the big ATV he kept for traveling around the property.

Gunora was exactly as I left her, still clinging to her blade.

Mason took one look at the ancient, wizened crone and said, "Who in the hell is that?"

"It's Gunora. I'll explain later. Just help me get her home."

Mason lifted her into the back of the ATV, though I knew what it cost him. Gunora still reeked of magic. I tried to broaden my ward to shield him too. He shot me a brief smile when he felt the gentle touch of my magic. Then he started the engine and we raced back to the house.

I sat on the plush chair by the window, my legs crossed under me, hands folded and tucked tight against my chest as if that could keep away the horror of what I was seeing.

I watched her sleep.

She changed again without waking. The wrinkles smoothed out. Hair darkened from white to rich blond. Cheeks filled out and turned rosy. Her breathing eased, and suddenly Gunora lay sleeping like a princess waiting for her kiss.

The light faded. Mason came in and turned on a light on the nightstand.

"Any more changes?"

"Yes. It doesn't stop."

"Anything we can do?"

I shook my head. He could see I didn't want to talk about it, so he left. Later, he brought me dinner—a steaming bowl of venison stew and bread still warm from the oven, but my stomach churned and I couldn't eat. I left the food on the dresser untouched.

Sometime after midnight, I woke with a start. I'd been dozing in the chair.

"Water." The cracked voice said. Gunora was awake. I rushed to the kitchen, stamping my feet that were full of pins and needles from sleeping on the cramped chair.

Grim hissed at me as I hurried by with a glass of water.

Back in her room, Gunora was sitting up in bed. She accepted the glass and drank half of it without stopping. She put it on the nightstand and we faced each other.

She looked refreshed, propped up on pillows. Youth and vitality seemed to ooze from her pores. Her blade lay on the bed, tangled in the sheets. She picked it up, and I let her have it. I wasn't afraid anymore. She'd had every right to attack me for what I'd done, but we were so far past that now.

"How long have you known?" I asked

She hummed and stroked the blade, then looked up as if she'd forgotten me.

"How long what? Oh, this?" She ran a hand down her stomach. "Sometimes I forget. When I'm in this form, I mean." Her hand continued down the length of her thigh. "It's easy to forget when I'm young and healthy." She cocked her head, in that way I'd seen her do with the young Vikings who came to watch the Valkyries train. "Do you know that in my mind, I still see myself like this. Always. Young, strong…beautiful. Do you? I mean, you were never really strong or beautiful, but you were young once. When you close your eyes, do you still feel it?"

I ignored the jibe. It was Gunora's superpower.

"Tell me when," I urged. "When did you know you were sick?"

She lowered her eyes. "Since before I started training as a Valkyrie. But the changes accelerated during our last year at the academy. That's why I went away."

I closed my eyes and said a small prayer. *Dear All-father, protect this daughter and help her into the light of your hall.*

Valkyries were strong, bold and tough, nearly unkillable as long as they stayed in Asgard and ate the Golden Apples. Age barely touched them. Wounds healed quickly. Sickness was almost non-existent.

Except for one disease—Maid Mother Crone.

It was a biological curse, set on one of our sisters long ago by a vindictive giantess who could not best the Valkyrie in battle, and so she cursed her with the illness.

There was no cure. MMC started slowly, not detectable until the girl reached maturity. Then, for no apparent reason, she aged quickly, becoming the matronly mother figure within hours. She might live in that form for years, but eventually the aging would speed up and she'd become a crone before her time.

The fun didn't end there though. At some point, the crone would shift into the maiden again. Then the changes started coming faster. She might live as a maid for weeks or only days, then become the mother, and once again the crone. Every change drew on her well of magic, draining the source of her life. Near the end, the shifts were like a seizure, coming fast and hard. And when these seizures took hold, the Valkyrie succumbed to the disease.

From what I'd seen, Gunora was near the end.

I sat on the edge of the bed. I wanted to take her hand, to give what comfort I could, but I knew Gunora would see any such care as weakness.

"Did Dana know?"

Gunora laughed. It was a sweet tinkling sound. "Of course. She sent me to find a cure. That's why I was away from Asgard when you…did what you did."

When I killed her brother and burned the only bridge back to Asgard she meant. The thought still burned like a thousand tiny flames.

"I took enough Golden Apples with me to keep me healthy while I searched. But of course those are long gone now."

The Golden Apples of Asgard were famous for their healing powers, but they didn't bring immortality.

My mother and I returned to Asgard when I was eighteen because her cancer was too far advanced for Terran medicine. The Golden Apples didn't cure her cancer, but they slowed it. For forty years, she lived with it. She still had some bad days, which she tried to cover up by saying she was just tired. But I saw it in the lines around her eyes. She was in pain. Most days though, she was just fine. When I'd left Asgard ten years ago, my mother had still been alive, eating her apple every morning for breakfast.

That could have been Gunora if I hadn't locked her out of our home world. She could have had years—decades—of good health before the MMC caught up with her. Instead, she spent the last ten years scouring Terra for a cure that probably didn't exist.

And now she would die away from her family and friends. And soon.

"Do you know how Verna died?" Her question pulled me back to the present.

I shook my head.

Aaric often spoke about Verna's great prowess on the battlefield or the funny stories she told in the mead halls. But he never told me how she died. I only knew that he took his own life by the blade so he could be with her again in Odin's hall.

"Verna killed herself. Impaled herself on her sword so she could die a warrior's death and be welcomed in Valhalla." Gunora smiled. "They don't let those who die of old age or disease into Odin's great hall, did you know that?"

She was chatty now. All traces of her earlier seizure were gone. She leaned over and picked at my dinner forgotten on the nightstand.

"Are you surprised that she had MMC?" she asked with a mouth full of buttered bread. "She hid it well, didn't she. It's the Valkyries' dirty little secret. We all know that inbreeding over generations has made the disease rampant, but no one talks about it. Girls just quietly disappear. But I wouldn't be silent!" She raised her voice and her eyes flashed. "Verna was weak! She broke Aaric's soul in two. She couldn't do what needed to be done to save herself. But I could. With Dana's blessing...I traveled to this world in search of a giant clan, descendants of the one who first cursed a Valkyrie with MMC. It wasn't easy. I won't bore you with the details of my battle with the giant. The bitch nearly killed me. In fact, I think I was actually dead at one point." She smiled again. "But only for a moment. And it was worth it because I found the cure." She leaned back on the pillow and scarfed down the entire bowl of congealed stew like a starving prisoner. My thin, damp t-shirt hugged her like a second skin. When she was finished, she wiped her mouth with the back of her bare hand.

"Imagine now, I return to Asgard in triumph, with the knowledge to cure myself, only to find the road home gone. And here's the irony, little cousin." She sat up and leaned forward. "The key to my cure lies with another Valkyrie, the one thing you denied me. But now, here you are." She let out a giggle that ended in a cough.

"I'm here." I shoved the glass of water at her, but she waved it away. She lay back and closed her eyes.

The speech had cost her. Her breathing became harsh, and I worried she was going to shift again.

I gripped her hand and squeezed. "You should rest."

She shook her head. Her glacial eyes bore into mine.

"I knew right away it was you who destroyed the bridge. Heimdall was inconsolable."

I nodded. Heimdall had been a friend once, until that fateful day.

Gunora continued. "When I found him, he was blubbering drunk, weeping by the stump of his precious Bifrost. He told me what you'd done. He cried so many tears that the whole valley is now a lake. But I didn't cry because I knew there was still one Valkyrie left on Terra. And that's all I needed. You are all I need."

"I'm here," I repeated. "I'll help any way I can."

She squeezed my hand and pulled me in closer.

"You were wrong. I don't want vengeance. I really do want your blood. I need it."

I pulled my hand away as the spasms clenched her, but she got herself under control again and reached for me. "My blood…mixed with your blood…"

What? I jerked away. She either didn't notice my reaction or didn't care. She rambled on, her voice as frail and strident as a newborn bird's.

"That's all it takes. An easy rite. Blood…a few power words…to pass this curse on to you…and I'll…I'll be free." She held her blade, ready to cut me.

I scrambled off the bed to the other side of the room. She'd just laid out the horror of her plan. So simple. So wrong.

Gunora's selfishness had always had a careless edge, but surely she wouldn't stoop to sacrificing another for her cure.

Before I could gather my wits, Gunora screamed. That odd light inside her flashed and maid became mother. Before she could even take a breath, she shifted to crone and the light died. She fell back against the pillow. Her sword clattered on the floor.

I stared at the shrunken creature lying in the bed. Part of me still couldn't believe that this old woman could be Gunora. Her breathing was so shallow, I thought she must be dead. But, no, I keened the spark of life still glowing inside her. It was a pale flame and rank with decay, but she still lived.

I remembered other Valkyries who'd suffered from MMC. Beatrice had died horribly. The changes came so rapidly at the end that she could do nothing but writhe in her bed, too exhausted to even scream. Emmi had simply disappeared. The girls on the training grounds had whispered that she'd thrown herself off the wall surrounding Asgard, and the city guards had buried her broken body where they'd found it.

Gunora wouldn't kill herself. She was too stubborn for that. She'd done the impossible and found a cure. But it wasn't really a cure. It was passing the buck.

I could see her reasoning. I was responsible for her exile, and in her eyes, I was the least worthy of the Valkyries anyway. Why shouldn't she pass the disease onto me and live out the rest of her life?

I should kill her. Right now.

The thought rang through my brain. It would have been easy to pick up her sword and plunge it into her heart. She would kill me if she got the chance. She'd been planning on it. And Gunora always got what she wanted. Always. She didn't care who she hurt in the process.

I took a deep breath and pulled myself away from the brink.

I wouldn't kill her. And she wouldn't kill me.

I tucked the sheet around her wasted shoulders and turned out the light.

Tomorrow, we'd find another way. Together. Because that's what families do.

Gunora slept through breakfast the next day. Mason and I spent a quiet morning on the patio. We ate a late breakfast while I told him about Gunora's affliction and her nefarious plans to pass the disease onto the only other Valkyrie she could find. He listened with his eyebrows slowly creeping up to his hairline. When I was done, his hands gripped the chair as if he was about to propel himself upwards so he could go smother Gunora with a pillow that instant.

"Don't worry." I squeezed his hand. "She won't hurt me."

"How can you be so sure?"

"Because I took her sword away and locked it in the armory. She can't beat me in a hand-to-hand fight. She's too weak. Besides, beating me up wouldn't solve her dilemma. She needs my blood."

Mason growled low in his throat. "Somehow, that doesn't make me feel better. I should stay home tonight."

The first of Oscar's many campaign events was that evening, and he'd be staying at Tor Tower, the alchemist stronghold in the city. It was home to the Alchemist Party offices, but suites were available for use by the ministers and other high-ranking alchemists. Oscar wouldn't be pleased that I was already begging out of an event, but he'd have to deal. I wouldn't leave Gunora alone.

"I'll be fine," I said. "Dutch will be here too."

Mason ground out a nonverbal response.

"And I'll have Berto check in regularly," I said. "I'll be safe as houses." I tilted my head to the side. "You know I never understood that saying. Why should houses be safe?" I was trying to lighten the mood. It didn't work.

Mason scowled. "This house should be safe. For you, for me, for the goblins and the others."

He was frustrated. I could see in in the tense line of his shoulders. If Oscar hadn't made a big deal of this campaign event, there would have been no question about staying home with me.

"It'll be okay. I promise."

He growled again and I shushed him with a kiss.

"Aren't you the cute couple," Gunora said from the door to the kitchen. She was still wearing my shorts and shirt, but she was in matron mode and they were tight across her chest and hips. She held up a cup of coffee. "I hope you don't mind. Some really pale dude offered it to me."

"That's Dutch," I said. "He works here."

Mason rose from his chair. He nodded toward Gunora in a gesture that was almost a bow. His old world manners kicked in when he was upset, but his eyes spoke of violence.

"If you'll excuse me, I have work to do." He left through the living room.

Gunora flopped into the chair he'd vacated. "He doesn't like me."

"He's just worried," I said.

She sighed. "Because of me."

"Because your treatment plan involves some blood rite that will pass your disease onto me!"

She sipped her coffee but wouldn't look at me.

Behind us, Tums and Tad rolled down the grassy slope toward the driveway. Their squeals of glee were matched by Princess's excited barks. Gunora turned and watched them with a strange expression on her face. If I didn't know her better, I might have thought it was longing.

"You really have set yourself up a nice little life here." She turned to take in the house with its turret-like towers on either end. "Good coffee too." She held up the cup. "I haven't had real coffee in a long time." She drained the last gulp and set the cup down on the table.

She leaned in and spoke fervently. "My plan was never to inflict my problems on you. The plan was to go home and find some old biddy on her death bed already. Maybe old Hildr. Remember her? She was the one who used to yell at us for eating the plums in her orchard. It's not like she could eat them all herself. Half of them rotted on the trees. She was a cranky old crone back then. If she's still around, she might actually enjoy MMC for a while. At least she'd get a few brief episodes of maidenhood again." She sat back with a smile.

"Until it kills her," I said flatly. "In any case, that's a moot point, since there's no road home."

Gunora waved her hand like that didn't matter, then said, "Where's my sword?"

The change of subject was abrupt enough to give me whiplash.

"It's safe," I said. "I put it away so nobody gets hurt."

She curled her lip in a sneer, and I held up my hand.

"Before you spout some threat about how you don't need a sword to hurt me," I looked her right in the eye and she shut her mouth, "I have something to say and you're going to listen for once."

She narrowed her eyes. At least she was listening. Whether she would hear me or not remained to be seen.

I took a deep breath. "I'm not going to let you blood me for some heinous rite." She opened her mouth and I held up my hand again. "And I'm not going to let you do it to some other poor Valkyrie either. But I will help you find another way. Together we'll find a real cure."

For a long minute she said nothing. Then her whole expression changed. For the first time, I saw something resembling hope on her face.

"You really believe that?"

I couldn't destroy her fledgling hope, so I squashed down my own misgivings.

"I do believe it. I have a friend at Abbott's Agora who's a whiz with this kind of stuff. He'll know what to do."

Gunora sniffled. "Thank you." Her fierce outer layer was finally cracking. She wiped her nose on her arm, and I handed her a napkin.

Then we sat and listened to the children playing in the yard.

LATER THAT AFTERNOON, Gunora stood by the desk in the living room, examining the bookshelves. Grim, who didn't like strangers, normally left every time she entered the room. But this time, he rose from his perch by the fireplace, arched his back and hissed at her.

"What's his problem?" Gunora asked. Then her eyes rolled back in her head and she collapsed in a ball of light.

When the fit ended, crone-Gunora lay in a heap on the floor.

Grim primly stepped over her and marched outside.

I carried Gunora to bed. She was as light as a pile of bones. Thin bones.

I really wanted to go to Abbott's Agora and consult Nesi's books. We needed to find a cure fast. But I didn't feel comfortable leaving her alone. I decided to let her rest for the afternoon. If she was still too weak the next day, I'd go to Nesi's on my own.

By early evening, Gunora was feeling better. She hadn't changed, but even in crone form, she seemed to have some energy. I suggested a short walk down to the barn so I could check on my critters.

The goblits had a soccer game going in the car park. Princess was so excited to be included, she could barely contain herself. She saw us coming and zoomed around our legs, nearly toppling Gunora.

"Hey!" I grabbed her arm before her frail legs gave out.

"This wasn't such a good idea," she said.

"I'm sorry. They're just a little rambunctious, but they'll behave now, isn't that right?" I raised my voice so the goblits and hound would know I meant business. The kids nodded, quiet now. Princess whined and bowed. It was a trick she knew was adorable, so she did it every time she thought she was in trouble.

"Just take me back to my room." Gunora clutched my arm. "I feel like I should lie down."

We turned and shuffled back to the house.

Once she was settled again, I made dinner and brought her in a plate. She was already asleep. I ate by myself at the breakfast nook. I texted Mason to ask how his evening was going. He sent back a picture of himself with Oscar and another alchemist minister. They were all dressed in suits and ties and looked wonderfully important. I suspected Mason was hating every minute of it.

Later, I fired up my old computer and searched the Ley-net for any information on MMC. There was very little, and most of that referred to the myths about the triple goddesses who symbolized the female life cycle. I didn't see how they could help.

Frustrated, I shut the computer and went to bed. Sleep wouldn't come though. I tossed in the bed. I played word games in my head. I recited the old dead US states in alphabetical order, forward and backward, a mindless game that never failed to put me to sleep. Finally, my mysterious violinist came to my rescue. The sweet music filtered in through my open window, and in minutes, I was asleep.

SOMETHING COLD AND hard pressed against my throat. Instinctively, I jerked away and felt the blade nick my skin. Gunora stood over me, holding a small, sharp kitchen knife. The frail crone arms were gone. She held the blade in a strong grip. Blond hair cascaded over her shoulder to fall between us. The maid was back.

"I told myself I couldn't do it. But…turns out I can. This is the only way. And you never really fit in. You're barely a Valkyrie at all. But maybe you have just enough Aesir blood to take this curse from me."

Her eyes were glazed and manic. Princess had eyes like that right before the zoomies took over and she went tearing around the house. On the hound, crazy eyes were adorable. On Gunora they were terrifying.

She jumped on the bed and pinned me. I squirmed, trying to kick her off, but she pressed the blade hard against my skin and I lay still. I could feel blood trickling down my neck and onto the pillow. It was an easy jab to sever my carotid artery.

"I thought about what you said. It was a nice gesture." She smiled, but there was no warmth in it. The only light came from the moon shining through my window. It cast her in a ghoulish glow.

"Gunora don't—"

"Shut up! You don't get to speak. I'm in charge here! And I say that I don't have time to search for another cure. Why should I wait when I have all the Valkyrie blood I need right here?"

Her hand was shaking. Desperation, fear and exhaustion had combined into a kind of mania. She was one step from falling over the edge. I just needed to give her that last push.

"Okay!" I raised my hands in surrender. "I'll do whatever you want. But if you kill me here, you won't get your ritual."

Her hand wavered. She lowered the blade.

I kicked up with my knee, knocking her off balance, then slammed my fist down on the side of her head.

"Dutch!" I screamed as I untangled my legs from the sheets. Before I got to the door of my bedroom, he was there like a tall pale specter.

He skidded to a stop. "What is it?"

I pointed to Gunora. "Get her out of here. I don't care where you take her. Just make sure it's far." She'd collapsed on the floor, out cold. A cut on her forehead bled profusely. She must have whacked it on the nightstand when she fell.

Gods love him, Dutch didn't question me. He picked her up as if she weighed no more than a child and threw her over his shoulder in a fireman's carry.

"Wait!" I called out. Dutch paused with one foot in the hall. "Get her sword out of lock up and leave it with her for when she wakes up." Dutch hesitated. I thought he'd question me, but he just nodded and disappeared with his burden.

Giving Gunora back her sword wasn't just an act of mercy. Being parted from her sword for too long would drive her mad. I didn't want her to have any reason to come looking for us again.

When I heard Dutch leave through the front door, I sank to the floor beside the kitchen knife stained with my blood and cried.

ason was too much of a gentleman to say, "I told you so." But he was thinking it.

As soon as Dutch left with Gunora, Berto came up from the gatehouse to sit with me. I was glad for the company, even if the Guardian wasn't the gabbiest guest. In fact, he stood by the back door staring into the night as still as…well, a gargoyle. I had no doubt others were watching the front of the house too.

I wouldn't be sleeping again that night so I sat on the couch holding a cup of tea that had long since gone cold. Grim, Princess and Jacoby all sat in silent vigil with me. Princess spread herself on the couch with her head on my lap. I absently stroked her mane. Jacoby kept sighing and patting my hand like an old grandmother. And Grim? He was pissed. He sat on the mantle above the cold hearth and stared out the patio doors. His tail swished like the pendulum on a clock. My hand kept going to the bandage on my neck. The cut was small and had already stopped bleeding, but it could have been so much worse.

An hour later, Mason burst through the door. His fancy suit jacket and tie were gone. He looked like he'd run the whole way instead of driving.

"Are you okay?" He pulled me into his arms without waiting for an answer.

"I will be. I'm sorry you had to come all the way back here tonight." I could feel the tears coming again and held them back by sheer force of will. I didn't want to cry in front of him. I'd been through much worse than this, so why couldn't I hold it together?

"I'm glad to be home, believe me. Come on. Let's go to bed."

He picked me up and I cuddled against him. He was warm and solid.

"Wait." I put one hand on his chest. "I have to know. What did Dutch do with her?"

Mason didn't say anything until we made it to the bedroom. Then he set me on the bed and said, "She's gone. Dutch will to dump her in the Barrows, and I've already revoked her visa. She won't be getting back into Montreal."

I lay back on my pillow, feeling suddenly drained. Barrows was good. It was the shanty town outside the fae gate, way over on the other side of the island. Without access to the city, Gunora would have to cross two rivers and fifty kilometers of the Inbetween to get back here—an impossible journey for a lone woman on foot.

I was safe. For now.

Oscar must have put a bug in Dutch's ear. Two days after Gunora left, I found him looking through my closet with a frown. His long craggy face frowned really well, like the disapproval of my habits had settled into the creases on his cheeks.

My closet held only one dress. The rest was an assortment of weapons, jeans, leather jackets and work shirts. Most of my clothes were piled on the small dressing table in the corner.

"How do you find anything in here?" Dutch asked.

I pointed to the three piles of laundry. "Those are clean enough to wear again. Those are iffy, but might go another day for a messy job, and those—"

"Those are disgusting enough to walk to the washing machine on their own," he said with one raised eyebrow.

"Something like that." I grinned and he favored me with a reluctant smile. Saving me from a maniacal cousin had finally broken the ice between us.

He picked up one of my grimy work shirts. It was splattered with elkthorn syrup, a concoction I brewed to keep viper slugs off a certain customer's prize tomato plants. Elkthorn smelled like urine with a touch of rotting corpse in the mix, so Dutch's look of revulsion was entirely excused.

He sighed and dropped the offensive shirt. "You know I can do your laundry for you. I do all of Mason's and my own. It wouldn't be a bother."

I squirmed on the spot. He was right, but it didn't make me comfortable.

I'd forbidden him from doing my laundry, not because he wasn't capable. I just felt that a grown-up should do her own laundry. When I got around to it.

Dutch inspected the rest of my dressing table. He picked up my tiny makeup bag with one mascara, lip gloss and concealer, and actually tisked. Then he eyed me up and down.

"What are you, a size eight dress? Size nine shoe?"

I nodded. He had a keen eye.

The next day, I found my closet filled with dresses and smart business suits. And my dressing table suddenly had enough makeup to cover a zombie apocalypse film set.

The dirty laundry was gone. I decided not to make a fuss about that.

Moving in with someone was hard. Mason and I were learning to dance around each other in the bathroom. His light snore woke me sometimes and I, apparently, was a blanket hog.

The situation was made harder by the fact that we weren't really alone in this relationship. Mason had Dutch and his Guardians. I had Gita and my menagerie. And the goblins were never far away. Not to mention the fact that I'd brought home a murderous relative only a week into our new co-habitation.

But we were learning. Adapting. Still…some days I missed my little apartment and piles of questionable laundry.

I stood gazing into the well-stocked closet like a pheasant staring down the barrel of a hunter's shotgun.

In less than two weeks, Mason would announce his bid for Prime Minister. He was already preparing for that by meeting with influential business people, Hub officials, ministers from the Alchemist party, and celebrities. I was supposed to make many of those appearances with him, and I wasn't such a bumpkin to think that I could rub elbows with Montreal's elite wearing jeans and t-shirts. But all the new clothes and accessories were a bit overwhelming.

"I have no idea what to do with all this stuff," I complained to Mason.

He watched me from the bed, wearing nothing but shorts. It was very distracting.

Even from across the room, I could tell his magic was calmer. He'd spent hours every morning with Errol, learning how to filter the thousands of tiny magics of everyday life, and he was a quick study. Already, the rough edges had been smoothed from his aura.

"I believe that Dutch has also taken care of that," he said. "He hired you a stylist."

Stylist. Just the word gave me hives. I flopped dramatically on the bed next to Mason and flung the sheet over my face.

"It'll be okay." He rubbed my shoulder. "Maybe even fun. Aren't girls supposed to like playing dress up? Didn't you have Barbies when you were a kid?"

"I did. But they were eaten by my t-rex doll."

"Of course they were."

I groaned again.

"Is everything okay?"

I whipped the sheet off my head. My hair was loose and it stuck to my face with static. I wiped it away and looked up at Mason. He watched me with that dark, penetrating stare of his, like he could see right inside my skull.

"Tell me." His fingers kneaded my shoulder and I scooted closer.

"Dutch did my laundry."

"Oh. Should I fire him?"

"You're making fun of me!"

"Just a bit." He leaned down and kissed the back of my shoulder.

"I'm just used to doing things for myself."

"You won't have time to do it all, whether you like it or not. You'll need help. Dutch is help. It's what I pay him to do and he's good at it."

"Fine. I'll wear the pretty clothes," I grumped.

"Not just yet. It's much too hot for clothes." He pulled me toward him, lifting me so I sat on his lap and nestled against his bare chest. We'd only just rediscovered each other after what felt like weeks apart. And so, for the next few hours we forgot about clothes, media appearances, mad cousins, and the rest of the world.

OUR FIRST PUBLIC event was an appearance at the symphony hall for a production of Brahms Second Symphony. We'd be on full display in the alchemist box. Mason said only that formal attire was required. I had no idea what that meant. While I stood in front of the closet-from-hell, dithering over one fancy dress or another, Chantal arrived. My new stylist.

"Sit." She put down two heavy leather cases and pointed at the bench facing my dressing table. Then she fluttered around me like a pixie on crack, examining my "bones and lines" as she put it. And with her delicate features, willowy frame and slightly pointed ears, I suspected she did have some fae blood in her lineage. I keened little power coming from her, but what she did with foundation could only be called magic.

"First we must lose these." She wrinkled her nose and lifted one of my braids.

"You can't cut my hair." I folded my arms over my chest, and crossed one knee over the other. I would have turned myself inside out to get away from Chantal's prying fingers. It was no use. She gently uncrossed my legs, and unfolded my arms.

"You must sit straight, yes?" she said in her faint French accent. "Only then can I truly see you. You want to look nice for Mr. Mason, yes? For all the others who will see you on his arm and admire the beautiful couple, yes?"

"Yes, yes, yes," I grumbled.

"And what is this?" She clucked over the scab on my throat.

"It's nothing." I tried to cover it with my hands, but she pulled them away and clucked some more.

"No worries, we will cover it up, yes?" She beamed and opened one of her cases. Out popped three tiers of creams, powders, brushes and pencils.

"Oh, yay."

Three hours later, Chantal had transformed me. She not only trimmed my hair and added layers so it fell down my back in a rich mane, but she also covered the dark circles under my eyes and even my scar. I turned left and right, inspecting my throat in the mirror. It was like the wound had never happened. That was good. I didn't want to think about Gunora anymore. She was dead to me. Once again, I was the only Valkyrie on Terra. Time to move on to other things, like getting Mason elected.

I sat through the rest of Chantal's ministrations. She plucked and lined my eyebrows, shadowed my eyes in smoky kohl, and dressed me in a coppery gown that hugged me in all the right places and flared into a ruffled skirt. I stood before the full-length mirror and swished it from side to side. The material had a pearly sheen, and when I moved it shimmered. The highlights softened me where I needed softening. The shadows accentuated curves I didn't even know I had.

"The color suits, yes?" Chantal fluffed my hair that matched the same copper highlights as the dress.

"Mason won't even recognize me."

"This is a good thing." Chantal winked. "Never let them think they know you."

I didn't recognize the woman staring back at me from the mirror. She was confident, elegant and put together. I could only hope to live up to her promise.

Chantal followed me out to the great room where Jacoby waited. He was full of nervous energy and dancing from foot to foot. Someone (probably Dutch) had cleaned him up. Instead of his usual scruffy bear backpack, he wore a neat brown leather vest with a pocket for Errol. Even the fringe of fur around his eyes had been combed.

"Wow! Kyra-lady. You looks just like a girl!"

"Thank you, Jacoby. You look very nice too."

He ran a hand over his new vest and beamed.

Errol poked his grizzled head out of the pocket and whistled through his mustache.

"Thank you, too." I nodded. "You guys know your job tonight, right?"

Jacoby stood straight, like a soldier receiving orders. "Stays close to Mr. Mason!"

"That's right. Don't get in anybody's way, but keep Errol close to Mason."

People exhaled magic with every breath. It came out of their pores and hung about them like a miasma at all times. Mason had only begun to master the keening. It would be easy to become overwhelmed in room full of posturing politicians and media types.

Errol had a much finer hold on his magic than I did. He would be sure to keep Mason warded, so I could concentrate on smiling, shaking hands and making nice—not something I excelled at.

Jacoby took my hand in his fuzzy fingers. "Don'ts worry, Kyra-lady. No one ever notices us. We stays close and keeps Mr. Mason safe."

"That's good." I rubbed him behind the ear, careful not to mess up his coif. "Do you know where Mason is now?"

"Outsides." Jacoby pointed to the patio.

"Okay. You go tell Dutch we're ready to leave."

Jacoby bounded off. Chantal hovered around me, tweaking the line of the gown even as I strode through the patio door.

Outside, Mason leaned against the low balcony wall, talking on his widget. The glow of the setting sun framed him, and a light wind tossed his hair. His suit was a throwback to another era, with a long coat tail, cummerbund, ruffled shirt front and white tie.

"He looks amazing, yes?" Chantal whispered in my ear. "This style, it will remind them of where he comes from. Of how *long* he has walked this earth, yes?"

I nodded. Power could be flaunted in many ways. Age had its respect, but there was something to be said for keeping up with the times too. Regardless, Mason did look amazing. His black hair and olive complexion were smart against the white shirt. The dark suit jacket didn't hide the bulk of his shoulders. It was custom cut to flex when he moved, showing off the line of muscles across his shoulders and back.

He heard us coming and turned, widget still pressed to his ear. His eyes didn't widen when he saw me. They smoldered.

"I'll call you back." He disconnected.

Chantal backed away, leaving us alone.

Mason continued to stare. Every muscle in me was clenched up as I stood under his inspection. I crossed the flagstones, feeling awkward, gangly, and somehow naked. His eyes never left mine. When I reached him, he took my hand and breathed a kiss across my knuckles, a throw-back to his days of chivalry.

"You're beautiful." A dark light glinted in his eye. "I only get to see your hair down when we make love. I'm not sure I like sharing that sight with others."

"Oh, well, we could just stay in. Watch a movie. Make popcorn?" I ran a hand down the exquisite gown. My palms were damp.

"I wish we could." He smiled sadly. "I hope this won't be too hard on you. The press will be there. We'll both be in the spotlight. Can you handle that?"

"Of course." I lifted my chin just a bit. In reality, there was nothing I wanted less than to be in front of the cameras. But Mason had risked his life for me, more than once. He'd never protested when I needed help. Never. Now he needed me. He wanted to make changes in our city, and the only way to do that was from inside the bubble of power. He needed to be elected. And if that meant I had to play the dutiful girlfriend for a few weeks, then so be it. I could give him that.

Mason saw right through my charade of confidence.

"I'll make it up to you. I promise." He squeezed my fingers. "Now let's get out of here before I tear that dress off you and mess up all of Chantal's artistry."

CHAPTER

14

The evening of the big reveal arrived. The last ten days had been a whirlwind of press events, photo opportunities and town hall forums, all leading up to this gala where Mason would officially announce his bid for Prime Minister of the Alchemists. As Mason's official plus-one, I'd been on point at all times. When I closed my eyes at night, I saw flash bulbs going off. Emil had pared down my schedule to the bare minimum, but I still spent mornings chasing vermin or wrangling errant brownies. Then I'd rush home to wash blood, dirt, and slime out of my hair before letting Chantal work her magic. It was exhausting.

Mason worked even harder. In his rare moments of down time, he practiced warding himself with Errol. The little bodach was never far away, boosting Mason's protection when his energy flagged.

The gala dinner would celebrate the renaming of the Montreal Opera House to Icewolf Opera House in honor of Leighna Icewolf, Queen of the Fae and founding member of the Montreal Triumvirate. Mason and I sat at the head table. I fidgeted with my napkin and gazed at the assembled guests. They were a good mix of fae, humans and alchemists. My keening had picked up a few shifters on the way in too. Since Leighna's death, tension between the factions had been high. It was nice to see everyone come together to honor her. Diplomacy had always been Leighna's strength. Once more, she brought peace to the squabbling crowd.

Along with celebrating the deceased queen, the gala was a fundraiser for new infrastructure. The Alchemists always had plans to bolster the efficiency of the ward, to improve our roads and electrical grid, but all that cost money, so they never went to the bargaining table empty handed. This fundraiser was unusual in that it had bipartisan support from the fae and humans.

After last year's insurrection, all parties recognized the need to plug leaks in the ward. Queen Leighna's brother Alvar had punched a door in the ward to access Underhill, the fae home world. And while that door had been sealed, it brought to light other deficiencies in our system. After a close inspection, Alchemists had found several weak spots, places around the island where the ward's coverage was thin enough that a strong mage might damage it.

We'd beaten back the opji vampires who banded with Alvar, but they'd had a taste of us, and many security specialists expected them to be back for more. No one wanted to relive the early days after the war, when opji attacks were common and we had no defenses to hide behind.

So fundraising. Fun.

Merrow, the new Fae Prime Minister, nodded to me from across the table. Someone came up to her and offered his hand to shake. Merrow stared at him until he lowered it. She didn't touch others unless she was trying to kill them. Her dark, fierce eyes were deeply set against a pale gray face. Glossy black hair was cut short to reveal ears that swept back from her face in long points. This wasn't a glamor. This was one of her two forms. The other was a monstrous, bone-plated beast with wings. I'd seen her take on a dozen opji vampires in that form. But today she wore her diplomatic face. It was only slightly less scary than her fighting face.

She took a seat farther down the table and I was glad we weren't seated close enough for conversation. I was the only one who knew that under duress, she'd betrayed the queen to the witch, Polina. It wasn't a piece of news I planned to use against her, but it made conversation between us awkward. I nodded, plastered a smile on my painted face, and made small talk with the fae minister to my right.

He was big and bluff, red-haired and ruddy-complexioned, with ears like cabbages and eyes that were just a bit too green. His magic smelled like pickled onions. He'd been around a long time and had the war stories to prove it.

"Aye! We taught those opji vermin a lesson they never forgot!" He punctuated the end of his tale by pounding a meaty fist on the table. The forks jumped. His glass of wine spilled. I stood up, pretending the wine had splashed me. Really, I just needed a break from the insufferable minister.

He pushed his chair back hard enough that it toppled. "My lady, my apologies. I didna mean to be such a bumblin' oaf." He reached for my hand, but I pulled away.

"Don't worry." I fluttered my napkin at him. "I'll just go tidy up." I turned and headed for the ladies' room before he could answer.

A small stage was set up at the front of the room beside the orchestra. Mason intercepted me as I passed by it. I spied Jacoby lingering in his shadow.

Good dervish.

"Are you okay?" Mason asked.

"I'm fine. I just need a break."

His hand slid around my waist, but he didn't pull me closer, and I didn't lean into his touch. Not here. Not with so many eyes on us.

"Did I tell you how incredible you look tonight?"

Chantal had dressed me in a long black sheath that flattered my height and lean muscle. His hand tightened on my hip. He leaned in and whispered in my ear, "But I miss your filthy jeans. They have much easier access."

A laugh caught in my throat when I thought of Chantal's face if I'd shown up to the gala in my work jeans.

Mason stood back and watched me with a half grin and one eyebrow quirked. When he looked at me like that, I lost all control of my limbs. My knees buckled and I pressed into him. My fingers dug into his starched shirt. He pulled me into the shadows behind the stage and circled me in his arms. His mouth found that sensitive spot under my jaw.

"I'm sorry. I know you hate this." His breath was hot against my skin. "It won't be for much longer. I promise."

"It's okay. Do what you need to do."

"Don't tempt me." He pulled away with a wolfish grin. "What I need is you."

"Tone it down, lovebirds." Oscar hissed from behind us. "It's time to change the world. Are you ready?"

Mason stood a little taller and nodded. Oscar strode onto the stage and stopped in front of a microphone.

"Is this thing working?" He tapped the mic with one finger. Speakers exploded with sound. The music from the orchestra wound down. The crowd quieted. Chairs scraped against the floor as people turned to face the stage.

"I want to thank you all for being here tonight," Oscar continued. "Queen Leighna Icewolf was a dear friend, and she loved music. I'm happy to see her honored with her name on this iconic building. Leighna also loved Montreal. The very spells rooted in our ward came from her magic. She had faith that the peoples of this great city could live side-by-side in harmony. She would be pleased to see us gathered here tonight to raise funds for badly needed repairs to our infrastructure. Montreal has a history of bipartisan politics. It's what makes this ward unique. It's the reason refugees swarm our gates." This got a boo from the crowd, and Oscar held up one hand to quiet them. "It's why fae, humans and alchemists can not only live together, but prosper!" There was polite clapping at that. "And though I enjoyed my brief tenure as interim Prime Minister, I will be glad to pass the torch to younger, more capable hands. With that in mind, I would like to introduce my dear friend, Henry Mason."

I squeezed Mason's hand once more and stepped back into the shadows, nearly tripping over Jacoby.

Mason crossed the stage to shake Oscar's hand, then pulled him into a hug and thumped him on the back. This brought a few cheers. Mason smiled and said something for Oscar's ears alone.

"Go get 'em, tiger," I whispered.

Jacoby tugged on my gown.

"I follows him?" His big eyes were all pupil in the dim light. Errol peeked from his pocket but all his attention was for Mason.

"No, stay here." It would look odd for the dervish to follow him on stage. No one in this room needed to know that Mason was weak right now. He'd have to fight through his magic sensitivity on his own for the next few minutes. I gripped Jacoby's shoulders as he leaned against my knees. Errol rapped my knuckles with his walking twig.

"Mftlbt." *He'll be fine.*

On the stage, Mason took over the microphone. He was made for the spotlight. It shone off his blue-black hair and highlighted the chiseled planes of his brow and cheekbones.

"Thank you for that warm welcome, Oscar." He showed his teeth to the crowd. Enough of the assembled guests would recognize that as a predatory expression instead of a smile. "You all know what I have to say, so I won't make you wait any longer. I am officially running for Prime Minister of the Alchemist Party. I hope to have your support on election day!" His last words were drowned out by cheering. From the corner of the room, where the alchemists were seated, someone whistled and thumped the table. Mason stood at seeming ease through this outpouring of support, but I knew the ramped up emotion in the room would be bombarding his keening. Errol mumbled a protection spell, but he was too far away. It would barely skim the edge off the magical deluge.

After several minutes of cheering, the crowd settled. Mason had gone pale. Sweat glistened on his forehead. I hoped everyone would think the spotlights were the cause.

Despite his discomfort, he pulled off his carefully prepared speech without a hitch. He spoke about infrastructure, refugees, resources, transportation, and food. Feeding an entire ward when agricultural space was policed by an angry god was rightfully at the top of any politician's agenda. As he went on, the crease between his brows eased. He spoke quietly but with authority. Instead of platitudes he offered real-world solutions. Hub should have a bigger presence in the shanty towns outside the ward gates. Refugees could be hired as day-laborers in the fields. New technologies from the alchemists meant the militia could more safely patrol our borders. The ill-fated train to Manhattan Ward would be put back online and Montrealers could expect great benefits from trade with our neighbors to the south.

I was proud of the thought and hard work that had gone into his campaign platform. I just hoped the people of Montreal would elect him and give him the opportunity to make those changes.

As he wound down his speech, a group of men caused a disturbance at the back of the room. Mason ignored them until they pushed through the crowd to stand in front of the stage. There were four of them, and they wore togas like frat house rejects.

Olympians.

Oh, dear Zeus, what are your children up to?

Security guards were already pushing through the crowd to detain them.

The tallest Olympian held a giant rod shaped like a lightning bolt. He pumped his fist in the air and the rod glowed bright blue.

"Will the Alchemists support the godlings to form a fourth political party?" He shouted loud enough that, even without a microphone, most of the room heard him. The guards surrounded the godlings.

"It's all right." Mason held out his hands in a placating gesture. "Please, let me address their concerns." The guards held back, but had batons out and ready.

"For those of you in the back who didn't hear the question, these men want to know if I support the right of the godlings to form a fourth party." Mason spoke into the microphone. "And yes, I do. I believe that all people should have representation in Parliament."

Someone shouted, "What about the shifters then? And the witches? Do they get their own parties too?"

This caused more shouting. Someone shoved a guard. He turned and lashed out with his baton. The other guards rushed the Olympians, but their leader squirmed away. He jumped onto the stage and waved his glowing rod.

"Zeus above all others!" A blue bolt of galvanic energy zapped the ceiling, setting the crown molding on fire. The flames quickly spread to the curtains that hung at the back of the stage.

"Fire!" someone in the crowd screamed.

The room erupted in chaos. One of the toga-clad rebels punched a guard, then fell under the lash of his baton. Another guard was jumped from behind. The Olympians had allies in the crowd. Fights broke out everywhere as regular guests screamed and stampeded for the exits.

Mason called for order, but no one paid attention.

The Olympian on stage shouted incoherently, waving his lightning stick. More blue fire burst from it. More screams came from the already panicked crowd.

Mason swung a fist at the Olympian, but he ducked under it and came up waving his staff again. Jagged blue bolts shot from the rod in all directions. People screamed and ran, trampling others.

The ceiling above the orchestra and stage collapsed with a crash and a bilious cloud of dust and debris.

"Mason!" I screamed and lunged for the stage, but two strong hands clamped around my waist and lifted me off the ground. I twisted to see my captor. It was Berto, Captain of the Guardians.

"Let me go!" I struggled in his grip. Berto spread his massive wings, knocking panicked onlookers aside. He flew over the crowd with me grasped tightly against his chest. He didn't let go until we were standing in the parking lot under the light summer drizzle.

I immediately turned to run back inside. Berto blocked me. His gargoyle face with the duck bill should have looked comical, but the dark determination in his eyes made him fierce. His wings were still spread wide, holding back the mass of confused onlookers.

"I have to get to Mason!"

Berto held up a hand to stall me. Then he fished a widget from his pocket and answered a call. He listened for a minute and grunted an agreement, then passed the widget to me.

"He wants to speak to you."

I grabbed the widget. "Mason? Are you still inside? Are you okay?"

"I'm fine. Everything is under control in here. Fire's out. But there are a lot of wounded."

Sirens filled the night. I gripped the widget like a life-line.

"I'm coming to help."

"No, Dutch is on his way to take you home." Mason sounded tired. That outpouring of magic couldn't have been easy for him. I glanced around the parking lot.

"Jacoby! Is he with you?"

"He's here. They're both here and fine. Errol will stay with me until I can get away."

That was something at least.

"Are you really okay?" My voice sounded small and lost.

He reassured me again, and then I had to let him go.

I handed the phone back to Berto.

"Thank you for getting me out of there," I said. Berto nodded. I wiped rain from my eyes, and my hand came away covered in mascara. The hem of my dress was drenched in muddy water. Chantal would be horrified by the mess.

"Kyra!" A familiar voice cut through the noise of the crowd. Berto stepped in front of me, then relaxed.

"Gabe!" I flung my arms around his neck. He hugged me hard.

"Are you all right? Hurt?"

I shook my head. "I'm fine. But Mason said there are wounded inside."

"Damn them to hell." He made a fist and punched the empty air as if wishing it were someone's face.

"You know them? The Olympians?" A sour spot formed in my gut. Gabe's family was one of the driving forces behind the godling uprising.

I grabbed his arm, digging my nails into his skin. "Tell me you didn't have anything to do with this!"

"Ow!" He shook off my grip. "No! Those damned Olympians are hotheads. We've been trying to work with them, but all they want is to blow up things, to make a big splash. They think no one will take us seriously otherwise."

"Hub is taking them seriously now." I pointed to where officers were dragging the handcuffed Olympians from the hall. The leader had lost his lightning toy and sported a pretty new broken nose. His toga was torn, exposing a thin, bare chest.

"Didn't anyone tell him the Ancient Greeks didn't wear togas?" I said.

"They're all idiots." Gabe glowered. "I knew they were up to something. Now they've set back negotiations by months."

"They'll be lucky if they don't end up on Grandill," I said, talking about the prison island that housed Montreal's worst offenders. I stepped back as a paramedic came out of the hall, pushing a gurney. A man with a blackened face lay on it.

What a great way to honor the queen who had brought peace and prosperity to this city.

Paramedics brought out more wounded. Some were ambulatory. Others were strapped to gurneys and loaded into ambulances.

Hub officers had also rounded up a bunch of the crowd. Those who had used the chaos to enjoy a good brawl would spend a few hours in lockup for their efforts. The detainees filed out of the building in handcuffs. A few looked defiant. Others were dejected. One tall, blond-haired figure in a red dress stood out from the others.

Gunora.

Then the woman turned and I saw a scared stranger. Not Gunora, just my stressed-out imagination making more problems. Gunora was banned from Montreal, she couldn't hurt me anymore. But as I rode in the car beside Dutch through the long journey home, I couldn't help thinking that every time Mason and I put down one threat a new one popped up.

15

A pebble hit me on the elbow, startling me back to attention.

"All right!" I said to Hunter and tossed him another stick. One tentacle rose and snatched it out of the air. He passed the stick from arm to arm, tasting it with his many suckers.

We were having a little family outing down by the stream that wound through the trees behind the gatehouse. I'd thought fresh air would do Hunter some good. Now I was stuck in a game of toss the stick. Jacoby snored on the grass beside me, his arms and legs splayed wide. Kur was also enjoying the outing. As an ice sprite, the summer heat began to wear on him in July. He was waddling along the riverbank, his fat little feet stirring up the muck. Oddly, no matter how much he played in the dirt, his feathery white fur was always pristine. Maybe he was made of Teflon.

Farther down the stream bank. Errol and Mason were practicing personal wards. That was what had caught my attention. Mason sat so deeply in a trance he looked like a gargoyle again. The cut of his nose was sharp. His eyelashes didn't even flutter. It was a face that could—and did—distract me.

"Ow!" Another pebble hit my arm. Kur made a little grunting noise and dove after the rock. I tossed another twig at Hunter.

Around us, the Inbetween forest breathed in and out in a steady beat. Sunlight shone through the branches, leaving round dapples like shiny coins on the leaves.

And *he* was watching us. The hidebehind. I keened his presence across the creek in a grove of cedars. I didn't get that I'm-hiding-because-you-are-prey kind of vibe from him. He was just shy and would reveal himself when the time was right. But for now he was happy to watch.

Yes, it really was a perfect morning.

The twins, Tums and Tad, came hurtling down the hill from the gatehouse.

"Miss Kyra! Mister Mason!" Tums shouted. Tad ran after him. Tums tripped and the two of them tumbled the last few feet to the river bank.

"Settle down boys before you hurt yourselves!" I said. They sat up with solemn expressions. Tad's pants were grass-stained and a stick poked out of Tums's ragged mop of hair.

"What's the problem?" I asked.

"Mr. Dutch…" Tums was still out of breath from his mad dash. "He says to come right away, Miss Kyra! And Mr. Mason too! He says…he says it's 'portant. Real 'portant." Tad nodded to show his support.

And just like that, our perfect day was over.

"Come, Miss Kyra!" Tums pulled on my hand. Tad copied his brother and grabbed my other hand.

"Okay. I'm coming." I laughed and extricated myself from the sticky fingers. "Can you boys bring Kur and Hunter back to the barn? Ask Muzzy or Gibus to help you put them away."

The boys splashed into the water to grab the two critters and ran back up the hill. Jacoby yawned and stretched.

"You'd better follow them," I said. "Make sure Hunter gets back in his tank. Then come and join us in the house." Jacoby nodded and trotted after the boys.

The disturbance had brought Mason out of his trance.

"Something the matter?" He rubbed the kinks from his neck.

"Dutch wants us in the house. Seems important."

Hand in hand, we climbed the steep hill to the road and followed it back to the house.

Inside, Berto and another Guardian were camped around the vid-screen where a news reel was playing. Grim sat by the unlit fire, but his attention was on the screen too. Dutch sat at Mason's desk with his widget held out in front of him as he spoke into it.

"I don't care if she's in a meeting," he said. "I need to speak to Captain

Lowe. Now!" Dutch could really hone the edge on his tone when he needed it.

"Yes, sir. Just a moment." This voice came through the tiny widget speaker, then it switched to techno-elevator music as Dutch was put on hold.

"What's going on?" I asked.

"Look." Dutch nodded toward the vid-screen on the wall behind the desk. The sound was muted, but a "Breaking News" banner scrolled across the bottom of the screen. A reporter stood in front of Hub Station, narrating the scene behind him. A Hub van was parked in front of the station doors. The words "Murder charges pending" scrolled across the scene.

I grabbed the remote to unmute the feed just as Dutch began talking into his widget again. He got up and went outside. I stood riveted to the scene unfolding in downtown Montreal.

"One Knacker was shot and killed at the scene." The perky reporter seemed thrilled to be on camera, despite the grim report. "At least two others opened fire on Hub officers, killing one and wounding another before militia secured the North Gate." The image on screen switched to an aerial view of the gate on Crystal Bridge that led off the island to the north. The shanty town known as the Barrows was surrounded by armored militia vehicles. Hub didn't screw around when it came to threats against the ward or the gates.

The image on screen shifted again, this time to a night scene, presumably filmed last night. Soldiers used battering rams to knock in doors and drag everyone into the street for questioning. Entire families huddled together while Hub cleared the area. The Barrows wasn't a sanctioned town. Its inhabitants had no rights under Ward law. Still the brutality of the scene made me cross my arms against my chest and shiver.

"I've got Captain Lowe." Dutch held out the widget. Mason took it and went outside to speak to her.

I watched the video, enraptured by the unfolding drama. The image shifted back to Hub Station, still night time. Red and blue lights tinted the scene in nauseating flashes. The chatty reporter narrated the clip.

"This was the scene early this morning around one o'clock when officers brought in the suspect, now being held on a possible murder charge."

An armored van pulled up. The back door opened and two soldiers jumped out. They wore full tactical gear—helmets and body armor—and held blasters ready. One pointed the gun toward the waiting crowd. Shouts could be heard in the background. The other guard pointed his weapon into the van.

Everyone stood still for a moment. Even the obnoxious reporter fell silent. Then Hub doors opened and an alchemist mage stepped out. I recognized him by the signature white coat and shoulder badge that ranked him as a Mage Protector, the highest alchemist rank within Hub militia. He approached the back of the van with hands extended in front of him as if he held an invisible ball. His lips moved as he chanted, too low for the reporter's camera to pick it up. But I knew what he was doing. If I'd been on scene instead of watching it remotely, I would have keened magic pouring off him. He was extending his personal ward to encircle the van and the prisoner inside.

Wow. That was one bad-ass prisoner to need all this extra security. Hub wasn't just worried about physical violence. They were worried the prisoner would blast their way out of the van with magic.

With the barrel of his gun, one of the guards made a motion for the prisoner to hurry up. A foot appeared, then a hand on the open door.

Gunora jumped down from the back of the van. She was in matron mode, strong, beautiful and defiant.

My mind froze. Dutch had left her in the Barrows only two weeks ago, and already she'd fallen in with the Knackers again.

"There won't be any bail this time," Mason said, right beside me. I'd been so focused on the vid-screen, I hadn't heard him come back inside.

"Did you talk to Captain Lowe?" I asked. It wouldn't matter. This was Gunora's second arrest. There was no doubt now that she was really working with the Knackers. And now a Hub officer was dead and another in hospital in critical condition. There would be no leniency this time.

"Yeah. She won't even consider it." Mason dragged a hand through his hair.

I nodded. My chest hurt and I realized that I'd been holding my breath as I watched the mage prod Gunora into the station. The soldiers had their blaster sights fixed on her.

"Do you think she did it?" Mason asked.

"I don't know. Probably." My chest felt hot and tight. Gunora wasn't my friend. She'd made that perfectly clear. But she was family, and I'd failed her. I'd sent her away when she needed my help. I hadn't tried hard enough to make her see that there could be another solution, another cure. So I would help her now, for Aaric's sake, even if the only thing I could do was bear witness to her end.

"Why are's you sad, Kyra-Lady?" Jacoby slipped his hand into mind. I squeezed it and pointed to the screen with my other hand.

"That's my cousin. Remember her?" Jacoby nodded. "She's in trouble."

"What is cousin?"

"Cousin is family." I smiled down at him. Jacoby had no dervish family of his own. Dervishes are usually solitary creatures. But that life hadn't suited him, and when I welcomed him to our odd-ball home, he embraced the idea of family with a solid grip.

"Then we shoulds help her!" The fringe around his eyes bristled.

"I'm not sure we can."

ontreal justice was swift. Three weeks later, three judges convicted Gunora on two counts of murder. Hub investigated for less than a week. The whole sordid tale came out during the three-day trial.

Gunora had been working with the Knackers to smuggle black market goods into the city—drugs and illegal magical artifacts. The first dead Hub officer was complicit in the deal but got cold feet at the last minute. He died by Gunora's hand, according to the prosecution. The second Hub officer succumbed to his mysterious injuries. The official autopsy proved he'd died by "no ordinary means." In other words, magic had killed him in some way they would never decipher. But the investigating officers had enough proof to tie his murder to Gunora too.

I sat in the courtroom for three long days. During his closing arguments, the prosecution painted Gunora as a conniving, controlling, bloody-minded witch—a being with too much magic and no sense of morality.

"He's aiming for a sentence to Grandill Prison," Mason whispered. He'd been with me at the trial as often as his schedule would allow.

The prosecutor took every opportunity to remind the judges about Gunora's deadly magic. I wasn't sure I believed them. Gunora had always excelled in the arcane arts, but I would hardly call her a witch. Valkyrie magic tended to be subtle and passive. Take away our swords and all we could do was sense magic and gently coax it to our will. My affinity for green magic came from the dryad side of my family.

But Mason was right. The prosecutor was setting her up to be sentenced as one who was a danger to the ward. Only hardened criminals with too much magic to keep in a regular cell were sent to the prison island.

My gut churned at the thought of Gunora alone in that hellish place.

She sat through the proceedings, ashen-faced and silent. Twice during the trial, she shifted forms. Once, when she spontaneously shifted from mother to crone, the prosecutor had been in the middle of a cross-examination. He paused to let the gasps from the spectators die down, then pointed at Gunora and said, "I submit to the court, proof of the accused's shape-shifting abilities."

I clenched my fists in my lap. If a convict could shape-shift, they faced automatic deportation to Grandill.

During the rest of the trial, Gunora's expression never changed, even when the lawyer tried to sway the three judges by describing the injuries to the dead men in detail.

After all arguments were made, the human judge turned to Gunora and asked, "Did you do this?"

Her advocate stood. "Your honor, my client does not have to—"

"Sit down." The judge's name was Ashlyn Meyers and she had been recently appointed to the bench by the new human Prime Minister. "I want to hear the defendant. Did you kill these men?"

Crone Gunora rose. She was frail and pitiful. Her eyes were ringed in dark shadows. Sallow skin hung from her jaws and cheekbones. She spoke only three words, and those barely above a whisper. "I did not."

In Montreal law, there were no juries. Every case was decided by a panel of three judges, one fae, one human and one alchemist. The decision had to be unanimous.

The judges deliberated for only an hour and returned with a guilty verdict.

"Sentencing will be August eighth." Judge Meyers banged her gavel, but the court had already erupted into excited chatter.

A guard jerked Gunora to her feet and snapped handcuffs to her wrists. She didn't react. But as he dragged her from the courtroom, her eyes never left mine until she was finally pulled through the doors.

By this time, the press had discovered that I'd bailed Gunora out of jail a few weeks ago, and I couldn't leave the courthouse without being swarmed by reporters.

"Miss Greene! Did you know your cousin was a killer when you offered her bail?" A widget was pressed into my face to record my sound bite. Mason growled and swatted it away. He took me by the elbow and dragged me through the court to the door used only by judges, shielding me from the rabid reporters with his body. We fled via the courthouse service entrance.

For the next two days I hid at the house. Most reporters wouldn't risk a trip outside the ward, so I was left in peace. I planned to stay there until the media frenzy died down, but the All-father didn't like that plan.

On the morning of August seventh, the day before Gunora's sentencing, Mason found me on the back patio. I'd been staring into the trees, trying to clear my thoughts. It wasn't working. Images of Gunora's eyes as I'd last seen them haunted me. She'd been scared. Really scared.

"Captain Lowe wants you to see Gunora," Mason said.

"What?" I turned to him, thinking I'd heard wrong. "Why?"

"Some kind of deal. She has info about the Knackers. Her price for giving it up is speaking to you."

I hesitated for only a moment. Then Aaric's face came to mind, his soft eyes pleading with me to get along with his sister, for his sake. In that moment, I hated Gunora for stirring up all these old memories.

I sighed and got to my feet. "Let's go."

Two hours later, I sat in a small interrogation room at a Hub satellite station.

"Stay behind the line." The guard pointed at a yellow line of tape on the floor. "And no touching. If you need anything, wave to the camera." He pointed to the camera mounted in the corner of the room.

Gunora's whereabouts had been kept secret to avoid hysteria. The press had hyped her as a mega-witch capable of killing with a touch. I didn't buy it. Gunora had touched me many times, usually with a fist, and I'd only suffered very natural bruises for it. But I nodded to the guard. I would play by his rules. He brought me a chair and placed it behind the yellow line. I sat and stared at Gunora.

She was sitting behind a metal table, wearing a gray jumpsuit that hung on her like a sack. Chains wrapped her wrists and ankles and were shackled to the table. They rattled as she shifted in her chair. She was back in maid form and her eyes were exceptionally dark against her pale face. Her hair had been badly cut to frame her face like dandelion flax.

"I didn't kill those men." Her words had a flat echo in the room. She stared at me, and in that gaze, I could almost imagine the witch that so terrified everyone.

The air conditioner kicked on and I flinched. The cooler air was a blessing though. My t-shirt clung to the small of my back.

Gunora continued to stare at me.

"Why should I believe you?"

"I had no reason to kill them."

"The judges, the prosecution, the detectives and every citizen of Montreal disagree."

"I was just in the wrong place at the wrong time."

"Okay. I'll bite. Why were you with the Knackers then?"

She leaned in. The chains screeched against the metal table. "I found it. The way home."

"You're lying." I folded my arms over my chest.

"Not lying." Gunora's lips curled up in a smile that had no kindness in it, no softness or pleasure. "There is a pass through Jotunheim that leads right into Asgard. Baldyr's treaty still stands. We can go home."

Jotunheim, land of the Jötnar or giants. It was true. The giants had once raided Asgard at will. My grandfather had made a treaty with them, to end the endless war between our peoples. Theoretically, it was feasible to reach Asgard from there.

"And exactly how to you plan of finding the door between Terra and Jotunheim?" I asked.

There were very few giants on Terra. Even if she found one, they guarded the secrets of their home world with fierce loyalty.

"The Knackers do have a giant. I found him." She leaned forward. Her words were heavy with desperation. "He's been fighting in the cages. He's also one of their bouncers. That's why I was there when Hub raided the club. I had nothing to do with those murders."

She leaned back in her chair. A small satisfied smile played across her lips.

I didn't believe her. Maybe there was a giant, but I didn't believe that she was innocent of her crimes. Murder would be easy for her. And if she'd set her ice-encased heart on going home, a few Hub officers wouldn't stand in her way.

"So this giant offered to take you through the carefully guarded door to Jotunheim and guide you across his land for free?" I sunk a barrel full of sarcasm in my tone.

"I was working on him. We would have made a deal. But now?" She waved a hand at the steel door that locked her in. She saw the look of incredulity on my face and rushed on. "Wouldn't you do anything to see your mother again? Visit with Grandfather if the old goat is still alive?"

That was a low blow. To see my mother's face one more time! Just the thought of it was like a sucker punch to the gut. Asgard was the shiny and impossible lure. My mother had been alive ten years ago, but cancer would make certain that her days were short. She might already be dead. I would never know.

Going home seemed like an impossible dream. Even if Gunora had found a way, all that was pointless now. Gunora was in lockup, the giant had probably gone into hiding.

I narrowed my eyes at here. "What do you really want?"

"I need your help to get out of here."

And there it was.

"Help you? You're kidding right? Even if I wanted to—which I don't—I don't have that kind of pull with Hub." But I had a sinking feeling about where this conversation was going.

"You might not, but your boyfriend does."

Yep, she went there.

"He's running for Prime Minister. No one gets elected without friends in the right places. I want you to use those friends to get me out of here. Tell them to exile me. Fine. I'll leave this godsforsaken city and never come back." She smacked the table with the flat of her hand, making the chains crash.

Normally, exile to the Inbetween was considered a fate worse that imprisonment. It was a death sentence. But for Gunora it might actually be a mercy. I closed my eyes and Aaric's face haunted me…his gentle smile that could turn hard when someone he loved was threatened. Aaric would never have left Gunora to rot in prison. But then, he had left her. When he took his own life, he hadn't thought about his sister any more than he'd thought about me.

I opened my eyes. "I can't ask Mason to intervene. I won't."

"Please." She reached for me, even though twelve feet separated us. The sharp edge was gone from her voice. I could feel it in the tension rippling off her in waves. "I need to go home!" A sob escaped her throat and she hid her face in her hands.

The air conditioner died, leaving the room silent, except for the tiny sniffles coming from Gunora.

"I can't help you." I waved at the camera and the guard opened the door. As I walked away down the long hallway, I could still hear Gunora screaming my name like a curse.

C H A P T E R

17

On a Thursday morning in September, I loaded gear into my truck, getting ready for another day of wrangling pests. The days were getting shorter and the goblits took advantage of the cooler weather to play soccer in the yard. Jacoby, who was supposed to be helping me, stole a few minutes to play. Arriz was never far away from his brood, but he didn't like to have idle hands either, so he raked gravel on the driveway where he could keep an eye on them. The sounds of squealing children seemed as natural as the birds chirping out a greeting to the day. A sudden longing for a family of my own stabbed me like a knife in my gut. Where had that come from? Mason and I were nowhere near ready for kids. I wasn't sure we ever would be. But in Asgard there were always young cousins running around, kicking up dust, giggling or shouting. I hadn't realized how much I missed that youthful excitability until the goblits arrived.

Gunora's recent intrusion into my life had stirred up memories of Asgard that made homesickness burn in my gut.

A month had gone by since her sentencing—a month since she'd been sent to Grandill Prison with the other murderers and violent criminals deemed too dangerous to keep inside the ward.

She was probably already dead.

I had no idea if she'd given up evidence against the Knackers as she promised in return for my visit to the prison. The news had moved on to more mundane events. The Triumvirate was in a deadlock about the current budget. The human minister shouted in the senate that we needed more armed forces.

112

The fae wanted extra funds allocated to food supply, and the alchemists fought for higher taxes to complete their infrastructure works. The unsanctioned godling party used the division to their advantage, and their popularity was growing.

I found it hard to care about any of it.

After Gunora's sensational trial, Oscar and his team of media spin experts had decided it was better for me to distance myself from Mason's campaign. I was happy to stay out of the limelight, though it meant I saw less of Mason. He didn't need me or even Errol anymore. He'd mastered his magic sensitivity and got on well with the crowds of well-wishers at each campaign event.

If there seemed to be an inordinate number of pretty women in the crowds around him, I put that down to chance. But then, good looks never hurt a politician.

I spent my days on the job. Most people I met would never link the glamorous woman they'd seen on the vid-screen on Mason's arm with the grubby, working girl who came to rid their basements of rats. That was okay too.

When I was working, I could keep the door to my thoughts firmly closed. But in the evening, and when I woke in the dead of night from yet another nightmare, my mind churned.

I badgered Jacoby into the passenger seat, waved to the goblins and set the truck on the road to Montreal. My hands gripped the steering wheel too tightly.

Last night, I'd dreamed of Gunora again. The dream had haunted my nights for weeks. She'd been running for her life on the prison island, then the images would morph in that chaotic way of dreams, and the runner turned into my mother, chased by monsters with claws as big as daggers. I woke boiling in my own sweat, with a scream gurgling in my throat. Luckily, Mason spent more and more nights in Montreal and hadn't seen me so torn up.

I was unsettled. That was the word for it. Not sad, mad or anxious. Just unsettled. I pounded my fist on the wheel and Jacoby jumped in his seat.

"Sorry. I mumbled. Why don't you find something on the radio." The dervish grinned. I didn't usually let him touch the radio dials, but I didn't feel like making conversation.

I went back to brooding. It's not like I had personally sent Gunora to the island. And she had tried to kill me! But the more time that passed, the more my anger at her faded. She'd been desperate and not entirely in her right mind. Maybe she really hadn't killed those Hub officers. All she wanted to do was go home and live out what little time she had left. It really wasn't a lot to ask.

Unease rumbled through me.

My widget chimed and I pressed the speaker button to answer it. My old truck didn't have the fancy hands-free gadget like Mason's so his voice came through on the small echoing speaker of my widget.

"Morning, sunshine."

"Hey," I said.

"Hey to you. How are you feeling?" His voice was overshadowed by background noises—horns honking and other voices.

"I'm fine." I'd told Mason that I had some kind of low-grade flu to explain my recent lethargy, but he wasn't fooled. "I'm on my way to my first job."

"Okay. Do you have a full day? I won't be home tonight." The background noises faded. He must have stepped inside.

"Oh." I didn't hide the disappointment in my voice.

"Oscar has me running all day. Then I've got some corporate bigwigs to suck up to tomorrow morning, so I might as well stay here."

Mason had a room at Tor Hall, but until recent weeks, he rarely used it, preferring to make the journey home. Now he stayed in the city most nights, though I couldn't blame him. I wasn't great company.

"I'm sorry." His voice dipped low like he was trying not to be overheard. "I'll make it up to you."

"I'll hold you to that." I was already wondering how I would fill the endless hours between work and bedtime. "I'll see you tomorrow?"

"I'll be home by dinner." There was a black pause. "Kyra, you sure you're all right?" I could hear the concern in his voice and stifled a sigh.

"I'm good. Just tired."

"Ok. I'll call you tonight."

He disconnected and I suddenly felt very alone. Jacoby, who had a touch of the keening, patted my arm and made cooing noises.

IT HAD BEEN a slimy day. An eldritch screech had nested in a mall in Carterville. About the size and shape of howler monkeys, screeches were covered in mucus instead of fur. They were usually docile creatures except during mating season, which happened to be the hottest part of summer. Then the females would attack anything that came near their eggs. I'd been called in to relocate the nest before someone got hurt. Unfortunately, the screech had nested behind a Fruit Juicee kiosk. Apart from eating all the fruit stock, it had attacked customers. The kiosk owner tried to kill it on his own. With a barbecue fork. It didn't go well.

When I arrived, paramedics were trying to staunch the blood flow from his severed arm. The screech was hoarding the limb and hissing at anyone who came close.

"Why did you only call me in now?" I snapped at the Hub officer on duty. She was a new recruit and turned red before stammering, "I…don… don't know. I just got here."

In the end, I couldn't save the nest. Once a screech gets a taste of human flesh, they can't be tamed. And so the slime. My jeans were caked in it, and my giddy sword would need a good cleaning.

And that had been only the first job of the day.

By 7:00 pm I was bruised, crusty and exhausted. I thought I might even be tired enough to sleep without the dreams tonight. But bed was still hours away. I needed to unpack and restock my kit, shower and eat first.

I parked the truck beside the barn and left Jacoby sleeping in the passenger seat. He might stay there all night, but he could get out if he needed.

The lights were on in the barn. Muzzy and Tak were probably still working on the evening feeding. But when I dragged myself inside, the barn was quiet and empty.

"Hello?" I called out. The bats ruffled their wings at the disturbance but nobody answered. I knocked on the door to Gita's room. Nothing. I cracked it open. The banshee was gone.

Now that was weird. Gita rarely left her nest. But then I remembered Arriz and his shy flirtations, and wondered if they were out somewhere together.

I climbed the stairs to the upper level and went out the garage. The garage doors opened to my new garden and the goblin cottage. Lights were on inside the cottage too, so I knocked.

Suzt answered the door. Her face was streaked with tears.

"Oh, miss Kyra! I'm so glad you're home!"

"What's wrong?" Alarm spiked in me and I was suddenly imagining the worst. Some great creature had lumbered out of the woods. Or marauders, or...

"It's the twins. They're missing!"

18

t took some time to get the whole story from Suzt. She blubbered more than spoke and had to stop several times to blow her nose.

Tums and Tad had gone into the wood that afternoon. The Inbetween was a terrible place, but the Guardians kept Dorion Park free of marauders and the worst creatures. As long as the boys stayed near home, they were allowed to play in the forest. And they always took Princess with them. The hell hound could take care of any nasties they met.

Tonight, they hadn't come home for dinner. Tums and Tads were growing boys. They never missed a meal.

"Da and the boys have gone looking for them, but the light's almost gone." Suzt squeezed my arms with both hands. "What if they can't find them before dark? They're just babies! Alone all night in the woods!"

I pulled her hands off my arm. "It's okay. We'll find them. I'm sure it's nothing. They probably lost track of time. You know how boys are."

I ran for the gatehouse.

Arriz would have been too proud to ask for help, but I wasn't.

I banged on the door. No one answered. I glanced at the trees. The sun still peeked through the branches.

So stupid!

The gargoyles wouldn't be awake for another half hour. I'd told Suzt not to worry, but as I watched the sun slip below the trees, my gut told me something was very wrong.

I turned for the house, already calling Mason on my widget. I got his voice mail and left and urgent message for him to return home immediately.

"Dutch!" I yelled as I opened the door. He was in the kitchen, wearing an apron and holding a dishrag. "I need you. You too." I pointed at Grim lying on his favorite table by the window. "Tums and Tad are missing. We need to go look for them."

Dutch dropped his apron on the table.

Grim jumped down. "Where?" he said.

"I don't know. Somewhere in the forest. Can you track them?"

"Maybe."

I glanced at Dutch. This was the first time Grim had spoken in front of him. Dutch took the idea of a talking cat in stride.

"I'll organize a search party with the Guardians," he said.

"Good. Grim and I will go out now. Call me as soon as the Guardians are awake."

I didn't wait for him to answer. I was already out the door with Grim right behind me. I stopped only to grab my sword from the truck. We ran through the gate in the hedge to the cemetery. There was no sign of Arriz or the others. I wanted to call him to find out where they'd already looked, but I didn't have his address. Did the goblins even have widgets? Why hadn't I thought to give them one before? Gita might be with them, but she never used her widget for anything but a flashlight.

Grim was sniffing the headstones.

"Can you get a scent?"

"I get many scents. The boys have been all over this yard. There are too many trails."

"Well pick one! We'll follow them all if we have to."

Grim cocked his head, but didn't didn't comment on my waspishness. He turned and sauntered out of the yard through the far gate.

"This trail is the freshest."

The light was fading fast now. We followed a path through the trees. It led to a pond in a small hollow. I'd once dumped a moon-frog there. It was the night I'd reconnected with Mason.

I glanced at my widget. Still no message from him. Where was he?

Grim hesitated at the boggy edge of the pond.

"It's too wet," he said. "The scents are all muddled."

My widget rang.

"Hello?"

It was Dutch. "The Guardians are awake. Berto has them working in widening sweeps from the house."

"Good. Have you heard from Mason?"

"I'm watching him right now. He's in the middle of an interview with MTL news."

"As soon as he's done, call him. And keep calling until you get an answer."

"I will." He hung up.

Grim was still trying to sort out the scent trail. Like his nose, my keening picked up too much information to be useful.

Three figures stepped out of the trees. I froze with one hand on the grip of my sword before I recognized Arriz, Gita and Muzzy.

"Did you find them?" I called out, but I could already tell from their expressions that the news wasn't good.

Arriz shook his head, the strain plain on his face. "It's too dark now. I told the boys to meet back at the house after dark."

Gita wrung her hands and let out a long mourning wail.

I wasn't going to wait until morning to search.

"There are gleams in the back of my truck. Jacoby knows where to find them. Go!" I urged. "I'll keep looking."

Arriz nodded and they hurried off.

"We keep going?" Grim asked.

"Can you see all right?"

He sniffed and twitched his tail. Of course the night sun would be able to see in the dark. I had a flashlight on my widget if I needed it.

"Let's go."

Grim led me away from the pond.

"You have a scent?"

"Not the boys, but there is a definite doggie smell this way." His nose twitched in distaste.

Princess!

For over an hour, we followed a path no wider than a deer trail. It was slow going. I felt eyes watching us from behind every tree. A new thought occurred to me. What if that hidebehind creature had taken the boys? I wasn't even sure what it was. Some fae creatures had dark appetites, and children were often delicacies. Arriz had said it was mostly harmless, but what if he was wrong?

I lost sight of Grim. He was much more agile than me and could slink past tangles of branches that forced me to go around. But I keened him up ahead. And more. I keened Princess too. She was nearby. Fear made her magic taste fiery.

I ran, not caring that low branches snagged at my pants and scratched my bare arms.

The trees finally gave way to a grassy meadow. I could hear the howls of an enraged hell hound.

A winged creature landed in the field.

Berto.

I ran past him, grabbing his arm as I went.

"It's Princess!"

We skidded to a stop at the edge of a pit dug in the grass. I shone my widget into the hole. At the bottom, tangled in a net of thick ropes, was Princess.

She was panting as she struggled to break free. She saw me and whined. I searched the hole. It was barely two meters across and about as deep. Just big enough to trap the hound.

The boys weren't with her.

My widget vibrated in my hand. I checked the call, expecting Mason, but it was Emil. I let it go to voice mail. Business could wait.

Berto had already jumped into the hole to cut the ropes and free Princess. Grim paced the perimeter of the trap.

"Anything?" I asked.

His tail thrashed. "Nothing. The trail ends here. Like they vanished into thin air."

I looked up. Maybe they had. Maybe whatever had taken the boys could fly, and it was taking them back to its nest to devour them right now.

But then why trap the hound, if it could just snatch them up? The hole and the net suggested planning.

I looked for tire marks in the grass. Maybe they'd incapacitated the hound and driven off with the twins.

My widget vibrated again. I answered it on impulse. It was Emil again.

"Kyra—"

"Emil I can't talk right now. Whatever it is, you deal with it." I almost hung up.

"Kyra!" His sharp tone stopped me.

"What?"

"A message came through the business mail tonight. Go look at it now. You really need to read this."

"Fine." I scrolled my emails. The second one from the top came from an address I didn't recognize. It had only two lines:

> *I have something of yours. If you want them back, bring your cousin to Dragon Pony Inn on Sunday at 7pm.*

My hand dropped. I could hear Emil's far-away voice calling, "Kyra? Kyra?" I hit end on the call. Then I doubled over and threw up in the grass.

I sat on the couch in the living room staring at the screen of my widget. I'd read it over a hundred times. The words weren't particularly menacing. There was no mention of kidnapping or murder. But they were implied—bring me your cousin or I'll kill the boys.

"Should we call Hub?" Dutch asked.

"No," Mason said. "They won't get involved." He was right. The kids were taken outside the ward and they were most likely being held outside the ward too. The Dragon Pony Inn was in Hedge, the town outside the South Gate.

Mason paced by the back door. He'd arrived just as we returned and sent the Guardians to patrol the park, just in case. Then he called Oscar. The old alchemist was already on his way.

Princess slept by my feet. She'd whined for half an hour and wouldn't stop licking my hand, as if she'd done something wrong. No amount of pets and hugs could convince her otherwise. She'd finally fallen into an exhausted sleep.

Losing the twins wasn't Princess's fault. It was mine. It was my connection to Gunora that put the goblits in danger. Someone wanted her badly enough to take on a hell hound. But who? One of the knackers? Or had Gunora reached out from her new prison home to orchestrate this whole thing?

That was possible. She was just cunning enough. But more likely, she'd stolen something of value from the Knackers and they wanted it back. They knew that I'd attended every day of Gunora's trial. And anyone who knew me even a little could guess that I'd do anything for my family of critters. But why take the boys, and not one of mine like Errol or Jacoby?

Whoever did it clearly expected me to break Gunora out of a maximum security prison. I could do it, of course. My sword could cut through anything. But how did they know that? Again, the possibilities circled around to Gunora.

"Who would do such a thing?" Arriz asked. The younger goblits had been sent home to Suzt, but Arriz and Dekar had stayed to talk strategy.

"The question we should be asking is why," Dutch said.

"It's an attack on Kyra and me," Mason said.

"How so?"

"Whoever took them knows that Kyra would go for Gunora. And the kids? They're my responsibility."

"They are not!" Arriz rose to his full height and pumped his fist in the air. "My family is my responsibility!"

"I brought you here," Mason growled. "I put you and your family in their cross hairs."

I rose from the couch and left the room. Let them covet blame all they wanted. That wouldn't help.

I needed weapons. I had a chest of knives in my room. I chose my three favorites and my sword. My utility belt was still around my waist, but I pushed aside the fancy dresses in the closet and dug out my old travel pack too.

A shadowy plan was starting to form in my head. I'd need more firepower than knives, but I didn't want to take the time to go back into the city for my guns. Mason had a gun safe in the basement. I went downstairs and found the keys to the safe where Mason hid them behind the electrical panel.

I grabbed a blaster and swung it over my shoulder. I added an extra battery to my pack and dithered for a moment about taking an old-style ballistics gun too. They'd worked well against the vampires, but the extra weight might slow me down. In the end I erred on the side of caution and added a holster with a pistol and a box of bullets.

I bounded back up the stairs, now full of energy.

I'd need food too. I stalked through the living room. Everyone fell silent when they saw me loaded up with my arsenal. I ignored them. In the kitchen, I threw some granola bars and bags of nuts in my pack and filled the canteen.

"You can't go after her." Mason was right behind me. I turned. Behind him, Dutch, Arriz and Dekar all stood by the breakfast nook, faces haggard and hopeless.

My heart thrummed in my chest, and I took a moment to calm it. Then I hiked my pack higher on my shoulder and lifted my chin.

"I can and you can't stop me."

He considered me for a long moment. "All right, then you can't sneak off alone."

I opened my mouth to deny the sneaking part, but he cut me off.

"We're going to fix this. If we have to, I'll sneak into Grandill myself to get Gunora," he said.

I got right in his face and raised my voice. "She's my cousin. My problem. I won't put you or your career in danger again. Not you or anyone else."

Grim jumped onto the counter to watch the drama unfold.

"You don't get to pick my battles," Mason snarled. "And besides, it looks like you need me." He jabbed a finger at the blaster hanging over my shoulder. "These don't even work on Grandill. The prison has a magic dampener."

"I...I didn't know that."

"Of course not. Why would you? Hub doesn't like to advertise its defenses. But I worked on the Grandill project when it was first built. You need what's in here." He tapped his head with one finger. "For instance, how do you plan on getting inside the ward?"

"My sword." I tried not to sound smug. Mason knew the sword could cut through anything.

"And what will you do when you set off every alarm in the place?" He raised an eyebrow. "How will you and your sword fight off a dozen guards, find Gunora and get her out without getting killed?"

"I haven't thought that far ahead, but I'm going!" My voice rose again. Even I could hear the hysteria around its edges.

"I'm not stopping you. I'm going with you." The fire in his eyes told me there was no point in arguing with him.

I let out a puff of exasperation and dropped my guns and my pack on the floor. I pushed past him. Arriz and Dekar parted to let me storm by. I stomped around the living room a bit, my thoughts about as loud as my footsteps. Mason let me get it out of my system for a while, then he caught my hands in his.

"I'm going with you," he repeated.

"You don't understand. She's behind this somehow!" I leaned my head against his chest. "I've been going over every possibility in my head and it's the only one that makes sense. I don't know how she did it, but Gunora's pulling the strings here. I can feel it."

"All the more reason you can't go in alone," Mason said. He tipped my face up to meet his gaze. I saw full understanding of the truth in his eyes—the truth we wouldn't speak aloud in front of the goblins.

By going to Grandill island, I'd be giving Gunora the two things she needed to survive—my blood and a Valkyrie blade.

"It's a trap isn't it?" I said.

My braids had long since come loose and he tucked a lock of hair behind one of my ears.

"Of course it is. But a trap only works if we don't know it's coming."

I nodded. Trap or no trap, we'd still go. Every time I closed my eyes, I thought of those two little boys and how scared they must be.

Grim jumped onto his favorite table and wound through the knickknacks to sit beside us and lend his silent support. His eyes shone like shards of amber. My hand ran absently down the soft fur on his back and for once, he didn't flinch away.

Mason turned to Arriz. "You might as well go home. See to the others."

Arriz's face was a storm of emotions. He didn't want to go home. He wanted to go find his boys. I couldn't blame him. But there was nothing to be done tonight. We had three days to free Gunora and take her to the kidnappers. They would keep the boys alive until then. I hoped.

Mason gripped Arriz's shoulder. "We will get your boys back. I promise this."

The goblin's lips were set in a grim line but he nodded.

"Come on, Da." Dekar tugged at his sleeve. Arriz shot me an angry glance and followed his son.

After they left, Mason poured whisky for the rest of us. It would be a long night.

Dutch leaned against the desk. He'd been running through the trees too. There was a smear of dirt across his pant leg and his hair wasn't in its usual slicked back perfection. It was the first time I had ever seen him looking rumpled.

"Why don't you use the election to get onto the island. Make it a campaign stop," he said.

"I've been thinking the same thing," Mason said at the same moment I blurted. "Absolutely not!"

I glared at Dutch for even suggesting it. He held up both hands in surrender.

I turned to Mason. "You can't be serious."

"Why not. We can at least tour the island to find out where she is."

"We don't have time for red tape and campaign tours. And I won't let you blow up your career to clean up my mess."

He crossed the room and sat beside me. His thumb caressed the skin beside my mouth and he smiled sadly. "How can I govern a whole city if I can't even take care of my own?"

I let out a humph. When he looked at me like that, I lost any chance of a coherent argument.

The sound of car tires on gravel broke the spell. I put a hand on his chest and narrowed my eyes. "Why don't we let Oscar decide?"

CHAPTER

20

bsolutely not." Oscar repeated my sentiment when we explained the plan. He glared at me then Mason. He didn't know which one to yell at first. "Putting aside the amount of energy and funds I've invested in your campaign," he jabbed a finger in the air, "Montreal needs your leadership. I won't let you throw away your career and put this ward in danger for some foolhardy exploit that's sure to fail."

"Please, tell us how you really feel," I mumbled. He shot me a black look. I raised my hands in defense. "I tried to tell him it was a bad idea. We should go in covertly. Break in, find Gunora and get out before anyone even knows we're there."

Oscar threw his hands in the air. "It's the rash leading the reckless." He stomped over to the patio and stared at the dark sky. A warm breeze blew through the open door, tossing wisps of gray hair around his ears. One hand rubbed his lower back. Jacoby hopped over and took his other hand, patting it in sympathy.

Grim rose from his perch on the long table beside the window, stretched and delicately threaded his way through the knickknacks. He head butted Oscar's shoulder and the alchemist scratched behind his ears. Oscar didn't know he was absentmindedly petting a night sun jaguar and holding the hand of a fire-dervish with enough power to take out a city block. I let him keep his innocence.

An owl hooted from the garden.

Mason broke the impasse in the living room. "You know we're going to do this, with or without you, old friend. So if you want me to be Prime Minister, you should help us."

127

Oscar turned. In the dim light, I couldn't read his eyes.

"This city is in turmoil. You know that, right? That human minister, what's-his-name?" He snapped his fingers as if that might help his recall.

"Gill Phillips," I said.

"Right. I've had bouts of gas that were more eloquent that Gill Phillips." The new human Prime Minister *was* a bit of a pompous wind bag.

"And the fae?" Oscar paced, on a rant now. "Merrow is unbending. She will bring this city to civil war before compromising. I need you at the table as the voice of reason."

"So help us," Mason said. "If you don't, we'll get caught and that will mean the end of my campaign."

"That will mean the end of your life as a free man!" Oscar made that growling sound that meant he was thinking it over and didn't like the conclusion he was coming to.

"If I do this, you need to be home by Ward Day. That's next week. If you're not seen out and about for the festivities, people will talk."

Ward Day celebrated the founding of Montreal Ward, the day the magic shield was first turned on to protect the city from opji, marauders and encroaching magic. Any aspiring politician who missed the events would be booed out of the race.

"We'll be there," Mason said. "One way or another this will be over by Sunday."

Oscar grumbled some more.

"And you'll get serious about the election? Really serious, I mean. Your heart hasn't been in it so far and it shows."

"I've had some…issues to work out." Mason glanced at Errol who was sitting on the desk, smoking a pipe. "But that's done now. I promise."

Oscar stared at him for a heartbeat longer, then nodded.

"Fine. Let's break into a maximum security prison. Should be kicks and giggles for a Friday night."

Mason projected a map of Grandill on the desk. Errol marched along the edge of the desk, his walking twig like a third clopping leg. He muttered and pointed out landscape features as if committing them to memory.

Grandill Prison was actually two islands, shaped roughly like a coffee bean with one side about half the size of the other. The Charles River split the halves. The whole thing was separated from the main land by the St. Lawrence River on one side and the Beauharnois Canal on the other.

Once the island had been a thriving community of about a hundred thousand souls. Now only two-hundred inmates occupied it, plus the dozen or so guards who lived at the administration building on the north end.

Getting there was the easy part. The island lay fifty kilometers southwest of Montreal, a straight shot down the Ottaway River at its junction with the St. Lawrence. I'd passed it on my forced journey by boat when Polina's goons had kidnapped me last spring.

"I've only seen it from the water." I traced the Beauharnois Canal and shivered at the memory of marauders spilling out of the ground like army ants to attack our ship. "Either of you been there?"

Mason shook his head. "Not recently. I helped to surveil the land for the original ward, but I wasn't part of the actual construction."

"I've been there. Long time ago." Oscar's eyebrows were scrunched up like fuzzy inchworms. "I was on the team that installed the ward's generator. It's here." He tapped the map. "And it hooks up to an apex stone here." He pointed to a spot on the mainland. "That tower is heavily guarded. No point in trying to breach it there."

"Is there a back door?"

"Here. Where the old drawbridge used to be." Oscar pointed to the opposite end of the island. "It's a smaller fortification but still guarded. I can't see a viable entry point."

I had a way in, of course. My sword would cut through the ward like a hot knife through butter. But that wasn't something I liked to advertise. Not when the city's entire defense depended on the invulnerability of its ward.

Mason knew what I was thinking. He slumped in a chair and said, "You might as well tell him. If we're going to get this done, he needs all the facts."

Oscar turned to me with a quizzical look. I bit my lip. "You know my sword has some…uh, magical properties?" Oscar encouraged me with a nod. "Part of that means it can cut through anything."

"Anything?" Oscar's inchworms were creeping up again.

"Well, I haven't tested it on every substance in the universe," I shrugged, "but so far, yeah. Anything."

He thought about that for a moment, and his eyebrows threatened to crawl off the top of his head as understanding dawned.

"It can cut through a ward?"

"Uh-huh."

We let him rant and curse and pace for a full minute before he returned to the map.

"Do you have any idea what that means? Our enemies are always looking for a way to break us! What if the opji find out about this?"

"Relax. It's a Valkyrie blade. It needs a Valkyrie to wield it."

"Oh, that's much better! So all they need is to kidnap you too. Or worse, threaten Mason or that furry little dervish you're so fond of." He jabbed a finger toward Jacoby asleep on the couch. "Or any one of your precious rescues. This whole ridiculous endeavor proves that you would do anything to save them."

He had a point. But my vulnerability wasn't the question here.

"Oscar, stand down." Mason pointed to the map. "Let's solve one problem before we make another. Kyra is safe. The sword is safe."

"Are there more of these swords?" Oscar wasn't ready to let it go. "Does this cousin of yours have one too?"

I nodded. "Hub would have confiscated it. I guess it's in lockup now."

Another minute passed while he paced the room, cursing my ancestry under his breath.

Mason caught my eye and winked.

Oscar finally got a grip on himself and returned to the table.

"When this is done, you and I are going to have a serious conversation. And I want access to that sword. And you. That's my price for helping with this madness." He folded his arms over his chest.

"Agreed." I didn't like the idea of becoming the alchemist-inventor's guinea pig, but I was in no position to argue.

"Fine. If you want to breach the ward, this is the best place to do it." He jabbed a finger at the map. It was a spot on the eastern edge of the island, halfway between the old locks where the marauders attacked and the back-door guard station. "It's the only true blind spot on the surveillance. But I can't see how that will help. The entire island is patrolled regularly. Their systems will notice a gaping hole in the ward. It might take minutes or hours, but it won't be enough time to find your cousin."

"Okay, put a peg in that idea. We'll come back to it." Mason stood and leaned over the table. "Let's assume we can get inside the ward undetected. Then what? What will we find?"

"The island is about two-hundred square kilometers." Oscar drew a line with his finger across the map. "A lot of ground to cover. And she'll probably be hiding."

"Hiding from what?" Mason asked.

"The other inmates. The last report I read showed three major camps on the island, here, here and here." He pointed to three spots on the island. "Most inmates fall into one of these cliques, if they aren't killed first."

"Why these sites?" Mason asked. "What's special about them? Are they defended?"

"The camps grew up around the drop points. Hub dumps food and necessities twice a month in three drops. The gangs formed to protect these rations. The bluecaps are here. They're your best bet for cooperation."

"Really? I thought they avoided humans as much as possible." I didn't really know much about the bluecap race of dwarves. There were none living in or around Montreal as far as I knew.

"They do. But they're political prisoners. Of all the convicts on the island, they're the ones least likely to shoot first and ask questions later."

"Shoot? You mean they have weapons?"

Oscar rubbed his hand over his fuzzy eyebrows. "I meant shoot metaphorically. But yes, you should assume they have weapons. Not blasters, but knives, spears, bows. Even if the guards wanted to, they couldn't stop them from making weapons."

"And they don't want to," Mason said. "Keeps the food bill down."

That was harsh. I rubbed my stomach where acid was burning a hole in me. This was starting to feel real.

Oscar continued with his lessons. "The bluecaps were the first inmates. Sent to Grandill for rebelling against the original Triumvirate. About three dozen of them remained at last count. They're small and magically inert, but bloodthirsty if roused. Then there's a herd of kelpies that were banished years ago for dragging humans into the river and eating them. They're on the west end, and they keep mostly to themselves, except when they run out of rations. The last faction is a mixed crew of shifters and fae, all murderers of the worst kind, led by some guy named One-eye Jack. A real piece of work by all accounts. If Gunora got herself accepted into any one of these groups, she'd have a fair chance of surviving. But which gang? Who knows?"

I studied the map details. A picture of this hellish prison was forming in my head. "Gunora is sick. Her magic has a distinct flavor. I'm fairly certain that I'll keen her if we get close enough."

"That's the other fun thing about Grandill," Oscar said. "The ward isn't just a barrier to keep prisoners in. It's a magic dampener."

Right. I'd forgotten about that fun detail. I thought of the horrible null rings that had been used against the dragons and shuddered.

"So my keening won't work?" I asked.

Oscar frowned. "Maybe, maybe not. Innate magic is affected less. Shifters can still shift but it's a painful, drawn-out process. Witches who draw power solely from the environment are out of luck."

"So even if you have innate magic, it will replenish slowly," I said.

"And Kyra's keening might not be strong enough to find Gunora," Mason said.

"Bingo and bingo." Oscar pointed finger guns at me then at Mason.

"Terrific." I'd been leaning over the map. Now I stood straight and stretched the kinks from my back, wishing it was just as easy to smooth the kinks from our sketchy plan.

"That also means the gangs will have trouble tracking us," Mason, my glass-is-half-full guy, said. "So we stake out each camp until we find her."

We stared at the map in silence. None of us wanted to admit that it could take days. It wasn't a plan. It was plan-adjacent.

Mason rubbed a hand over his face. He looked worn out. "Can you work with Berto and the others?" he asked Oscar. "Go to Hedge and find the kids in case…" He didn't finish that sentence, but he didn't have to. We all knew what he meant. In case we didn't make it back. If we didn't find Gunora and break her out, the Guardians were the goblits best hope.

Oscar nodded. He was rereading the ransom note with a frown. "We can start in at this Dragon Pony Inn."

"And look into the giant. Gunora mentioned him more than once." Giants were rare. I didn't know of any living within the boundary of the ward. If there was one in Hedge or the other shanty towns outside the ward, someone would have noticed.

"So that just leaves the problem of the gaping hole in the ward," Oscar said finally.

A creaky voice came from the balcony. "I can help with that."

C H A P T E R

21

The hidebehind was, well…hiding behind the bit of wall between the patio door and window. I hadn't keened him there. And from Grim's irate hiss, I suspected he hadn't sensed anyone lurking either.

The creature was taller than me, lean and twiggy. Dark, opaque eyes watched us from a thin face of mottled gray skin and a darker slash for a mouth. His arms were thin with knotty joints. Legs too, but these bent behind him like a grasshopper's. Long gossamer wings folded along his back. He flexed one wing and ran his leg across its edge like a bow on a violin string. Haunting music filled the night.

"It was you!" I said.

The hidebehind smiled and played on.

"The lady likes my song?"

"Yes." I breathed out a sigh. The music tugged at some elemental part of my soul.

"I give it as a gesture of goodwill. We trade? I help you. You help me." He cocked his head to one side, still sawing out the potent music.

Mason also seemed affected by the sound. He stood by the couch, one hand clinging to the armrest as if his knees were about to give out. On the table, Grim wasn't so impressed. His back arched and fur stuck up like bristles on a brush.

Oscar stepped forward. "Who are you? Are you fae?" He turned to me. "Kyra, don't bargain with the fae."

"Not fae." The hidebehind stopped his song, and I felt the loss like the death of a dear friend. "My name is…" He shook his head. "You could not pronounce it. You may call me Cricket."

I took a step toward the patio. Cricket didn't retreat, but his back leg planted itself as if he were ready to bolt.

I stopped. "You're a hidebehind."

"Your people gave my people that name many, many lives ago. When the first human men came to these woods with their axes and their fires."

Interesting. You could tell a lot about a creature by how they described their first encounters with humans. They came with arrows and spears? That meant the two races had been overlapping for millennia. Humans brought guns and magic? That probably meant the first encounter happened in the last century. Axes and fires meant humans first encountered hidebehinds in the eighteenth century when lumberjacks and trappers roamed the lands west of the big cities. The fact that he didn't mention traps and knives, meant that this was a tree dwelling creature. I'd have to search the old almanac database to see when they were first mentioned.

Mason recovered from the effects of the music and strode forward to stand at my side.

"What makes you think you can help us," he said.

"And why should we help you?" Oscar added.

The hidebehind glanced at one, then the other. His gaze settled on me.

"I watch for many nights now. I see you don't chase away the goblins. I see them welcomed here. Tonight I hear you make plans. I see you search for the lost children."

"You were eavesdropping?" I asked.

Cricket looked up at the roof line. "I did not drop from eaves. I came from forest."

"Did you see who took the boys?" Mason asked.

Cricket shook his head. "I only know the trees were angry. Very angry. They like children." He smiled, then frowned. "They didn't like those who intruded into the wood. But they are gone now." He crossed his twig-like hands over his chest.

"Never mind." I waved my hand at him. "Continue. How can you help?"

He nodded. "I hear you need to hide magic. I hide magic."

I turned to Mason and said, "That could come in handy."

He nodded, then motioned for Cricket to come inside. The hidebehind's eyes widened. He took a hesitant step over the threshold.

Grim hissed and jumped down from the table. In a moment he disappeared into the hall leading to the bedrooms.

"What's his problem?" Oscar asked.

"He's just being a cat," I said. If Grim had detected any danger from the hidebehind, he wouldn't have left us. But without the spitting feline, Cricket seemed more at ease. He stepped into the middle of the room, careful not to bump into any furniture with his long body and spindly legs.

"Camouflage is good, but it's not really magic that we need to hide," Mason said.

Cricket cocked his head. "I hide hole for you. In magic ward. No one will know it there."

I frowned. It was a terrific offer, if he could do it. But I wanted to be sure he understood the ramifications. "We could be gone for days," I said. "And if you're caught, the Grandill guards will kill you."

He nodded solemnly. "I accept these terms."

"And in return? What do you want from us?"

Cricket spread his arms wide. "I want what you give goblins. I want to stop running. I want a home."

I studied him for a moment. Cricket was a nervous creature. He looked fierce because of his sheer size, but I could see how fragile he was. Long, thin limbs were easily snapped in a fight. His wings were beautiful but as insubstantial as gauze. And unlike some insectoids, he had no carapace to protect him. He kept his long arms bent and his hands clasped before him, less like a prayer and more like a steadying gesture. His back legs were poised to flee.

"I'm sorry," I said. "I can't make that bargain with you."

Cricket lowered his head. I laid a hand on his arm. It was warm and rough like an oak branch in the summer sun.

"I can't make that bargain because you're welcome to stay with us. No strings attached."

He looked up. His onyx eyes were glassy. "You mean that?"

"You have a home here as long as you need it." Mason grinned. "Welcome to the Kyra Greene Wildlife Sanctuary." I could have kissed him.

"You no need my help?" Cricket asked.

"Yes, we do," I said. "But if you decide to help us, it will be because you want to. You have a home here either way."

He considered my words and nodded sharply. "I help."

A Kelpie Tale

August 29, 2076

Here's a story I heard around a campfire long ago.

There once was a shepherd named Daniel, who lived with his sheep on the moors of Scotland. Daniel thought sheep were boring. He dreamed of being a horse wrangler, like the cowboys he read about in America. Those were real men. And horses were beasts to be tamed. Sheep were already tame and all they did was eat grass and get stuck in ravines so that Daniel had to search all night for them.

Then one day, while he was tracking down yet another lost ewe and cursing the beast for its stupidity, he spied a herd of horses in the valley at the bottom of a ravine. They were the most beautiful creatures he'd ever seen. Their sleek bodies shone like gold in the sun.

Daniel forgot his sheep in an instant. And for the next week, he forgot everything else. He even forgot to eat. He followed the herd over craggy dunes and across heathered moors. Every time he approached them, the horses would gallop away, but never far, as if they taunted him to follow. The great stallion, king of the herd, watched Daniel with his black eyes.

Daniel became obsessed. He would not rest until he rode that stallion. He followed the herd until the moors ended. And then he followed them onto the rocky sands of the shore. With the ocean at their backs, the horses had nowhere to run.

"Now I've got you!" Daniel said. The stallion bowed to him in defeat and Daniel mounted onto his back. The great horse reared and neighed. Daniel clung to his mane and shouted with triumph. No cowboy had ever ridden a beast as magnificent as this.

And then the kelpie stallion ran into the waves and Daniel drowned. The whole herd feasted on his flesh that night. The next day, the kelpies trotted back into the moors, looking for another shepherd who dreamed of greatness.

What's the moral of the story? Don't get too big for your britches, I suppose. But critter wrangler rule fifteen says: always look a gift horse in the mouth. And if it has sharp teeth, never, never get on its back.

So yeah, kelpies. There's a small herd of them taunting folks in the shanty town outside the ward. And a few folks were dumb enough to ride them…right into the river. It seems the kelpie modus operandi hasn't changed in the last thousand years. It goes something like this.

Step 1: Lure an unsuspecting dupe to get on your back.
Step 2: Run into the nearest large body of water.
Step 3: Wait for the frail human to drown.
Step 4: Feast and repeat.

This is one of the more difficult cases I've had to deal with. Hub wants to call in the militia, but I'd like to find a less drastic and bloody resolution. I was hoping my crew here could offer some advice for dealing with a kelpie infestation. As always, my thanks in advance for any help.

COMMENTS (3)

Why are you worried about those murdering beasts? I'm with Hub. Shoot them all.
AllTheGoodUsernamesWereGone682 (August 29, 2076)

— • —

We had a problem with kelpies a few years back. Now we plant nightshade and horse nettle around our property. They're toxic to horses. Doesn't kill them right off, but turns their stomachs sour. Enough that they moved on to sweeter pastures.
Homesteader75 (August 29, 2076)

Homesteader75, FYI, Water hemlock will take care of them much faster. And permanently.

Homesteader893 (August 30, 2076)

The alchemists shared property. They had apartments in the city where party members could crash for days or weeks. They had a fleet of cars, trucks and boats that could be signed out for business or personal use. Mason had rescued me once in one of those boats. They were sleek, metal cruisers that could go forty kilometers an hour against the current and were similar to the boats Hub militia used to patrol the waters around the ward.

This boat wasn't one of those.

"It actually looks sad." I scrutinized the collection of rotting wood that was supposed to be our getaway vehicle.

It had oars.

"I hope you're not expecting me to row." I scowled.

"Only if we run out of gas." Mason patted the small outboard engine mounted to the stern.

"Gas? Real gas? Where did you even find it?"

"Alchemists can get just about anything."

I rounded on Oscar who'd driven us to this secluded inlet on the edge of Dorion Park. "Why don't you have some kind of fancy boat for us? You know, something that can grow wheels and climb out of the water itself. I thought that's what you did."

"I don't swim. Think of all the monsters under there!" He pointed at the water and shuddered. The sun was low on the horizon and the water reflected it back with golden tipped waves. There *were* monsters in the depths of the river. I'd seen them.

"Which was exactly why I don't want to make the trip in that leaky bucket." I nudged the boat with my toe and it creaked against the dock.

Oscar looked sheepish. "I did bring you this."

He pinched a small locket between his finger and thumb. It hung on a leather thong that he draped over my head. The locket hung nearly to my waste. I unclipped the lock and it opened like book to reveal a small golden gemstone inside, oblong like a capsule.

"What is it?" Mason held out his hand. Oscar shook his head.

"Sorry, old man," he said. "You're too human to use this. It's pure magic. Concentrated."

He shut the locket and closed my fingers over it.

"When you get inside Grandill ward, if things get rough, you have one dose. Bite it to break the shell, then swallow the whole thing. It should be enough to use whatever innate magic you have without killing you."

I held my fisted hand close to my heart. The locket was warm, but I couldn't keen anything from it.

"Doesn't feel magical."

Oscar winked. "That's the real trick. Any two-bit alchemist can concentrate magic. But containing it is another matter."

"Good to know." I dropped my little prize inside my shirt.

"And this one's for you." Oscar held out a walkie-talkie. Mason took it and frowned. "It's old tech, I know. But sometimes the old ways are the best. The militia still uses analog out there because the Inbetween interferes with the Ley-net. I have a friend of a friend whose wife contracts for the militia." He waved a hand. "Anyway, it's not important how I got it." He tapped the walkie-talkie. "But I programmed that bad-boy with the militia channels. You should be able to hear their command center and any audio traffic with the patrols. Just don't hit the talk button, and they shouldn't even know you're there."

"Nice." Mason smiled and pocketed his new, old-fashioned toy.

Jacoby sidled up beside me and slipped his hand in mine. "Pleeeeeeeease, Kyra-lady?"

"No. We went over this already." I crossed my arms and stood firm.

Throughout the entire ride to the dock, Jacoby had pestered me about joining our raiding party. Already, I thought we were too many. With me and Mason and Cricket, the boat would be cramped.

"I comes too!" Jacoby whined.

"Not this time." I stroked his fuzzy head.

"But Errol goes!"

Mason had more or less mastered his keening, but Errol had other talents. When you needed to disrupt an electrical grid and make a lot of noise doing it, Errol was your guy.

"He has to come. You don't."

It was bad enough I had to put Errol in danger, I wouldn't risk Jacoby too. Not again.

"*I* has to come!" The dervish stamped a foot. Wisps of smoke rose from his ears. "I takes care of Errol. Kyra-lady gaves me that job! Kyra-lady says keeps Errol safe. And I do. I do! It's my job!"

I wiped a hand over my eyes, already feeling tired and the journey hadn't yet begun.

I *had* told Jacoby to keep Errol safe when we broke into Pierre's lab to find the bloodstone. Jacoby had kept his word. He sacrificed himself to Pierre's vile machine to protect the little bodach. As a result, his soul had been lost in the Nether for months.

But that hadn't deterred Jacoby from his mission. If anything, nearly dying had hardened his resolve. It had solidified the idea in his mind that he was Errol's lifelong bodyguard. And now we were taking Errol into danger and leaving him behind.

I sighed. I had planned to leave Errol with Cricket, but maybe this was a better solution.

"You can come," I said. Jacoby instantly brightened, shucking off his tantrum like an unwanted shirt. "But only to get Errol to safety. Once we're inside, you take Errol and hide until we return. Understood?"

"Yes!"

I watched Jacoby dash to the end of the dock with a sinking feeling. I had forced him to make that promise to me once before and it hadn't gone well.

We loaded our gear into the boat. Cricket, looking awkward and worried, lowered himself onto the rocking deck. Jacoby jumped on board, making the boat swing precariously. He wore his favorite bear backpack and Errol rode on the bear's head.

Princess was over-excited and overheated. Drool hung in strings from her muzzle as she ran up and down the dock. Since returning from the Nether, her left ear had started to droop. Just the tip. When she ran, it flapped like a hand waving goodbye. With her ferocious bone plating, she looked monstrously cute.

I snapped a leash onto her collar. I didn't usually insult her with a lead, but I also didn't trust her to go home quietly with Oscar.

"You have a three day window," he said to me as if I could have forgotten the hours that marked the lives of Tums and Tad. "After that it's time to quit these gallivanting adventures."

"Last gallivant, I promise." I hugged him and kissed his cheek. His frown softened.

"Just come back safe."

"We always do."

I climbed into the tiny boat that was already too cramped. Mason yanked a cord to start the outboard. I had expected the roar of a combustion engine, but after the initial rev, the engine settled down to a gentle *putt-putt*.

Mason grinned. "They'll never hear us coming."

"That's because we won't get there this century." I felt even less secure in the boat.

"Nonsense." Mason patted the outboard troller. "We'll get twenty kilometers an hour with this baby. Just fast enough to get us there after dark."

"And if we run out of gas?"

"That's where these come in." He pointed to the oars. Terrific. At least we had the current on our side. If nothing else we could float to Grandill.

"Let's just get going." Already we'd had to waste hours of precious time because we couldn't approach Grandill in the daylight.

Oscar untied the boat while Princess paced on the dock. She sensed an adventure in the making and was starting to realize that she wasn't included.

"Hang onto her!" I shouted to Oscar.

Mason used the manual tiller to steer us gently away from the dock until we could turn around.

"Aroooooo!" Princess's desperate plea was loud enough to drown out the engine. I turned back in time to see Oscar plunging into the river as he tried to hang onto her. Princess leapt into the air. Bone-white wings flashed in the afternoon sun. The leash trailed behind her.

"What the?" Mason cut the engine. Princess flopped into the boat, making it rock violently. Her big paws scrambled on the splintered boards. Cricket squeaked and tried to squeeze himself into the V at the front of the boat. Jacoby climbed right into my lap and gripped my knee in both hands.

"I guess she really didn't want to be left behind." Mason laughed. Princess licked his cheek, then shook her head, sending a spray of drool over the rest of us.

"I'm fine!" Oscar called from the shore. He clung to the dock, standing hip deep in water. His normally frizzy hair was plastered to his round head.

I wiped my face on my sleeve and calmed the over-excited hell puppy.

"How does she still have wings?" I ran a hand along her pearly wings and they disappeared.

In the Nether, we'd all had wings. But that was a spirit realm where we could shape ourselves to suit our needs. My wings disappeared the moment I stepped through the door to Terra. I'd assumed everyone else had lost their access to flying too.

I turned to Mason, who'd restarted the engine and now manned the tiller as the boat floated downstream. "Do you still have wings?"

He closed his eyes, and the muscles in his shoulders bulged as he tried to access his phantom limbs.

"Nope. You?"

"No. Why did Princess get to keep them?"

"Must be a hell hound thing."

"Maybe." Hell hounds were the guardians for doors between dimensions. Hopping between worlds was probably no different than taking a trip to the corner store. Maybe she'd had wings all along.

"She really coming with us?" He waved to a soggy Oscar.

I shrugged. "I guess so. There's no way we'll get her home now."

The river was narrow and shallow here, just deep enough for the draft of our small boat. Princess launched herself into the air again and fluttered overhead like a great bumbling bee, sometimes soaring high, sometimes diving until she almost hit water. I watched her with some envy. Having experienced the joy of flight, it was hard not to be jealous.

Mason navigated around rocks and snags of brambles until the stream opened into the wider Ottaway River that would eventually join with the great St. Lawrence Seaway. He turned the boat south and we putt-putted through the twilight.

The wind had died and the water was eerily calm.

"Hold on!" Mason said. The boat shot forward. Cricket's bony hands were clamped onto the gunnels, his black eyes wide and mouth hanging open. A quick glance behind me showed a deep wake and a grinning Mason.

"I might have made some modifications to the engine," he said.

"I see that." I couldn't help grinning too. It was a warm evening, the kind that made you think winter would never come. I unbound my braids and let the wind run its fingers through my hair. Jacoby's vise-grip on my knee loosened as he started to enjoy the ride too. Only cricket didn't relax. He closed his eyes as if silently willing the ordeal to be over.

Princess eventually tired of keeping pace with the boat and crashed to the floorboards. Panting, she hung over the edge of the boat and nearly tipped us before I hauled her into the middle.

"Sit and stay." I admonished. She licked my chin, then curled into a ball on my feet.

Even with Mason's ramped up motor, it would take us over an hour to reach Grandill.

"You might as well get some rest," I said to Jacoby. The dervish nodded and tucked himself into the crook of Princess's back leg. He laid his head on her stomach, and the rise and fall of her breath lulled him to sleep too. Errol stayed awake. He sat on the bear's head and watched the light fade.

Perrot Island slid by on our left. There was no shoreline. The dense forest hung over the water. Mason's expression was grim as he scanned the site of the alchemist stronghold.

"Are there sentries?" I asked.

"The apex compound is heavily guarded," he said. "But that's on the other side of the island. Out here?" He shrugged. "No need for security. But someone's bound to be outside, digging a pit or blowing crap up."

The alchemists had claimed Perrot Island because it was outside the ward, and they could conduct their experiments in secrecy and without endangering anyone else. They also maintained the generator that fueled the ward and linked the apex towers around Montreal. All that tech and the main buildings were on the north side of Perrot Island. We watched in silence as our boat crept by in the narrower southern channel.

Thunder cracked like a whip. Princess woke with a snarl. I glanced up. Thin clouds covered the darkening sky. Was a storm coming?

Crack! Crack!

Two more thunderclaps jarred my bones.

Oh, no.

Mason and Cricket were peering at the sky, but I searched the flat expanse of water looking for telltale signs.

Crack!

There. A hundred meters away, a tiny splash broke the surface of the river.

Princess let out a rumbling growl. She'd seen it too.

"What is it?" Mason asked.

"Not good."

Something bumped our boat, sending us rocking.

Mason stared into the dark water. His right hand held a knife and his left had gone to stone.

"Kyra, tell me now. What is it?"

"Bildad. I think."

"How big?"

"Not very. About the size of a beaver, with a face like a hawk."

Mason's shoulders relaxed, so I added, "They work in packs. That clapping sound you heard? They make it with their flat tails. It's a call to arms, sort of."

The boat tipped again and I heard a splash near the bow. The water churned with bodies. Two small hands with long fingers grabbed the rim of the boat. A sleek head popped up. The creature chittered. Its wickedly sharp beak opened to show tiny sharp teeth.

That was just unfair. A creature shouldn't have a beak and teeth. I hit it with the flat of my sword. It squeaked and fell into the water. More bodies were scrambling to board. The boat rocked wildly.

"Don't let them tip us!" I braced my feet. In the water, the bildads would have all the advantage. They were expert swimmers and could see in near darkness. Princess snarled then yipped when a billdad pecked her.

"Ow!" Mason swore and brought his stone fist down on a furry head.

Jacoby had his own small knife and was jabbing at the horde of critters.

There were too many. For every one I pushed back into the water, three more tried to climb aboard.

"Errol, shield Mason!" I shouted.

The bodach's clung to Jacoby's backpack. "Hgtmg?" *Why?*

"Just do it!"

I called to the green growing things—the grasses that swayed in the current, the trees hanging over the water. I let their magic fill my bones and blood until my skin tingled. Then it burst from me in a silent wave of power.

The billdads shrieked and fell away. Mason crumpled to the bench, rocking the boat dangerously. Cricket fluttered his wings and hovered in the air.

I pointed to the back of the boat. "Jacoby, grab that tiller and keep us in the middle of the river." Jacoby jumped to obey.

I grabbed Mason's shirt and hauled him upright before we all took a swim.

"I'm sorry." I wiped cool sweat from his face. He was pale but awake. "I had to do it. Billdads are extremely sensitive to magic. It was the only way."

"S'okay." He slurred and squeezed my hand.

In the darkness, I heard angry chitters and one clap of a tail against the water, but the billdads decided to find easier prey.

The current carried us downstream toward our next fight.

CHAPTER

23

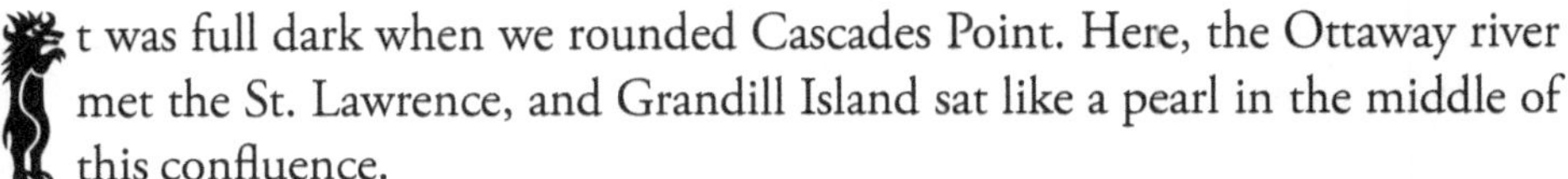

It was full dark when we rounded Cascades Point. Here, the Ottaway river met the St. Lawrence, and Grandill Island sat like a pearl in the middle of this confluence.

I remembered coming to Cascades as a child. It had been a provincial park back then, a perfect setting for a mother-daughter picnic. We skipped rocks on the water and watched fishermen launch their boats down the ramp. We walked along the narrow causeway that marked the entrance to a once busy canal. But the Flood Wars had changed the landscape. The causeway was gone, washed away along with the tiny islands that once dotted the point. Much of the land, including the canal, had eroded, widening the river between the mainland and Grandill.

Mason shut off the engine and we coasted into the reeds at the edge of the point until the bottom of the boat scraped against a sandy shore.

It was time.

I took a big sip of water from my canteen, not knowing when I'd have another chance. Then I re-wrapped my pack in the waterproof covering Mason had provided. It didn't hold much—some dried rations, first-aid kit, water and knives. But we'd be taking a swim before this was over and I didn't want to lose any of it.

Mason gave me a jar of black paint. "Cover any exposed skin."

I opened the lid and sniffed. Not too bad. It smelled like chamomile with a faint whiff of tar. I dabbed it on my face and hands. It dried almost instantly, but left my skin soft and pliable.

"What is this?" I looked at the small jar. It had no label.

Mason grinned. His white teeth stood out against his blacked-out face. "Alchemist special."

"Yeah, yeah. You guys get all the cool toys." I pulled a black knit cap over my auburn hair. The others didn't need disguising. Cricket's bark-like skin would let him hide in any forest. Jacoby's brindled fur would too. And Princess? I studied her face. The bone-white plating really stood out. Any stray bit of light would reflect off it like a beacon. I scooped another gob of black goo from the pot and slathered it over her face. She squirmed and pawed at it, but enough remained to give her a mottled look.

Mason used an oar to push the boat out of the shallows until he could restart the trolling motor. It was near silent and we slid through the water barely disturbing the tall grasses, like an alligator stalking prey.

Then we rounded the point.

This was our first good look at the prison island. The flood-lit administration building lay along the shore less than half a kilometer into the channel. From Cascades Point, we were far enough to be undetected, but the building still seemed dangerously close. The island's apex tower stood out like a beacon. Its stone glowed brilliant and red against the night sky. That was hooked up to Montreal's apex through Perrot Island, which extended and boosted the ward to protect the prison. The only bridge onto the island was another two clicks south, but it would be heavily guarded.

The prison's ward hummed along my keening sense. I could almost taste it. I shot a glance at Mason to see how his fledgling keening was dealing with the enormous magic output so near at hand. His lips were pressed thin and his eyes were flinty, but he was holding it together. Errol saw me watching and nodded his head. For the last few weeks the bodach had always been close by, ready to boost Mason's shields in case of a sudden overload. But we needed Errol elsewhere tonight. Mason would have to fly solo.

I pulled my thoughts away from that concern. I had enough worry to keep me occupied in the here and now.

I scanned the administration building and the prison gate.

"How many guards?" I'd spotted only two.

"Two outside the gate and two more there." Mason pointed along the road that led to the bridge. We both looked at the apex tower. There were probably more guards in the crow's nest.

Princess was bored with this game of sitting still. She flopped her paws onto the gunnel. The boat pitched sideways, and one of the oars fell out of the oarlock with a splash.

I froze. The sound had seemed disproportionately loud in the quiet night. Mason grabbed Princess by the scruff and yanked her down into the boat. The hound rolled on her back and Mason scratched her belly to keep her quiet. We all ducked low, hoping the shadows would hide us.

We waited.

No alarm sounded. After a full minute, Mason risked lifting his head to study the compound, then flattened himself to the boat deck again.

We floated by the north end of the island until trees blocked our view of the administration building and guard towers.

In the open water, the wind picked up, sending a chill down my spine. This was the most dangerous part of the expedition. We had about five kilometers of open water to navigate, right in full view of Grandill. And the current shifted here, pulling us toward the island. The trolling motor was near silent as we headed into the main expanse of river. This river was a busy throughway for cargo ships. But a tiny boat, at night? No, we didn't look suspicious at all. The trick was to stay far enough from the island that if we were spotted, the guards would think we were just homesteader fisher folk.

"Are you ready?" Mason asked the hidebehind. Cricket nodded.

"Jacoby won't be too heavy?" I asked, second guessing the plan we'd gone over a dozen times. Cricket's wings bristled and he gave one shake of his head. I'd insulted him.

I turned to Jacoby. Errol clutched the threadbare fur on his backpack. I tried not to think of this as déjà vu. Things wouldn't go bad this time.

"Remember. As soon as Errol is done, you two hide. When it's safe, cross the river and meet us back at Cascades Point. Got it?"

Jacoby nodded. He didn't like water. It was the antithesis to the fire that was always burning inside him. But he'd do it because I asked. My stomach turned in knots, and my legs felt as weak as a newborn calf's.

This was the moment of no return. Once Cricket left with Jacoby and Errol we could only go forward with this mad plan. And it was madness. We were giving Gunora everything she wanted. But I'd give her that and more if it meant getting Tums and Tad back.

Grandill slid by on our right, slowly. Ever so slowly. Mason fought the current, and I could hear him swearing in French. The water was choppy, and the wind cut through my light jacket. The boat hit the swells. Water sprayed with each bone-jarring slap. Within moments, I was soaked to my skin.

I wiped my eyes and kept them fixed on shore, waiting for some diligent guard to send up a flare, alerting the tower to our presence.

Movement caught my eye. This was it. Out here in the Inbetween, ward laws didn't apply. If they thought we were a threat, the guards would shoot us. No questions, no chance to plea bargain. But the figure standing just inside the tree line wasn't a guard. He was too small. A brownie, maybe? Or it could be a dwarf, goblin or one of the smaller trolls. He was too far, and the shadows too dense for me to get a good look. The figure stood with two hands raised as if to press them against the ward that could only be inches from his face.

I tried not to feel sorry for him. He was there for a good reason.

I could feel his eyes watching us hungrily as we passed.

Cricket stirred in the bow of the boat. The tip of the island jutted into the river. We would never be closer than this.

There was no time for goodbyes. The hidebehind grabbed Jacoby in his gnarled fingers. He flexed gauzy wings and took flight.

I held my breath. And I held onto Princess whose muscles tensed as she readied herself to join them.

"You stay with us," I whispered. The hound whined and wagged her tail.

Clouds hid the moon, but the floodlights at the prison gate haloed over the rise, and for a moment, Cricket stood out in stark relief. Then he dove to fly low over the water. His camouflage kicked in, and it seemed like they winked out of existence.

Mason hit the switch that engaged his alchemical modifications and the boat sped on. There was no point in hanging around to see if Cricket and the others landed safely. They would already be skulking around the edge of the ward, hiding in any crevice or hollow they could find. I worried less for Cricket. His camouflage would protect him as he headed east around the island to our rendezvous point.

But Jacoby and Errol would be heading west, toward the gates and the administration building. Jacoby would get Errol as close as he could, then hide while the bodach created a distraction. Errol was tiny, but his magic clashed with electricity in a spectacular way. When he was in a temper, he could knock out the grid for a whole city block. I could only hope that his distraction would be enough to gain us a few minutes of blackout time—enough to cut through the ward.

On the far side of Grandill, we passed the tunnel that once led from the mainland and went under the locks to the island. The tunnel was now a mountain of rubble blocking part of the canal. When I'd been captive on the cargo ship bound for Toronto Ward, marauders had spilled from the ruined tunnel to attack the ship. I watched the shadows between the rocks, looking for any movement, but our luck was holding, and we passed it like a ghost in the night.

After the locks, the canal was blocked by the old hydro-electric dam. Another guard tower had once stood beside it, but the marauders had burned it during their raid and it hadn't been rebuilt yet. That didn't mean the site was unmanned or unarmed.

We floated by the massive hydro-electric station, its ancient bones like the remains of a leviathan. The rumble of water rushing through the dam masked our motor. Nothing moved on land.

With the power station and Grandill behind us, I breathed easier. The mainland on this side had survived the Flood Wars with only minor devastation. We sailed on until we found a small rivulet that cut inland, then drove the boat up it for another three kilometers until the stream became too shallow. We beached it on the rocky shore. Leaving everything but our small packs and my sword, we headed over the stream bank. Princess zig-zagged over the barren landscape with her nose to the ground. A ten minute hike brought us back to the canal.

Across the water lay Grandill Prison.

We were clear on the other side of the island, far from the prison gates. Between us and those gates stood acres wilderness and hundreds of murderers, rapists and other vicious criminals.

And a freezing cold canal.

We would have to swim it.

I was already wet and shivering, and we had no time to waste. I followed Mason down to the water. There was no beach here. The trees grew roots right into the canal. The overhanging branches gave us good cover as we waded out.

Princess whined and paced in the shallows.

"Come on," I urged. "It's only water." When she saw we were determined to press on with this insanity, she followed.

The shelf below us dropped off, and we were suddenly paddling in deep water. This far north, the water was always icy, it didn't matter what time of year, but once my legs went numb, it wasn't so bad. Princess found her sea-paws and paddled by with her tongue hanging out.

The narrow canal quieted the choppy waves. The only sound came from the wind rustling the trees. I tried not to think of the things that our passage might be stirring up in the murky depths.

Deep currents pulled us downstream. We had to cross quickly, not just to keep out of sight from any patrols, but so that we didn't end up too far from our rendezvous point with Cricket.

Mason was a powerful swimmer. He cut through the water with swift strokes. I was no slouch either. In my teens, I'd won a few swim meets, and in Asgard swimming had been my escape from the grueling hours of training. But I couldn't keep up with him.

A rogue wave shot up and splashed me. I gagged on the brackish water and kicked frantically. Princess bumped against me. I grabbed onto her mane.

Mason saw me fall behind and turned to wait.

"We're almost there." His voice was no louder than a whisper of wind. I was trying to hold in a cough and nodded. I wiped my eyes, worried that Mason's magic black paste wouldn't survive a bath in the canal.

My arms were lead weights, but I continued to put one in front of the other.

On the other side, there was no shore, no sandy ground to rest my numb feet, only an ancient retaining wall that rose into the sky. I clung to the slippery rocks. The wall hadn't looked too high from the far side, but now, already tired from the swim and limbs numb from the cold water, it seemed insurmountable.

Mason waved at me to catch my attention. His eyes were black sparks against his blackened face. He pointed downstream to a section of crumbling wall. Stones had shifted and fallen, leaving decent footholds. Driftwood had snagged against the protruding rocks.

Mason boosted Princess onto the pile of debris. She shook, spraying us with water.

I glanced at the impossibly high wall again. Even with footholds, it would be a difficult climb.

"She'll have to fly it," I panted, wishing I had wings too.

Mason braced himself against the wall and gave me a boost up.

My icy fingers struggled to grip the slick stones. My right foot slipped on age-old algae, and I cracked my knee against the wall. Pain shot up my leg. Pain was good. It blasted through the cold and revived my frozen nerves.

Princess whined and I shushed her.

"You wait here until I call you." She licked my chin and I hoped she understood.

Another slow step upward and I breached the water line. Now the rocks were dry and I climbed more quickly. I could hear Mason pulling himself onto the debris pile.

I ignored the ache of cold fingers on stone and climbed. One hand. One foot. Another. And another, until my head poked over the top of the wall. I waited. Nothing moved. Fifty meters of rocky ground led to the ward. Its magic hummed in my teeth, and I took a moment to brace my psychic shields. Then I hoisted myself up and rolled onto the uneven ground, making myself as small as possible.

Princess landed beside me with a thump. I dragged her down until she lay flat too.

Mason's head crested the wall and he pulled himself up. I pointed to a cluster of bushes and rocks to our left. He nodded and we crab-walked over to them. The shadows were barely big enough to hide in.

"You okay?" I gestured toward the invisible ward. Its magic screamed. His expression was tight and grim but he nodded. One more reason to get through the ward quickly.

He took out Oscar's radio and turned it on low. A squelch of static came through the speakers, then quiet voices. It was the guards at the gates. No one seemed alarmed. After a moment he shut it off.

So far, we hadn't been discovered. Now we just had to wait for Errol to make his move.

Mason checked his compass. It was an alchemical gadget that used apex stones as a reference instead of the Earth's magnetic field, which had become unstable since the Flood Wars. He'd destroyed his original compass when he learned that Gerard Golovin had created it, using the spirit stone of a dead fae as a battery. But since then, he'd revamped the design with a less heinous fuel source.

He studied the digital face, then clicked it shut. "We're in the right spot. Cricket should be here."

"He'll find us," I said with more confidence than I felt.

The night was deathly still. Then footsteps scraped on the gravel, and every muscle in my body tensed.

Peering through the thin foliage, I spied a lone guard making his rounds along the outside of the ward's perimeter. He had a blaster slung over one shoulder, but his relaxed gait told me he didn't expect to use it.

The footsteps faded. We waited. My leg cramped under me, but I didn't move. I could barely see Mason in the shadows, but I felt his calm presence beside me and took comfort from it.

Away from the water, the night air was warmer. My wet clothes clung to me, but the chill had left them. I pulled the damp hat lower over my brow and tucked in my loose braids.

The ward loomed ten steps ahead of us. I couldn't see it, but its presence was like a gnat buzzing around in my brain. I gripped Mason's hand, hoping to imbue him with some of my magic, or barring that, my unyielding confidence in him. He gave me a small smile, and mouthed, *I'm okay.*

A low harmonic sound like a violin being tuned cut through the silence, and I let out a breath I hadn't realized I was holding.

Cricket stepped out from another stand of bushes. I beckoned him to join us.

"All is quiet," he said as he slipped into our hiding spot. In a moment, he looked like just another tree trunk.

"Quiet is good," Mason said. "It means they haven't found Jacoby and Errol."

"They won't." I said that to still my worry, but found I believed it. My dervish could be silly and capricious at times, but when the danger became real, he'd proven more than once that he could handle himself.

Princess jumped the moment before a burst of magic surged from the ward. A bang shook the night and rattled my teeth. The glow from the far side of the island went out, leaving the night inky black. Mason made a gurgling sound and fell among the brambles. Seconds later, a flare burst over the island like fireworks. I heard shouting. Feet pounded on the gravel as the guard returned at a run. He passed by our hiding spot without even a glance.

Whatever Errol had done, it was effective.

"We have to move now!" I grabbed Mason's arm. He groaned. Getting to his knees seemed like torture.

"Go!" He shooed me toward the ward. I hesitated. It was too much magic for him. He'd overload for sure. He waved me away again. "Go!"

I ran for the ward. The best I could do now was get him through and away from the unsteady magic.

Errol's attack didn't disable the ward, but we hadn't expected it to. The prison would have hefty backup generators. But the diversion gave me time to work. With any luck, no one would notice this second disturbance in the field of magic.

I unsheathed my sword. It was vibrating with excitement.

Hold on. You'll get your taste.

I pressed the tip of the blade against the invisible shield. It was like pushing through thick gelatin. The air sizzled where blade met magic. A heavy hand gripped my shoulder. Mason panted as he tried to protect himself from the onslaught.

A little further. I pushed. The blade slid through the ward. I cut downward. We were almost there. Princess whined at my side. Shouts came from my right.

My arm froze in the downward cut.

"Keep going," Mason hissed. The shouts grew louder. I could hear gravel crunch under heavy boots. The guards were almost upon us.

Cricket flexed his shimmering wings. They spread wide enough to encircle us all.

"Be still," he said. I stopped. Mason dug his hands deep into the thick ruff of fur around Princess's neck. Cricket closed his eyes and I felt a shift in the air. It was amazing. One moment his magic tasted like tree-bark and loam. The next it had the same ozone zing as the ward.

He was camouflaging us!

Two guards ran by. This time, their blasters were primed and ready. But they didn't even glance our way. All their attention was on getting back to base and the disturbance at the gatehouse.

Thank you, Errol.

The guards disappeared into the shadows.

"Hurry, now," Cricket said, but I didn't need any urging. I dragged my blade down and around, cutting a hole big enough for a man to slip through.

I shoved Mason toward it. He ducked and rolled onto the grass on the other side.

"You'll be okay?" I said to Cricket. "We'll be as fast as we can."

"You go. I will keep door safe."

I prodded Princess until she crawled through the tiny gate, then followed her. The magic of the ward shivered over me like wet noodles down my back. On the other side, I shoved Princess and we ran for cover.

As soon as we were safely hidden in the trees, I turned back, but I couldn't see Cricket or the hole in the ward. He was true to his word.

"Can you mark this spot on your compass thingy?" I asked. Cricket's camouflage was so good, I wasn't sure we could find the breach again.

"Already done." His voice was gravelly. "Lets get away from here." Mason had lost some of his face paint, and his skin peeping through seemed unnaturally pale.

We stumbled through the trees, no longer worried about stealth. We had no real destination in mind. Our only plan was to make contact with some of the inmates and find news about Gunora.

The trees were tall and broad and almost prehistoric, an effect of the Inbetween's magic that had reshaped the island before Hub turned it into a prison.

"Do you feel that?" Mason breathed deeply as if filling his lungs after a long run.

"I don't feel anything."

"Exactly. The magic is dampened. I feel like I can breathe for the first time in weeks."

Tentatively, I let down my shields. They'd been wrapped around me so tightly and for so long that it took a moment to release them. Then I felt it too. The magic in this place was dull, like a painter's watercolors that were all smeared together and had lost their beauty.

"I don't like it." It was like losing my sense of smell, disorienting and somehow sad. I gripped my sword tighter. At least that still hummed steadily in my hand. It had enough of its own magic to sustain it through this unnatural drought.

We emerged from the trees onto a dirt road. My clothes had mostly dried. My jeans were stiff, but my boots still squelched with every step.

While we'd been under the cover of the trees, the clouds had broken up and a thin moon gave a bit of light, just enough to illuminate a boy standing in the road.

He looked no more than six years old, but his gaze was steady and unwavering. His slight frame was dressed in clothes that were too big for him and much mended. Thick black hair curled around his shoulders in waves. A shock of white hair on his forehead glowed in the moonlight.

Then he seemed to melt, and the next moment a fluffy pony stood in the road—a gray with Appaloosa spots across his rump, black mane and that same white forelock. Stubby white wings curled from his back. He was terribly cute—until he grinned. Two rows of razor-sharp teeth filled his mouth.

Horses weren't supposed to have sharp teeth.

Princess growled low in her throat. I held her back and could feel the muscles of her shoulder tensing under my hand.

The pony tilted his head and studied the hound, not afraid, but curious. Then he turned and trotted a few steps down the road, his feet clip-clopping on the hard-packed dirt. He stopped when he realized that we hadn't moved. His tail pointed straight to the sky and he tossed his head. He took another few steps and turned back again.

"He wants us to follow him," I said, as if meeting a shape-shifting boy-pony was a normal occurrence.

"I see that. Do we trust him?" Mason asked.

"It's what we're here for."

"Fine, but don't get any ideas."

"Whatever do you mean?"

"I mean your rescue instincts kicked in the moment he batted his big brown eyes at you. We're not here to rescue him too."

"Of course not." I smiled sweetly. He knew me oh-so-well.

Mason took my hand and we ran after the trotting pony.

24

I studied the pony as we followed him down the twisting road. The stubby wings flexed like bellows as he trotted. They didn't seem strong enough to support even his small body.

"What is he?" Mason kept his voice low, but it seemed unnaturally loud in the quiet woods.

"I'm not sure. Kelpie or pegasus would be my guess." But neither of those races quite fit the pony-boy. Pegases didn't usually shift form. Not that I knew of, anyway. And kelpies didn't have wings.

"Anything we should be worried about?"

"Well, kelpies like to lure people into the water and drown them." I paused. "Then they eat them."

"Nice. Carnivorous horses. What twisted mind came up with that?"

I grunted an agreement. Wild horses were dangerous enough without pointy teeth. Still, he was just a wee thing.

"If we run into a herd, we might be in trouble, but I think we can handle one pony."

It was Mason's turn to make a grunting sound. He knew critter wrangler rule ten as well as I did: cute can kill as easily as ugly. He didn't know lucky number thirteen though: where there's one carnivorous horse, a herd will follow.

The path narrowed. Maples flanked each side and their branches hung low over the road, making it seem like we were about to enter a tunnel. I didn't expect there would be cars on the island, so no need for wide roads, but the lane way was barely wide enough for us to walk side by side. The pony disappeared into the treed tunnel. I stopped and held Mason back.

Instinctively, I tried to let out my keening. Nothing. The empty feeling left me panicky. My imagination filled in the blanks, and I was suddenly sure that we'd be facing an army of vampires, ogres or werewolves on the other side.

"What's the matter?" Mason rubbed the back of his neck like it prickled.

"Phantom limb syndrome," I said. "My keening is gone, but I feel like I *should* be able to sense something. I guess this is what mundanes call the willie-nillies."

"There isn't anything mundane about you." Despite our circumstances—the urgency of our mission and the possibility of a coming fight—he took a moment to tuck a strand of my hair under my cap, then leaned in to kiss me gently. My hand rested on his chest. My keening might not pick up the beat of his heart anymore, but there it was, steady and strong under my fingers.

He nodded toward the tunnel. "If things go sour in there, we run. No heroics. Agreed?" His eyes bore into mine. I nodded. "And whatever happens, I've got your back."

Unreasonable hot tears prickled my eyes. "When this is done, we're going to sit at home by the fire for a month. Two months at least. I promise."

He laughed, a deep, low sound that rumbled under my hand. "I know you well enough not to hold you to that promise." Then he squeezed my butt and nudged me forward. "Ladies first."

I rolled my eyes. "Such a gentleman."

Under the arching branches, the night became even darker. A blister was forming on my right heel where my wet sock rubbed, and I limped on in the dark. Princess stuck by my side, her fur bristling. A branch snagged on my knit cap, triggering my heart to beat against my ribs. I imagined clawed hands grasping at me from the shadows. I was blind and deaf without my keening, unable to sense the hundreds of little lives scurrying in the leaf litter or crawling through the branches overhead.

Then we were through and the moon lit up a cluster of ramshackle huts built around a large fire pit. A dozen people milled around the low-burning fire. My eyes ranged over them. They were hard faces. None were friendly and a few were outright hostile. They ranged in age, from young to very old, but the only child was the pony-boy, now back in his human form.

No one spoke. Hands gripped weapons—spears mostly and a few knives. They seemed ready for violence.

Mason called out, "Who are you?"

"The question is, who are you?" This came from the man standing next to pony-boy. He was tall and straight-backed but thin and wasted looking. Skin hung off his cheekbones in craggy folds. Black hair had mostly gone white and hung in lanky, unwashed locks. He was missing an eye and didn't bother to wear a patch. His long-sleeved shirt was too short in the arms and looked like it had once belonged in a boardroom but was now faded, stained and worn ragged. He brandished a stout walking stick in one hand, and I had no doubt that it could easily be turned into a weapon.

"Didn't hear tell of any newcomers arriving today," he said. The others fanned out behind him. I spotted at least half a dozen shifters in the crowd by the tell-tale golden glow in their eyes. There were also a couple of goblins and one particularly nasty looking fae with tentacles and skin covered in oozing moss.

"We're looking for a friend," Mason said. "A woman. She would have arrived within the last month."

"That doesn't tell me who you are." He ground the walking stick into the dirt.

I stepped forward. "My name's Kyra. This is Mason. We don't want any trouble."

The man rubbed his beard with his free hand. "Seems to me that if you didn't want trouble, then you shouldn't be breaking into prisons. The boy here said you came from down by the river. I'm curious about how you got there without none of us knowing."

Blood pooled in my legs. I hadn't considered that the inmates would be curious about how we gained access to the island.

"We bribed a guard," Mason said, and I shot him a sharp glance. "I'll tell you which one, if you help us find our friend."

The man considered us for a moment. "My name's Jack. Folks call me One-eye, but not to my face."

"Don't believe them, Jack! They're spies." A skinny being stepped into the firelight. He was tall for a goblin, but uglier than most with a nose that drooped over his too-wide mouth.

"Shut it, Malcolm." Jack snarled. "I decide who is a spy and who isn't.

Now go make sure the others are ready. We leave in twenty minutes."

The goblin glared at Jack. Jack stared him down until he blinked and backed away.

"Crimbils," Jack said. "Always too big for their britches."

Malcolm was a crimbil. The name pinged a memory, but I couldn't quite place it.

"Come and sit by the fire." Jack waved a hand to a bench beside him. "You both looked like you've been dunked in a bog. What's with the black makeup? Is that a new fashion in the big city?" He made a twirling motion around his eye with one finger, and I realized that we must look a mess. Most of the black paste was gone from Mason's face, but it ringed his eyes. I probably looked no better.

I sat, but Mason remained standing. Pony-boy threw himself in a boneless heap at Jack's feet.

"My son, Raven," Jack said.

"We met." I nodded to the boy. He stared back with an uncanny gaze. There was an old soul behind those eyes.

A young woman handed us cups of something that smelled yeasty. She had pointed ears and vividly green eyes. I smiled and nodded, not quite thanking her, just in case. She smiled back, showing inordinately sharp canines.

We were in a camp of convicts, many of them not human. We had no friends here. I tried to remember that as the fire warmed my feet and I began to relax. I longed to kick off my boots and dry my socks, but there was no telling when we might have to make a quick escape.

I took a sip of my drink. It was warm and loamy and tasted faintly like beer, if beer were brewed from shoe leather.

Around the camp, people were stirring. Spears and knives were being sharpened. Packs were packed. A group of three men lay down in the cool grass and started to shift to wolf form. Their legs twisted and bent, reforming into the canine angles. Fur grew on their skin like sprouting mold. It seemed to take forever. Screams of agony filled the night, but none of the others paid any attention. I'd seen wolves shift a dozen times, but it had never been as painful to watch.

"It's the dampening ward," Jack said when he saw my look of revulsion. He waved vaguely at the sky and the invisible prison bars. "Makes it hard to shift. Not impossible, just uncomfortable."

About as uncomfortable as being skinned alive.

I hadn't tried to tap into my own well of magic. Oscar had warned that it would be difficult to access, and after the discomfort of finding my keening gone, I hadn't wanted to try. What if I couldn't do any magic here? Not that my magic was much good in a fight, but it was part of me, a part I had been gently encouraging to blossom in the last few years. Finding out that it might be a withered stump was unsettling. I touched the locket under my shirt, glad for the magic pill Oscar had given me.

"You're expecting a fight," Mason said.

Jack nodded. "Always." He sat with his legs man-splayed, elbows braced on knees and hands dangling down between them. The flickering firelight accentuated the deep creases on his face and the empty eye socket.

"We're headed for the drop zone. Deliveries came two days ago and we got our share, but the bluecaps might have left something useful behind. No harm in checking." He glanced over his shoulder where his crew was already mustering. "We were planning to leave at first light, but there's been a disturbance at the gates. You wouldn't happen to know anything about that would you?"

Mason stared at him, the grim line of his mouth neither agreeing or disagreeing.

"Fine. You can keep that secret. But if you're responsible, I thank you. having the guards occupied elsewhere will serve us better." He leaned in and spoke in an exaggerated whisper. "Those bluecaps don't take kindly to us picking through their rations." Then he leaned back again, clapped his hands and smiled. "Now I've got to get ready. You're welcome to stay until morning, but they're a violent bunch." He waved to encompass his crew, the huts and the fire pit. "Most of them would kill their own grandmothers for a hot meal. I can't promise your safety while I'm gone."

He made a move to rise, and Mason said, "We'll be leaving as soon as we find our friend. Have you seen her? She's nearly as tall as me. She might be blond."

"Only one newcomer in the last month." Jack leaned in and whispered, "A witch."

Mason sipped his beer and heroically didn't wince at the taste.

"Can we speak to her?" I asked.

"You can try. She ain't here though."

"Do you know where she is?"

"I do."

I was starting to feel like we were getting the run around.

"Would you take us to her?"

Jack leaned back, stretching his long legs precariously close to the fire. "I might be persuaded to. Why don't you start by telling me how you really got in here, and don't bullshit me with that story about bribing a guard. I've been here long enough to know the guards are incorruptible. Believe me, I've tried." He smiled and I saw the predator lurking in his eyes. He was a shifter of some sort. Not a wolf, I thought. He was too lean and wiry for that.

"I told you, Papa." Raven pointed at my sword. "The lady cut a hole in the magic with her big sword." The boy had been sitting in the dirt beside Jack, playing with a roughly-carved wooden car. He dragged it along the ground on its roof as if he'd never seen a real car in action. And I thought, maybe he never had.

Jack fixed his eyes on me. "Is this true?"

I bit my lip and nodded. Mason stood behind me and put both hands on my shoulders as if feeling a sudden need to protect me.

Jack watched us, then took a wheezing breath and rose.

"Raven, take that hound and find her something to eat before she starts digging up the bones of the dead."

Princess, having been unsupervised for a few minutes, had grown bored and started gouging out holes in the middle of the clearing. Raven glanced at the hound and hesitated.

"It's all right," I said. "She's very friendly. Her name's Princess. Here." I grabbed a stick from the kindling pile and handed it to him. "You throw that for her a couple of times, and she'll follow you anywhere."

The boy reached for the stick, then ran off to play.

Jack wasn't smiling when I turned back to him.

"Now you come with me."

JACK WALKED US down a path toward a stream. The firelight barely penetrated the trees here, and the water rushing over rocks drowned out the noisy camp. It would also mask our conversation from anyone trying to listen in. He glanced around to make sure no one was within earshot. Then, with icy determination in his eyes, he said, "Now you're going to tell me exactly how you breached a secure ward. And I'll know if you're lying. It's my special talent." He grinned. His teeth were startlingly white and a sharp contrast to his grubby face and puckered eye-socket.

"I'm Valkyrie." I kept my voice low and waited a beat for Jack to acknowledge that he knew what a Valkyrie was, but he just stared steadily from his one eye.

"My…uh…sword has some unusual properties. One of them is that it can cut through just about anything." I left out the part about the sword needing a Valkyrie to wield it. Experience had taught me that bit of knowledge was better kept a secret.

"So you cut open the ward?" Jack's eyebrows shot up. "How do you expect that to turn out? The guards will find the breach in no time." His gaze shifted to Mason then back to me. "Was that the reason for the explosion we heard earlier?"

Mason cleared his throat. "A diversion only. And no one will find our breach."

Jack pursed his lips, considering us.

"Did you see this witch who arrived last month?" I asked.

"I did."

"What did she look like?"

Jack fished around in his shirt pocket, pulled out a small twig, and began to chew on its end.

"I didn't get a good look at her, mind. She seemed tall, but she was standing a ways in the distance, talking to a couple of bluecaps, so perhaps she only tall by comparison. She wasn't dressed like a witch, to be sure. More like you are. Black jeans and a coat too heavy for the day, but she'll be happy to have that in a few months, I suppose."

I tried to rein in my frustration at his rambling.

"But what did she look like? What color was her hair?"

Jack tucked his chin and curled a lip. "White, of course. Didn't I say so? She was old. Very old. With a face like boiled leather. Frail looking too, but perhaps not so frail as that, because she scared those bluecaps off quick."

So Gunora had arrived in crone mode.

"You said your friend was blond. What do you want with the witch?"

"She's a shifter, of sorts," I explained. "She might look young or old."

"Where is she now?" Mason asked.

"Probably with the kelpies. Witches always end up with those bastards."

"Will you help us find her?" I asked.

"She your kin?" Jack squinted his eye at me as if deciding what to think of someone who would be kin to a witch.

"Yes."

He nodded like it all made sense then. Family was important to Jack.

"We'll be heading toward the kelpie territory," he said. "Your little interference at the gates will keep the guards busy. Buys us some time to raid the other drop zones. But I don't see why we should risk bringing you along."

"We can pay you," I prodded. This brought a rueful smile to his face.

"With what? Credits? Gold? What use would I have for such things?" He waved a hand at the camp behind him. "I'm king here in my little kingdom."

I nodded to acknowledge his kingship.

"What do you want."

Jack leaned in, a feral grin on his face.

"When you leave, I want you to take someone with you."

"I won't release any prisoners." I crossed my arms over my chest as if that made me more fierce. Jack wasn't impressed.

Jack used the twig to pick at his teeth. "But you'll take this cousin of yours with you, I expect."

"My cousin is sick, dying actually. That's the only reason we're here." Jack didn't need to know about Tums and Tad. I got the feeling the less he knew about us, the better.

"We're all dying, darlin'. Some of us are just better at it than others." Jack laughed. It made a wheezing sound through his chest.

My wet toes curled in my boots. I was tired, hungry and had a blister the size of a dragon egg on my heel. I was in no mood for banter.

"We won't be taking any other prisoners with us." I kept my voice even. Mason moved closer to my side, and I was glad for the weight of his hand on my shoulder.

Jack's expression lost its humor, and the determination in his eye matched mine.

"Not a prisoner. I want you to take the boy. He's the only true innocent on this island. He was born here, you see. To the authorities, he doesn't even exist."

Mason narrowed his eyes. "Why him? Why not you?" He wasn't buying what Jack was selling and neither was I.

Jack sighed and his shoulders slumped. It could have been a trick of the light, but he suddenly look years older. Ancient and worn down, in the way a mountain wears under eons of wind and rain.

"I'm set in my ways," he said. "Life's not so bad here, really. Not when everyone knows you're strong enough to leave you alone. Besides, I don't have too many years left in me. Better to live well-fed in here, than to starve out there. But the boy has a whole life ahead of him."

I glanced toward the camp that I could just spy through the trees. It was bustling with activity as Jack's crew got ready to raid. Raven was engaged in a fierce game of tug-the-stick with Princess. Dressed in clothes that were too big for him, he looked small and thin to the point of fragility.

Jack gripped my arm, startling me.

Mason was suddenly between us, and he wrenched Jack's hand away. "Don't touch her, old man."

I saw something untamed and untamable in Jack's gaze. His pupils flashed gold for a moment, and I got the feeling we were being analyzed as prey, the way a hawk watches an unsuspecting mouse when it sniffs the open air.

Mason stood taller and stared him down. If he were a cat, he'd be puffed up to twice his size. A low threatening noise came from his throat, but Jack didn't back off.

"Promise to take the boy when you go, and I'll get you to the witch."

The implications of what he was asking washed over me in a wave, and Mason's teasing words echoed back at me.

We're not here to rescue him too.

This wasn't just about breaking a convict out of prison. Jack had said it. The boy had no identity outside of Grandill. He didn't exist. We would be responsible for him. *We* would be parents.

As usual, Mason understood my thoughts without having to ask. He squeezed my shoulder and said, "It's a deal."

"Have something to eat." Jack said. "You look like you need it. We leave in five minutes. With any luck, you'll be drinking tea with the old hag by breakfast."

Back in the camp, the wolves were resting after their painful shifts. The crimbil leaned against one of the huts, not disguising the fact that he watched us. Others were mustering. Jack was taking a small army with him to fight the kelpies.

The young woman who'd brought us drinks approached.

"My name's Lily. Jack said to offer you weapons if you don't have none."

She smiled shyly, showing off her rows of piranha teeth and fangs.

"I think we're set. Thanks," I said.

Mason slung an arm around my shoulder. He seemed relaxed here under the magic-dampening ward, like infiltrating a high-security prison and putting his career and our lives at risk was infinitely easier than living with his new-found powers.

"Can you tell us what we should expect out there?" Mason pointed in the vague direction of the woods.

Lily's grin was hard-edged and humorless. "If we see the kelpies, we'll fight them. The kelpies have been asking for it. They take our people. Last year they took…" Her eyes went glassy, but then she hardened her expression. "They took someone dear to me. No one is allowed to go outside the camp alone anymore. Not since last month."

"What happened last month?" Mason asked.

Lily glanced around to be sure no one paid us any attention. She leaned in and whispered. "They took Silvia, Raven's mom." She paused. "Jack's woman."

I closed my eyes and took a deep breath. By the One-eyed Father, we'd walked into the middle of a war.

"And Jack didn't go after her?" Mason asked. I knew what he was thinking. If someone kidnapped me, he'd stop at nothing to get me back.

Lily shrugged. "She's a kelpie. And she has a history with them."

Well that explained Raven's horse form. He was half kelpie on his mother's side. It didn't explain the wings. Those must come from his father. I assessed Jack again. He still gave me shifter vibes. Maybe a hawk?

"She left him for the kelpies?" I asked.

"Jack thinks so."

"But you don't."

"Nah. She'd leave Jack. He's a right bastard. But she wouldn't leave Raven."

I looked over at the boy who was sitting beside Princess, stroking her back. Poor kid. His mother had been gone for a month. No wonder he looked so solemn.

"Right then. Gather round folks." Jack's voice boomed.

The entire camp gathered around the fire. Many of the residents were quite old, or maybe old before their time from eking out a hard existence on the island. They were grizzled veterans of past battles. I could tell that much from the scars they wore and the hard looks in their eyes. Most weren't decked out to fight, but a squad of at least a dozen were armed and ready to leave.

"Let's go over our tactics before we head out." Jack squatted with a great cracking of his knees. He grabbed a stick and drew a shape in the dirt. It was a crescent, fatter at one end. "This is for our new friends' benefit." He caught my eye, then Mason's to be sure we were paying attention. "This is the island." He didn't wait for us to agree, but drew three circles on the east, south and west ends and a smaller circle at the north end. He pointed to that one. "The gates and admin building." He jabbed the stick in the larger circle that covered most of the eastern end of the island. "We're here. The bluecaps are here." He pointed to the south. "And kelpies across the river there." He scratched a line in the dirt, splitting the island. I remembered the map we'd studied before leaving home. The kelpie camp was on a smaller island that was separated from the main island by the Charles River. It was hard to tell from our map, but it had seemed to be no wider than a creek.

"Your witch is either dead in the wild or with the kelpies." He traced a line from our base, along the edge of the bluecap territory, to the Charles. "We can cross here. The kelpies will be watching. If the gods are watching too, you might live long enough to speak your piece."

"How can you be so sure she's with the kelpies?" I asked.

"Because she's not here. And the bluecaps don't take kindly to witches. The kelpies are the only other choice."

"When you say bluecaps, you mean actual bluecaps?" I wanted confirmation of Oscar's intel. Bluecaps were a dwarven clan that had been barred from entering Montreal since its earliest days.

"Small fellows about yay high." Jack held his hand three feet off the ground. "Hair so black, it looks blue. Vicious little buggers. We'll stay out of their way, if we can."

"What about this territory?" Mason pointed to a large swath of land in the middle of the island that none of Jack's circles touched. "Why can't she be here? Maybe she struck out on her own?"

"No one lives in the drop zone," Jack said. The guards clear it every week after rations are dropped. They give us a few days to take anything we can get. Then they come in with guns and shoot anyone remaining."

"Why?" I couldn't keep the incredulity out of my voice.

"So none of us have a chance to build a stronghold around the drop points. They don't want one faction ruling by right of resources. This way they keep us scrambling, you see?"

I did see. It was a brutal way to live, made more brutal by being forced to fight for scraps of food and equipment. Mason's nostrils flared, and I knew he was thinking the same thing.

"So we go around the drop zone," he said.

"That's right. We'll stop to raid the bluecap rations on the way. After that, I'll get you to the ford in the river," Jack said. "But that's where our bargain ends, you remember. You rescue your friend on your own. We won't be fighting any battles for you." He spat out the twig that he always seemed to be chewing and stood up.

I pretended to consider the map.

"That's all right. I don't expect you to fight. Of course, if we die in the kelpie camp, we can't keep our end of the bargain." I looked Jack in the eye and gave him a sly smile.

He stared right back, then snorted. "You must have some fae in you, girl, to twist a bargain into a pretzel like that."

Jack's crew melted into the forest as soon as we set out along a narrow trail. Lily remained with us and walked with another fae named Bear. I suspected they were a couple, and they seemed particularly attached to Jack. The wolves scouted ahead, dashing between trees as silent as shadows, and I had to hold Princess back to keep her from following. The others, some human, some fae, flanked us ahead and behind. In the dark, I couldn't see them. The crimbil came too, and he didn't miss a chance to sneer at me in particular as he passed us. I wondered what I'd done to piss him off.

There was also another mated pair of fae whose names I couldn't remember. And Raven. No one seemed to expect him to stay home despite the expectation of violence.

Princess whined at my heel. She sensed excitement and action in our near future and didn't like being held back.

"I'll take care of her," Raven said. "Come on, Princess!" The boy shifted in an instant. It would have been incredibly fast, even if we weren't under a magic dampener. Then fuzzy pony and furry hound bounded up the road, enjoying the simple pleasure of having young, strong bodies.

"That's amazing," I said. "He changed so fast!"

Jack chuckled. "He's an amazing kid. You'll see."

I got the first glimpse of sadness in his eye. When we left, we'd be taking Jack's son with us, if everything went to plan. That couldn't be easy.

As the sun lightened the sky, I didn't want Princess getting too far ahead, so I gave a low whistle to call her back. She stopped in mid-stride, turned, and trotted back to duck her head under my hand and grin up at me with her tongue lolling.

"Yes, you're a good girl." I scratched behind her ear.

A second soft head butted my other hand, and I looked down to find Raven under my fingers too. I wiggled them through his soft mane. "You're a good boy too. Now stay close, both of you." Pony and pup gamboled off again.

"He's taken to you," Jack said around his chew stick. Up close, I got a good look at it. He was chewing on a willow twig. Willow bark was a staple in my first aid kit as a pain reliever. What was so wrong that Jack needed a near constant supply of willow bark?

"You haven't told him he's leaving, have you?" I asked.

Jack tilted his head so he could see me better with his one eye. "Not yet. He's had enough to deal with these past few weeks."

Jack was keeping information from us. I let silence work his magic and he eventually continued.

"It's his mother, you see. My wife, Silvia. She's taken up with the kelpies. I haven't told him she's not coming back yet."

"Oh, is that all." I let sarcasm drip from my words.

Mason had been listening to our exchange and spoke up. "Are you planning to take her back from the kelpies?"

Jack's lip curled. "I don't take women against their will. If she wants to come home, she knows she's welcome."

Unless, of course, she was being held against her will by the kelpies.

Malcolm, the crimbil trotted down the path toward us. He gave a brief report to Jack from the scouts. We were about to enter bluecap territory, but the road ahead was clear. The crimbil turned to trot away, but not before baring his teeth at me.

Jack nodded toward Malcolm's retreating back. "Remember, you've got no friends here. That one would skin you alive and eat your entrails if given half the chance."

"He won't," Mason said. His eyes were hard as granite.

"So you say." Jack's breathing had become labored. Each breath came out with a little wheeze on the end. He waved us ahead and slowed to walk with Lily at the rear of our procession.

"Now I remember," I muttered to Mason. He raised an eyebrow in question. "Crimbils. They're changelings. A type of fae that steals children and puts one of their own in the cradle to be raised by unsuspecting humans."

"Like a cuckoo bird that lays eggs in another's nest," Mason said.

"Like that, only way nastier. They often grow up to be serial killers and psychopaths, and no one can figure out why because they came from such wholesome, caring families."

Mason glanced backward to make sure the others were out of earshot and said, "Sounds like an excuse to me. 'Oh, he was such a quiet boy. We don't know how he could kill all those people,' said the mother of every serial killer ever."

"Maybe. But Crimbils have excellent glamor and often pass for human their whole lives."

"Until they're convicted and get sent to a prison with a magic dampener."

"Until then." I agreed. It probably burned the crimbil to lose his glamor.

We walked in silence for a few minutes, then Mason said, "What do you think about this Silvia. Did she go willingly with the kelpies or is she their hostage?"

"I don't know. They usually take humans, not other kelpies. And Jack doesn't seem like he'd be the easiest guy to live with, but…" Lily was right. I didn't know Silvia, but I couldn't imagine a mother abandoning her child in this place.

Mason nodded like he knew what I was thinking.

"If we ever get to the kelpie camp, maybe we can find out the truth," I said.

Raven, at least, deserved that much.

We walked for over an hour, meeting no one on the dirt track lined with end-of-summer weeds. In my mind, I heard a clock ticking away the minutes until we had to produce Gunora or lose the twins. I wished we could pick up the pace, but neither Jack nor his crew seemed in a hurry.

The novelty of our adventure finally wore off, and Princess panted at my side. Raven dragged his pony feet too. We stopped for a rest and to let Jack and Lily catch up.

"There's a creek up ahead," Jack wheezed. "Raven, take the hound to drink."

Raven trotted into the weeds. Princess gave a short "Aroo?"

"Go on." I waved her off. We followed at a slower pace.

Mason walked on ahead with the fae scouts, but I hung back with Jack. His breath came in puffs like a steam engine. I wasn't sure he'd survive the trip across the island.

"When are you going to tell Raven about leaving with us?" I asked. Jack spat out his used stick and patted his pocket for another.

"When the time is right."

I didn't want to lecture him on how to be a parent, especially since I couldn't claim any great expertise on the matter, but it seemed to me that the longer he waited, the worse it would be.

I tried not to think about what I had gotten myself into, taking on a shifter child who had never lived in the civilized world, one who'd been taken from his home and his family…No. I would focus on getting Tums and Tad back first. The rest would work itself out. I had to believe that.

"Can you tell us what to expect when we reach the kelpie camp?"

"How much do you know about kelpies?" Jack said.

"A little. They're horse shifters. Kind of like Raven, right? But they don't have wings, as far as I know."

Jack nodded. "That's right. Raven's mother was a kelpie. But the boy is one of a kind." A smile softened the hard angles of his face. Then he checked himself and came back to the problem at hand.

"Kelpies are carnivores, you see."

"So I've heard."

"Oh, it's true enough."

"They like water too," I said.

"Only so's they can drown their prey. And they're as fast in the water as out. Don't let yourself get cornered by one in the river."

"But will they talk to us? Can we even get near the camp without being attacked?"

"If you show them you have something to trade, they maybe won't kill you right off. Maybe."

"I might have something worth trading," I thought of Mason's alchemical toys. Surely the kelpies would find those interesting. Or the walkie-talkie. Being able to listen in on the guards had to be worth something. If not, I might be able to trade the dose of magic Oscar had given me.

"Who should we speak to when we get there?" I asked. "Who's in charge?"

"Felix." Jack put so much loathing into the name, I didn't have to ask if they were friends. "He's not a kelpie, but a nuckelavee."

A ripple of fear ran through me. Nuckelavees were to horses what werewolves were to dogs. Maybe they had similar forms, but no one would ever mistake one for the other. They were creatures of violence. Born from violence. I'd never met one in all my years of critter wrangling, but by the One-eyed Father, if the old stories about nuckelavees were even half true, we were in deep trouble.

"You know this Felix." It was a prompt, not a question.

"I do." Jack nodded slowly and twisted the willow stick between his teeth. "We have a history. And if he did steal my Sylvia, I'll kill him myself. But she loved us both once, and I wouldn't fault her for going back to him."

"So how do you kill a nuckelavee?" I asked.

Jack stroked his beard, considering. "Like most beasts, I suppose. Beheading is always a winner. They don't like fire—kelpies or nuckelavees. In a pinch, you could keep cutting away bits with that sword of yours." He nodded toward my blade and smiled, like it was all a big joke. "Eventually, he's bound to stop moving. Of course, that assumes you can get near enough to do any of that."

"Killing him is a last resort," I said. "We just want the witch."

"That's too bad. No one would miss the old bastard. Not even his own kelpies, I reckon."

"Don't nuckelavees have wings?" I asked, watching Raven flap and hover a few inches off the ground before pouncing on Princess.

"They do. Sometimes. They've got a human form, a horse form like a kelpie, and a third hybrid form, their fighting shape. It'll scare the piss out of you. Big and butt ugly—legs of a horse, body of a man—sort of—and wings of a bat." Jack squinted at me and spat out his chewing stick.

I wanted to ask more but we were leaving the forest. The road opened up to a vast empty ground, covered in scraggly grass. The sun was just topping the trees and already warming my shoulders. The others waited for us near a heap of junk piled in the clearing.

"What's this?" I asked, holding a hand over my nose.

"Drop zone," Jack said. "One of three. It belongs to the bluecaps."

"Why does it stink so much?"

"Because they dump garbage here too. The lazy guard scum are supposed to pick it up, but they never do."

Even in the cool, predawn air, the stench was overwhelming. And they wanted to scavenge here?

"Ugh." I took out my bandanna and wrapped it around my face. It didn't help much.

Mason stood with the fae scouts, as his eyes scanned the many shadows made by the garbage heaps. He was expecting something or someone to attack. I had the same feeling, like hidden eyes were watching us. Princess, of course, was already digging up something dead and smelly to roll in.

"Princess! Leave it!" I called. She looked up from her buried treasure and snorted out a snootful of dirt.

In front of us, wooden pallets were piled in a careless heap to one side. Burlap rags still clung to many of them as if they'd been wrapped in the material at one point. Strewn around the rest of the clearing were crates, torn open and demolished and bits of clothing trampled in the dirt along with other debris—metal, wood, glass. The wind shifted and the distinct aroma of rotting fruit wafted over us from the even bigger pile of garbage behind the pallets.

"The bluecaps have done a good job of picking it over already." Jack frowned. The sun was just rising over the trees behind him and his gray hair seemed to ring him like a halo.

"But they left a lot of good wood left behind." He waved a hand at the piles of discarded crates and pallets. "Their carelessness is our gain. Winter will be here before we know it. Oy! You over there!"

A head poked up from rummaging in a junk pile. At first I thought it was a child, but when he turned, his blue-black beard was plain in the morning light. A second head popped up beside him. The bluecaps saw us and their axes came out. They jumped down from the crate they'd been pilfering and stood in a threatening stance, weapons held in both hands.

From the corner of my eye, I spied Lily readying an arrow to fly. At my side, Princess vibrated with a low growl. I sank fingers into her ruff and she pressed against my leg.

"Something's not right," Jack said in a low voice. He nodded toward one of the wolves. "Circle behind. Where there's two bluecaps, there's more. Be quick and don't engage unless they do."

The wolves faded back into the trees the way we'd come. The rest of us stood our ground, weapons at the ready. The crimbil sported a spear with a nasty point hardened by fire.

Jack had explained that we needed to skirt the bluecap territory to reach the kelpie camp, but the bluecaps didn't look accommodating. The one on the left was older, his face craggy and beard long. He raised his axe and growled out a challenge. The younger one, had a less impressive beard, but his axe looked just as sharp.

We were at an impasse.

Then a little black form went racing toward the bluecaps. Raven's hooves thudded dully on the packed ground. The older bluecap hefted his axe. My fingers clenched Princess's fur as if I could stop Raven's forward motion by squeezing them tight. Raven skidded to a stop, inches from the bluecap. The dwarf raised the axe…but only to get it out of the way. His thick lips spread in a grin. Raven, who stood taller, butted his head gently against the dwarf.

"Och! Quit it you wee beastie." The bluecap protested but didn't push the pony away.

Lily lowered her arrow by a fraction. Princess tore away from my grasp and ran at the bluecaps. She just dashed around them, then settled at Raven's side. Those two were becoming inseparable.

The bluecaps, nonplussed by hell hound antics, turned their attention back to us.

"The boy's welcome here. You are not," the lead dwarf shouted across the expanse. He raised his axe above his head to emphasize his point.

"Come now, Cletus." Jack took a step forward. "We're not here for a fight." He stepped forward again and the bluecaps menaced him with their axes. Jack stopped. "Look, we don't want anything from you. You see? We just want to get through. We've got business with Felix."

"If that's so, why's that damn elf pointin' an arrow at my heart." Cletus swung his axe toward Lily.

"Because we're not dumb enough to travel through the drop zone unarmed." Jack raised an eyebrow.

"Tell 'er to lower 'er bow an' we'll talk," Cletus grumbled.

There was a tense moment when I thought Jack would disagree, then he nodded.

An arrow burst through the air, glinting in the sunlight and struck Cletus in the shoulder, toppling him backwards into a pile of junk. Jack whirled on Lily, but her arrow was still nocked in her bow.

Her eyes were wide. "It wasn't me!"

The other bluecap had flattened himself to the ground as more arrows sailed over his head and into the mound of broken crates at his back.

I heard a yelp of pain.

Princess!

The hound fell onto a wooden pallet that splintered under her weight.

She didn't get up.

CHAPTER

27

I tried to run to her, but Mason held me back.

"Wait!"

I bristled at the command. My hound was hurt, and my only thought was to get to her.

"Look." Mason pointed to two figures stepping from the shadows between us and the bluecaps. One was tall and lanky and nearly naked. Hair the color of September wheat hung in thick waves to her shoulders. The other was a sleek palomino mare at least sixteen hands high. Froth flecked her lips as if she'd just been run hard. Gills puffed open and closed on her long neck.

These would be the kelpies then.

"Petra!" Jack snapped. "You have no business here. Leave off!"

The human kelpie turned to us and smiled. She'd been pretty once, I suspected. But years of hard living and sun had weathered her.

"Anytime bluecaps are plotting with your crew, we make it our business." Petra glanced over at Lily whose arrow now pointed at her chest. She made a quick lunging motion, snapping her teeth at the fae. Lily's hands gripped the bow hard enough that they shook. Bear stepped forward, casually flipping a wicked-looking knife in the air. Petra laughed—a sound like the braying of a donkey—and then she leaped onto the palomino's back. The kelpie turned and galloped at full speed toward Jack.

More kelpies burst out of the dump site with human riders on their backs. They looked fierce and wild in the first light of the sun, like avenging angels rampaging from the gates of heaven.

"Cover!" Jack yelled. His people turned and ran for the trees where the horses would have a harder time maneuvering.

"Run!" Mason grabbed my arm. We sprinted toward the bluecaps. Behind us the kelpies let out ululating cries as they stampeded. Shouts from Jack's crew answered. I heard the clang of steel weapons and cries of pain.

I pulled my arm from Mason's grip and ran for Princess.

She lay on her side in the shadows of broken crates. I dropped to my knees and cleared away debris. Princess panted and whined and tried to lick my chin. Blood had spattered the dirt. I couldn't see where it came from in all her fur. My hands shook as they roamed over her, fingers prodding. Then I spotted the broken arrow in the dirt, broken by the jaws of a hell hound when she yanked it from…where? She yelped again as my hand found the spot between her shoulder and chest. My fingers came away sticky with her blood.

"It's okay. We're going to get you fixed up."

She watched me with dark, trusting eyes.

I glanced behind me. Cletus was in bad shape too. The younger bluecap struggled to help him sit up. An arrow shaft protruded from Cletus's shoulder. Mason was already at his side. He was a decent field medic, so I turned my attention back to Princess.

Drool puddled under her muzzle. It was a reaction to the stress. She whined and licked the bone plating on her cheeks. Dehydration could be a real problem if I didn't get her fixed up soon.

"It's okay. I got you. You'll be fine. You'll be okay." I babbled more nonsense and scratched behind her ears. From my kit, I pulled out a questionably clean bandanna and pressed it to her wound. Princess grunted and laid her head in the dirt. She was trembling. So was I. But the bleeding had already slowed. My head knew she'd be fine, but my heart, like my hands, was still covered in her blood.

Raven pranced around us, his hooves stirring up dust.

"Stop that!" I snapped. The pony froze, his wings flexed as if ready to fly. *Keep your wits, Kyra. The boy is as upset as you are.*

I softened my tone and smiled. "I need your help. She's not hurt too badly, I don't think, but I need to stop the bleeding, and she likes you. Think you can hold this bandage to her wound while I see to Cletus?"

Raven shifted back to his boy form, clothes and all. I'd really like to know how he did that. He crouched in the dirt beside Princess.

I packed Princess's wound with some of Gita's herbal wound filler. It was antiseptic and would stop the bleeding. I pressed the bandanna over that.

"Hold it here," I said. "Firmly. Don't let her squirm away. Got it?" The boy nodded. His brown irises seemed to fill his eyes. "Good. You take it now." I guided his small hand to the bandanna. He didn't flinch at the feel of blood soaking through it.

I turned my attention to the bluecap. Mason had torn away Cletus's shirt and was prodding the shaft stuck in the fat part of his upper arm.

I dug my first aid kit from my pack.

"Let me help."

Cletus eyed me warily. Sweat oozed down the side of his face into his beard. He spat in the dirt, but gave me a curt nod.

I was vaguely aware that behind us, the kelpies cries and other shouts were fainter. The fight was moving away from us.

The younger bluecap paced beside his fallen mate.

"Ralus!" Cletus snarled. "Stop yer fussin' and get me some water."

Ralus jumped and ran to two large packs laying in the dirt. He came back with a small canteen. Cletus took a long swig, then passed it to me.

"For your dog."

"Thank you." He might be a murderer, but I liked the old bluecap already. I handed the canteen to Mason, then crouched to examine Cletus's wound. The arrow head was stuck in the fleshy part of his upper arm. But he wore a thick leather shirt so I couldn't see how deeply it was embedded.

"I'm going to cut away your shirt." I showed him my knife. "Is that all right?"

He glared but nodded again. Carefully, I split the leather. It was as soft and supple as flannel, well worn, but also well-made. The arrow was stuck in deep, past the barbed head, but not so deep that it hit bone. Still, it would tear when I pulled it out.

Under his dark beard, Cletus had gone pale.

"I have to cut out the arrow. It's going to hurt," I said. "Do you want something to bite down on?"

Cletus grabbed the shaft and yanked it out with a grunt.

Odin's eye! I wished he hadn't done that. He could have torn an artery. He'd certainly done more damage to the muscle.

Blood poured from the wound. It was dark, not bright red, so I didn't think he was in danger of bleeding out. I packed it with Gita's wound filler, then wrapped it with a clean bandage. My first aid kit was small, and it was the only bandage I had. I hoped we wouldn't need much more doctoring in the next few hours.

I put a hand to my eyes to shield them from the morning sun and scanned the debris field. Jack and the others were gone.

"You almost done there?" Cletus asked as I was tying the ends of the bandage.

"All done." I let his ruined shirt fall back into place.

Princess was standing now, drinking water out of Mason's cupped hands.

"How is she?" I asked.

Mason's face was streaked with dirt and sweat. Princess heard my voice and wobbled toward me, favoring her right front leg. Mason caught her before she fell.

"She's not going to get far."

I chewed my lip and gazed around at the collection of garbage. Now what to do?

"We can't leave her here," I said.

"You have business with the kelpies too?" Cletus asked. He was already on his feet, leaning heavily on Ralus.

Mason nodded. "We do."

Cletus nodded toward me.

"Well, I thank you for your aid, Miss…?"

"Kyra." I said. "And it was no problem. I wondered…" It wasn't a good idea to ask the fae for favors, but redcaps weren't like other fae. They were a pragmatic species.

"You wondered if we couldna care for the hound while you seek…" He waved a hand at where Jack and the others had disappeared, "whatever fightin' you be up to."

"Yes. It would only be for a few hours at most."

Cletus nodded wearily. "O' course. My wife's a healer. After she yells at me for gettin' shot, she'll take good care o' your beast. But you must bring her. She canna walk to our village, and I dunna have strength to carry her."

"Of course."

"You an' your man are welcome. An' the boy too." He looked fondly at Raven and I wondered how often the pony-boy had visited the bluecaps. "But Jack and his crew are not."

"Okay." I glanced back toward the trees. I didn't think Jack would be a problem. He was gone—run out on us and our agreement.

Mason picked up Princess and Raven danced around him anxiously. Now the question remained. With Jack gone, what would we do with his son?

BLUECAPS AROUND THE WORLD?

September 22, 2081

Unlike the bloodthirsty redcaps, who get their name from dipping their hats in the blood of their enemies, bluecaps are mostly a peaceful race. Peaceful, as compared to the other dwarven races, that is. They still like to carry a good axe and know how to use it.

Like many dwarves, the bluecaps were at home in the pre-war coal and gold mines. Long before the fae came out to the world, miners told tales of strange, flickering blue lights in the mines. After cave-ins, the blue lights sometimes led men to safety. In return, the miners left gold in a secluded part of the mine for these benevolent spirits.

Bluecaps are short in stature with hair and beards so black, they appear bluish. I've been told that in the darkness of a mine, their heads do actually glow with a faint blue light. I have not been able to confirm this theory.

Other than the flaming blue heads, their most distinguishing feature is their fingernails. These are long, curved like claws, iron-gray, and as hard as iron too. The bluecap never needs a shovel or pick-axe for digging.

There are no bluecaps in Montreal, not since the founding of the ward. But it is my understanding that they are still active in parts of Europe. Can anyone confirm this?

COMMENTS (6)

The laws of Terra have forbidden such destructive practices like mining. May the benevolent one also rid the land of these inferior races too.

MyGodHasOneFace (September 22, 2081)

MyGodHasOneFace, Let me educate you, since your parents didn't bother. Benevolence: the quality of being well-meaning; kindness.
BennyBlaster (September 22, 2081)

> BennyBlaster, you're going to hell.
> *MyGodHasOneFace (September 22, 2081)*

>> MyGodHasOneFace, I'll see you there. I'll be the one in top hat and tails ;)
>> *BennyBlaster (September 22, 2081)*

My grandfather used to tell tales of bluecaps, but I haven't seen any in my lifetime. I'm in the Breton Ward, btw. Have a blessed day!
cchedgewitch (September 23, 2081)

Now you're just making shit up. No such thing as dwarves with blue heads of fire. Get your head out of your arse.
BirdsArentReal451 (September 24, 2081)

rigged a kind of sling to help Mason carry Princess, then scolded the hound until she lay still in his arms with her head draped over his shoulder. It was a thirty-minute hike to the bluecap village, and I could see the strain around Mason's eyes by the time we arrived.

The bluecaps were much better established than Jack's camp, and I remembered that Oscar had said they were the first inhabitants of the island. A long, low stone building dominated the clearing with smaller wood shacks scattered about. A paddock held a small herd of goats and a garden in full leafy bloom filled the rest of the available space. Dozens of bluecaps worked along its rows. A whole clan, by Oscar's estimation.

As we neared the big hall, one bluecap head after another popped up from pruning or hoeing to nod at Cletus and eye Mason and me suspiciously, though everyone had a smile or a word for Raven.

"So many," I mumbled.

Cletus heard me and grinned. "We're a bloodthirsty lot, for true. You're probably wonderin' how we can all be criminals. Rebellion, that's how. Damned fae." He spit in the dirt. "Right after the founding. We bluecaps dinna keep with the other fae. Caused a pretty revolt over it. That damned Sidhe, the one who calls herself queen, she wouldna recognize our right to rule ourselves. We cursed her for it." He grinned as if remembering a fond dream.

"You mean Queen Leighna?"

"Aye. That's the bit. An' then she kicked us out o' the ward. But we revenged ourselves on that queen." He made the word "queen" sound like an insult.

"She's dead." My chest ached just saying those words.

"Aye, she changed her tune when she realized we could dig under the ward. No one has ever been able to do that. Wha—?" He stopped short and gazed up at me. "Dead, you say?" He tugged on his beard, considering this news. "Humph. That's too bad. She was a formidable opponent. I'd hoped to spar with her again when we get out of here."

"When you get out?" I'd never heard of anyone being released from Grandill.

"Aye, our sentence is one-hunnerd and one years. Only fifty-one left."

"Only," I said faintly. "That seems a bit excessive."

"What's for ye, will no go past ye. Old bluecap proverb." Cletus waggled his iron tipped fingers. "Diggin's in our blood. When those fae learnt we could tunnel under the ward, the river an' all, they weren't none happy."

"So why don't you just dig under this ward?" I waved at the sky.

Cletus spat in the dirt. "Smaller island, but deeper ward. Diggin' out of this one will take longer."

That's when I noticed that some of those sheds weren't for gardening tools. A bluecap came out of one pushing a wooden wheelbarrow full of rocks. His face was black with dirt. He whistled and nodded to us before trundling into the trees with his load.

I decided I didn't want to know what kind of excavations were going on below the bluecap village. I glanced at Mason to see if he'd picked up our conversation, but he was focused on putting one foot in front of the other, carrying his hound burden.

Inside the main hall, bluecaps were relaxing with food and drink at long tables. Others were busy mending clothes, sharpening tools or with one of the many chores needed to keep a village running. The far end of the hall was given over to a giant hearth and butcher block style counters for cooking. Cletus showed Mason to a smaller table at the back of the hall near this hearth.

"Lay the hound there."

A stout older woman with coal-black hair turned from a bowl of peeled potatoes and wiped her hands on her apron. She saw Princess and frowned. Then she saw the bloody bandage wrapped around Cletus's arm, and the frown deepened to a scowl.

Cletus introduced her as his wife, Neva.

"What's this now?" Neva was already undoing the bandage.

"Arrow," Cletus grunted.

"Again? You've been shot again?"

"It wasna his fault," Ralus spoke up for Cletus, but Neva slapped him upside the back of his head.

"Ow! What's that for?"

"For talking' out of turn." She slapped him again.

"Ow!"

"And that's for not watchin' out for your uncle."

Ralus rubbed his head and grumbled. "Wasna my fault neither."

"And why's there a dog on my table?" Neva asked.

"She's mine, ma'am. She's hurt too. I hope she won't be too much trouble." I scratched Princess's ears. She lifted her head, then let it flop back to the table. Neva's whole demeanor changed.

"Aye. Well she's just a sweet beastie. Innit she? We'll see what can be done. Etta, fetch bandages and hot water."

A younger female bluecap jumped off the stool where she'd been sitting and handed a bundle to Ralus.

"What am I suppose to do with this?" He held the thing like it was a bomb. The bomb cooed.

"It's a baby, you daft man," Etta said. "You hold it." She giggled. She was pretty, dark haired and sturdy featured, with those tell-tale long fingers and iron-gray finger nails that marked the mining breeds of dwarves.

"A baby!" All the bluecaps turned to me. "I've never heard of a…I mean."

"You thought we sprouted like cabbages, did you?" Neva raised an eyebrow, and Etta giggled again. "'Tis true we don't spawn often, being long-lived as we are, but we do make babies just like you giant lot."

I could feel my face turning red. I hadn't meant to question their reproductive capabilities. It was just that bluecap babies—dwarven babies of any kind—were so rare, or at least so well protected that humankind never got to glimpse them.

The baby started to fuss, and Ralus looked panicked. Etta dumped a pile of bandages on the table and handed him an empty bucket.

"Here, go on and get the water." She reclaimed her bundle and the baby quieted, soothed by its mother's presence.

Neva inspected Cletus's wound and grunted her approval at my handiwork. There was little she could do except clean the wound and re-bandage it.

"Off you go." She shoved her husband away. "Be a good host an' see to your guests while I tend the hound."

Cletus grumbled, but he lifted a pitcher from the counter and headed to the far end of the hall where Raven and Mason rested. Ralus followed him with two fistfuls of mugs.

Neva was a good healer as Cletus promised. She deftly snipped the fur around Princess's wound and clucked at the ragged hole left from the arrow head.

"That's a nasty one. But it should heal without permanent damage. What kind o' dog is she anyway?" She gently touched the bone plating and Princess licked her fingers.

"Hell hound. She usually heals quickly, but here, with the dampeners? I'm not sure."

She gave a long-suffering sigh and re-bandaged the wound. "Aye, we all struggle in this place. Well, that's the best I can do. She canna walk for now. You'd best leave her 'til you're finished with whatever business it is you have."

Her eyebrow quirked up. She was fishing for information.

"We're looking for my cousin. She came within the last month. She might look like a young maid with blond hair, or an old woman, white haired and stooped. You haven't seen her, I suppose?"

Neva's eyes widened as she cleaned fur and blood off her blade. "A witch, is she? Not here. She'd be with the kelpies if she innit with Jack's crew. You mean to break her out o' their camp then? Or is Jack going after that slut o' woman he calls wife." She spat on the floor.

"Just my cousin. I need to find her soon. And Jack…I can't answer for him."

"You don't have to. Everyone knows about the bad blood 'tween him an' Felix. They were friends once, you know. Partners in crime, so to speak."

Neva handed me a mug and filled it from a pitcher. I expected ale—another dwarf stereotype that I'd have to shed—but was glad to find only water. I drank then, deciding not to miss my chance to get the real dirt on Jack and Felix. Any info I could pry out of the bluecaps might help me infiltrate the kelpie camp and find Gunora.

"But Jack's not a kelpie, is he?"

"Nay. He's somethin' else altogether. Felix too. They say he's a nuckelavee, though I've never seen his other form and I don't care to." She lowered her voice and glanced around as if saying the name might summon the beast. "But when he arrived here, Felix took charge of that murderous herd of kelpies. The woman, Silvia was part of it."

"And when was that?"

"Oh, fourteen or fifteen years ago, at least." She lowered her voice, and leaned in, a sure sign that she was about to reveal a secret. "Then Jack showed up and they fought over her. She played along. Encouraged them even. And so when the boy was born, no one knew who the real father was."

I snuck a look at Raven who was sitting on the floor with Etta and her baby. So Raven might not be Jack's son. That was an interesting tidbit.

"But Silvia went with Jack in the end."

"Oh, aye. She did. An' Jack built his own crew from the rest o' the scoundrels on the island. An' for years the two have been squabbling like schoolboys. Only now, after more 'n ten years with Jack, Silvia decided to return to Felix."

"What if Silvia didn't go willingly?"

Neva smirked. "Did Jack tell you that? Well, he would, wouldna he."

I just shook my head. I wasn't going to get into the details of Jack's personal life with her. Somehow, we'd become snarled in a soap-opera drama. I'd expected a straight-forward infiltration to grab Gunora and leave. I should have known better.

I helped Princess off the table. She stood on three legs and shook her ruff.

I refrained from thanking Neva and said, "She won't be too much trouble? We'll be back before sundown." I hoped that was true.

Neva had no chance to answer. A bluecap came running into the hall.

"Guards!" He panted. "Five minutes out!"

Mason rose to join me.

"They can't find us here." He grabbed my hand and looked around. There was no place to hide.

"Help me with this!" Neva shouted for Ralus. Together they moved the table and swept away the carpet to reveal a trap door. Ralus swung it open. Stone stairs crept into the darkness below.

"Get in," Neva hissed. "You too, Raven."

The boy didn't hesitate, but scrambled down the stairs.

Mason scooped up Princess and followed him. Etta shoved the baby into my arms.

"Take her, please! They canna find her!"

"I can't!" I tried to push the baby back at her, but she resisted.

"They'll take her from me. Please." Her brown eyes pleaded.

I grabbed the bundle and descended the stairs into darkness.

WE WAITED IN a cold room. Pots of preserves lined the shelves. The only light came from cracks between floorboards overhead. I sank to the stone floor with the baby in my lap. She watched me with big, dark eyes. Tiny fingers with claws like iron-gray pearls gripped the swaddling blanket. In the near darkness her fluff of black hair glowed faintly blue.

I looked at the other faces around me. Raven squatted on his heels, his eyes big and round in the dim light. Mason stood by the stairs, looking up at the closed door as if willing it to open, and Princess lay on the cool stones with her head on her paws.

The baby wiggled and I cuddled her close.

"When did we become babysitters?" I asked. Mason gave me one of his wry smiles and shook his head.

"I'm not a baby! I'm nearly thirteen!" Raven said a little too loud. I put my finger to my lips to shush him, then realized what he'd said. Thirteen? That couldn't be right. He looked no older than six or seven. Then I remembered Neva's story. Jack had wooed Silvia away from the nuckelavee thirteen or fourteen years ago. If that was true, something had severely stunted Raven's growth.

"Do you hide every time the guards show up?" Mason asked.

Raven nodded. "Papa says the guards will put me in a home for bad boys if they find me. Mama tried to make it a game when I was little. Hide and seek, sort of."

"I'm sorry about your mother," I said. "You must miss her."

Raven shrugged one skinny shoulder. "S'okay. Papa will get her back. If she wants to come." He saw my furrowed brow and continued, "Mama is sad a lot. She wasn't always like that, but I barely remember her before. Papa doesn't mind. He treats her like everything is okay, but…" He shrugged again.

"But you don't think it is."

He shook his head, eyes lowered. It sounded like Silvia battled a good dose of depression. I pitied the woman who had to live in this place, but I pitied Raven even more, old before his time, even if his body hadn't caught up yet.

The baby started to fuss, and I stuck my finger in her mouth. She had no teeth yet, but a strong jaw clamped down hard.

"Ow!" I pulled my hand away, and she let out a little mewl.

Upstairs I heard the clomp of boots and strange voices. Cletus answered, but they were at the other end of the hall and I couldn't make out their words.

The baby whined and squirmed. Princess's tail thumped on the stone floor.

The voices overhead paused.

"Quick!" I whispered, "find me some honey or jam. Something sweet." Mason and Raven roved over the shelves. The baby arched her back and let out a howl. Mason shoved an open jar at me. Honey. I dipped my finger into the pot, then stuck it in the baby's mouth. I remembered some warning about honey and babies, but it was too late to worry about that. And the little bluecap would be worse off if the guards found her.

She sucked my finger, making us both a sticky mess.

The voices rose and heavy footfalls approached the hearth end of the hall.

The floor creaked overhead. The bit of light was blocked by a boot. We all held our breath, and I begged the One-eyed Father to watch over the baby and keep her quiet.

We'd always known that getting caught was a possibility, but I hadn't really dug into that until now. What would happen if they found us? If nothing else, Mason would lose any chance of winning the election. Hard to be prime minister from jail.

The footsteps faded as the guards headed away from the hearth. We waited for several tense minutes in the dark. The baby squirmed and wriggled like a slippery eel. I could barely hang onto her. She opened her mouth and wailed. Her hair sparked bright blue like the flame at the center of a candle wick.

Then light poured into the room as someone threw open the trap door, and Etta bounded down the stairs, her face full of concern.

"I'm sorry. I tried to keep her quiet."

The baby reached for her mother, and I let the swaddling cloth fall away. Etta grabbed her baby and made those cooing noises that seemed to come naturally to all mothers.

"'Tis alright, little one. You're alright now." The baby gave a few more sulky cries as Etta mounted the stairs again.

Cletus waited for us in the light. "Those guards are in a right tizzy."

"Do they suspect someone is on the island?" Mason asked.

Cletus squinted. "Hard to say. They're a tight-lipped bunch. But I think it's best that you leave now."

C H A P T E R

29

eva overruled Cletus and insisted on feeding us before we left. The hall was subdued after the guards left. Nobody spoke while we ate porridge drenched in sweet strawberry preserves sitting at one of the long tables. It was warm and delicious. I hadn't eaten since the afternoon of the previous day and hadn't realized how hungry I was.

Princess shuffled over to sit beside me. She still wouldn't put much weight on her sore leg. Neva offered her some cold mutton. The hound let out a harrumph and settled at my feet, not touching the treat.

Mason and I ate quickly. We didn't want to impose on the bluecap hospitality any more than we needed to. We thanked Neva and Cletus and he offered to escort us to the end of bluecap territory.

Princess limped out of the hall behind me. I stopped and stared at her, hands on my hips. Short of tying her up, I wasn't sure how to make her stay with Neva. And I didn't know what kind of rope would hold a hell hound.

"I'll stay with her," Raven said. His hand rested lightly on Princess's back and the hound licked his chin, then looked at him in that adoring way she usually reserved for me.

I wasn't jealous. Honest.

"Your father won't be worried about you?"

Raven shrugged. "I go off on my own. He's used to it." From the reception he'd received at the bluecap village, it was obvious he was a frequent visitor. He coaxed Princess back inside the lodge and I fought the urge to follow them.

"Come on," Mason took my hand. "She'll be all right."

Cletus walked with us along a narrow trail. We were headed in a general northwest direction. He stopped at a seemingly random spot and pointed up the trail. "You'll hit a creek in a bit. Follow it upstream. It'll widen, but eventually you'll come to a ford. That's where the kelpies are."

"Thank you." I wanted to say more, but really, there was nothing left to say. We wouldn't meet again.

He nodded to me then to Mason. "You're fools for going into the kelpie camp, but if you get a shot at that bastard, Felix, I wouldna cry if you took it." He turned and disappeared back into the trees.

We moved out and were quickly swallowed by the dense foliage. The wind teased us with hints of brine and I knew we were heading toward the bigger expanse of the St. Lawrence again. The forest was thick on either side of the road, but I got no sense of eyes watching me like I did in the Inbetween. That could have been because my keening was dulled or because most of the creatures that lurked in the Inbetween couldn't survive with Grandill's lack of magic. And other than the prisoner settlements, I'd seen no remains of human habitations.

Once this island had been home to thousands of people—families, businesses. There had been community centers and hotels. Schools. Most of that washed away in the Flood Wars. Grandill had been underwater for years, and when the water receded, Hub took it over. The ward had been put in place almost immediately. There'd been little chance for the land to be repopulated, either by Terra or humans.

Mason and I walked side by side.

"Why do you think Cletus wants Felix dead?" I said in a voice pitched low enough for only Mason to hear. "Did he say anything to you?"

Mason nodded. "Seems the kelpies want more rations than Hub gives them. Especially meat."

"Meat? You mean they've been stealing from the bluecaps." I thought of all the work gone into the bluecap homestead, the gardens, the flock of goats.

"I mean the kelpies have been stealing bluecaps. Some of Jack's crew have gone missing too."

"Stealing? You mean…"

"To eat." His expression was bleak.

By Odin's one eye. My stomach flip-flopped at the idea. I knew the stories about kelpies. I'd even faced a herd before, but I'd never heard of them outright kidnapping people from their homes.

The possibility of Gunora still being alive seemed more remote with every passing second. And we were willingly headed right for their camp. Still, Mason and I had fought worse, and I would face just about anything for the chance to get the twins back. I kept their little faces in my mind's eye like a talisman to keep my courage from flagging.

We found the creek. The path ran alongside. It was a well traveled track, and I started scanning the trees ahead for a kelpie ambush. The sun was leaning toward evening and we walked through alternating strips of sunlight and deep shadows from the thick trunks. The constantly changing light kept my eyes from adjusting properly.

A flash of white ahead startled me. I ducked before realizing it was just the tail of a deer. The beast darted like a silent arrow through the bush.

The river widened. It flowed over a rocky bed and the sound of rushing water deafened us to anything else. I stepped from a swath of sunlight into shadow and froze.

A black beast stood on the path. His lips curled back from wet fangs, and a deep growl rumbled from his chest. The werewolf's head hung low, emphasizing the bulk of his shoulders as he crouched, ready to spring.

Another figure slipped from the shadows to stand beside him.

Malcolm the crimbil.

He held a bow with the arrow fixed on my chest. His face was flushed and he glared at us from red, manic eyes.

Mason stepped up on my right side.

"Don't move!" Malcolm swiveled his aim to point the arrow at Mason.

"Where's Jack?" I asked.

"Jack's not here. You got me to deal with now."

Mason inched forward, trying put himself in front of me.

"What do you want?" he asked.

The crimbil laughed. It was not a happy sound.

"What do you think I want? I want out of here!" He squinted his already narrow eyes. "You got in. I figure you can get out."

The wind puffed through the branches overhead, and sunlight broke through to dapple the crimbil and wolf in bright spots.

"We're not taking you with us," Mason said.

"But you'll take Jack," Malcolm sneered. "And that mongrel of his too, I'm sure."

"We're not going anywhere until we find our cousin," I said. "Help us get to the kelpie camp and we'll talk." The wolf started to circle around us. I ignored him. He wasn't the real problem. If he lunged, Mason could take him, but I wouldn't be able to disable Malcolm before he got a shot off.

Mason's left arm bumped up against me. It was hard as stone. He was letting me know he was ready to fight. I didn't know what it cost him to morph into stone in this low magic, but he wouldn't be able to keep it up for long.

Malcolm gestured with his arrow, pointing it back the way we came before fixing it on Mason's chest again.

"Turn around," he said. "Ward's that way. You'll show us exactly how you broke through it. Try anything and I shoot him through the heart. I figure I only need one of you."

I nodded. I'd agree to anything to keep him talking. Beside me Mason held up his one fleshy hand as if in surrender. "Okay, we'll take you, but you have to understand, it's not that simple."

"Move!" Malcolm's eyes bulged and spittle flecked his lips. The wolf shuddered as his muscles prepared to leap. He snarled at the same moment Malcolm let out a gurgled cry and pitched forward. The crimbil hit the ground with an arrow sticking through his neck.

The wolf whirled and barked once. His eyes shone yellow.

"Peter! Stand down!" Jack's voice came from the dark between the trees. The wolf dropped to his belly and whined.

Jack stepped into the light with Lily right beside him. She had a second arrow ready to fly and aimed straight at the wolf. Jack nudged Malcolm with a toe.

"Damned crimbils, never know when to stop." He turned to Peter the werewolf, who cowered like a kicked dog. "Get yourself home. I'll deal with you later!"

The wolf took off. Jack waited until he was gone and said, "He's not a bad lad. Just impressionable. Lets others rope him into stupid schemes. That's how he got caught and convicted in the first place." He glanced behind us. "Where's Raven?"

"He stayed behind with my hound at the bluecap village," I said. Jack made a face like he smelled raw sewage, and I added, "I hope that's okay."

"It's fine. The boy thinks I don't know, but he's over there all the time."

"Were you hurt in the kelpie attack?" I asked.

"Nah. One of the wolves took an arrow, but he'll survive. We gave as good as we got." He patted his pocket, looking for another willow stick. Considering the morning he'd had, he was in good shape. His sleeve was torn and dirt covered his shirt in patches. Lily sported a new cut across her forehead.

"You still going forward with your mad plan?" Jack asked.

I nodded. We had no other choice.

Jack stuck a stick in his mouth and grinned around it. "Let's go find your witch, then."

THE REST OF Jack's wolves flanked us in the trees. Jack fell back and Lily kept pace with him. Bear had taken the lead, and we followed a short distance behind him. He was as big as his name implied, with broad shoulders, blunt features and a blank expression. A killer's face.

Before we'd headed out, I spied a moment of tenderness between him and Lily. He passed her a canteen and she took a moment to caress his hand. A small smile flickered across his features.

I had no trouble imagining him beating someone to death with his meaty fists, but Lily was another matter. She was definitely fae, but other than her teeth she could have passed for a human woman. She was slight and small, not in the least bit threatening. Of course, I might have felt differently if I'd been faced with her magic too. But neither of them struck me as heinous criminals. And after meeting the bluecaps, I was beginning to wonder about the need for this island prison.

We continued on the path that ran beside the river. It led us down a slight incline, but we had to stop several times to climb over barricades or around sections of the trail that had been washed out.

"The kelpies do this," Jack said. "To keep traffic out of their territory." His breathing rasped. It was painful to listen to, though he waved me away whenever I suggested we stop to rest.

We walked on. That ticking clock in my head was getting louder. We had a little more than twenty-four hours to find Gunora and drag her back to Hedge and the rendezvous with whoever was holding the twins. Mason was feeling the urgency too. He picked up his pace and I followed. We were climbing over yet another barricade of broken sticks and rocks when Lily shouted. "We need to stop!"

I turned to find Jack bent over and red-faced as he tried to suck in air. Lily helped him to sit with his back against a tree. I looked ahead at the path. The light was starting to fade.

"What do you want to do?" Mason asked. I glanced back at Jack and Lily. We could leave them and go on alone. They wouldn't stand with us against the kelpies anyway, if it came to that. But it would be dark soon, and we could easily get turned around in this forest. I sighed.

"I guess we can take a short break."

The clock ticked louder.

JACK SAT WITH his back against a tree. His chest rose and fell steadily, but each breath came with a wheeze.

Mason and I found enough dry kindling to get a small fire going. Bear stood like a bouncer at a bar, ready to kick out anyone who intruded on our little impromptu camp. Lily stuck her metal canteen right in the flames, and when it was warm, she poured the water into a tin cup and added herbs from her pack.

"It's for his lungs." She stirred the tea. "The medics say there's nothing to be done for him, but this helps."

I sniffed but the scent of mint overpowered anything else in the brew.

"It's just mint with a bit of lungwort and plantain."

I'd been hanging around Gita and her concoctions long enough to know those were all herbs that supported lung health. And the willow bark sticks he chewed all day long would be blocking pain.

"Is it very bad?" I asked, nodding toward Jack.

Lily shook her head, but wouldn't say. Jack's concern for Raven's future made more sense now. Though Raven seemed like everyone's darling, Jack knew his time here was short. When he was gone, Raven would no doubt end up in Hub's care.

Lily nudged Jack and handed him the cup. He opened his one eye and nodded thanks. His breathing was already easing, but he sipped the tea.

The wind had died as the sun began to set. All was still except for the few buzzing insects that whizzed past my ears in a frenzy to live their very short lives.

"We were friends once," Jack said. His eye was still closed and he clasped the cup in both hands. "Felix and I. Back in the early days of the ward, before Hub gained control of the streets."

I almost argued that Hub still didn't have a good hold on Montreal, but I didn't want to interrupt. His speech seemed fragile, like a butterfly that lands on your hand and any movement might scare it away.

"We were wild boys, always chasing the next high, whatever that was. Then my family got caught up in a blood feud with…with another family." He smiled ruefully, maybe realizing that when we left the island (if we left the island), we could look up his arrest as a matter of record. "And you know, blood feuds never end well. So here I am." He spread his hands wide. His story sounded like a confession. "I wasn't too surprised to find my old chum here ahead of me. Felix had set himself up as king of a tidy little crew. I joined his ranks, but it didn't last."

"Because of Silvia," I said.

"Silvia." He said her name like an affirmation. "She was Felix's woman back then." He lowered his head and shook it as if trying to dislodge memories. But he was smiling. "Silvia was stunning…is stunning. Hair as red as the setting sun, skin like velvet. Beautiful, but frail. And that brute Felix tried to break her. He used her so badly…" His gaze was far away, on another place and another time. "But I couldn't accept it. And I took her."

"You took her? Like kidnapped her?"

"Not kidnap." Jack's voice rose. "Why do you keep thinking I'd take a woman against her will? She came to me. To get away from Felix. When you meet him, you'll understand why. Nuckelavees are cruel and ugly. Inside and out. I loved her, but I asked for nothing in return. I only wanted her to be safe. I like to think she loved me, but maybe she only stayed for that safe haven." Jack's hands were spread open on his lap now, like he'd just emptied them of a heavy burden.

Neva's story was true then, Raven could be Felix's son. I worked the logic through in my head. Raven got his horse form from his mother. But the wings… I glanced at Jack. He was definitely a raptor of some sort. If I had my keening, I could narrow it down.

But nuckelavees had a winged form too. They didn't shift into this warrior shape until puberty. Until then, Raven's heritage would remain a mystery.

I chewed on this for a moment. I'd made the deal with Jack in good faith. Bringing a shapeshifting child back to Montreal was one thing. Bringing a nuckelavee back was entirely different.

Jack found me watching him and the gaze of his one eye bore into me. "You'll keep the boy safe, won't you? You'll take him with you or…" He paused for a breath. "Or he'll end up in a Hub home, or worse. Felix will get him. Finally."

I nodded. I wouldn't leave Raven to the tender mercies of a nuckelavee, father or not.

But Mason was always more practical than me.

"The deal was you'd take us to the kelpie camp," he said.

Jack scratched his chest through his thin shirt and stretched out his legs. "And I did. You'll find them just over that rise."

A Near Miss with a Nuckelavee

April 29, 2077

Last week, I answered a Hub call about a creature lurking in Beaver Lake on Mount Royal. The hill in the middle of the city barely qualifies as a mountain, and the lake in its crater is no more than a glorified pond. But it's a major attraction for Montrealers. Hikers, walkers, and bikers all use the green space. So when reports of hikers going missing and only body parts being found came into Hub, I got called in to wrangle whatever was lurking in the depths of the lake.

Whispered rumors spoke of a ferocious beast—part man, part horse with eyes of fire and a tail made from the souls of the dead. Rumors tend to exaggerate.

After spending some time researching on the Ley-net, I suspected it was a nuckelavee. They're supposed to have three forms—human, equine and a horrifying fusion of both—a skinless creature that is half man, half horse and blended in all the wrong ways. From the descriptions of the Hub officers that were first on the scene, that last form was what waited for me on Mount Royal.

But when I arrived, the water was calm. The park had been emptied by Hub. Only a few stray leaves moved on the walking path. I staked-out Beaver Lake for three days and saw nothing. The captain in charge wanted to tie a goat to a stake and leave it there as bait. I convinced him not to.

The creature had moved on. I probably dodged a bullet with this one, but I can't help wishing I'd seen the elusive nuckelavee. Has anyone had a run-in with one of these?

COMMENTS (3)

I'm glad you're safe! *shiver* Nuckelavees are bad news.
cchedgewitch (April 29, 2077)

I've had experience with a nuckelavee, and the scars to prove it. Too gory to type here. I'll pm you.
hottrotter (April 30, 2077)

Skinless? That's too bad. The skin's the best part, especially with some of that Montreal steak spice you folks are famous for.
MyMommaIsAMutt57 (May 2, 2077)

C H A P T E R

30

The kelpie camp sat in a wide ravine where the island was split by the Charles River. The current slowed as it widened into a pool, and here, a dozen kelpies bathed in the last light of the afternoon.

I lay on my stomach on a rise overlooking the camp with Mason on my right. Jack wheezed on my left, and Lily lay beside him. The others waited in hiding until we scouted the camp.

Below us, a mare came out of the deeper water, her mane tangled around her like seaweed, gills puffing with exertion. She stood in the shallows watching two younger males fight. They reared and struck out at each other with sharp *thwacks* of their hooves. No one seemed overly concerned about the fight.

"Do you see your cousin?" Jack asked.

"No."

Beyond the pool a great fire pit smoldered. The land sloped up toward the trees. A couple of wood structures, no more than shacks, were built on the rise. The bank on our side of the river was littered with bones.

"Some of those are human," Mason said.

"That's right," Jack growled. "Animal, human, fae, bluecap. Whatever those murdering devils can get their teeth into."

I stared at the field of bones—femurs, skulls, clavicles. So many. My stomach roiled and I was glad it was empty.

Jack rolled and slid down the incline. I followed until we were out of sight of the kelpies. So far we hadn't encountered any scouts. The kelpies didn't seem too worried that anyone might attack their camp.

"They don't exactly play by the rules." Jack kept his voice low, but it still whistled through his teeth.

"How do you mean?" I asked.

"There were only a handful of kelpies who came here with Felix."

"I counted at least a dozen."

"And there's more than that. We keep an eye on them. Last count was over thirty."

"He's breeding." Mason's tone was flat and his eyes flinty.

"He is." Jack nodded. "There's worse. He keeps the females. But the males? They're a threat, so when they get too old, he kills them." He paused. "And eats them."

In the stunned silence that fell between us with those words, I could hear the horsey screams and splashes of the young stallions below. How long did they have before Felix thought they were a threat?

"And the Grandill guards don't stop him?" I couldn't keep the rage from my voice.

"The guards won't come into his camp anymore. Not for years. The last time they tried to take his offspring away two guards died. Their bones are down there with the others. The guards leave them alone now." He didn't seem too broken up about the dead and eaten guards.

"Come on. There's a better view from the other side." He scrambled down the hill, leaving Mason and I staring at each other in astonishment.

FROM THE WESTERN slope, we had a better view of the bonfire as the river curved around the camp.

"Still no sign of Gunora," I whispered to Mason. He squeezed my hand. I was waiting for him to tell me it was time to abandon this folly. It *was* time. Gunora was probably a pile of bones by the river. But Mason knew me well enough—I wouldn't give up until I was sure.

I spied a human figure coming down the slope from the shacks. He was naked and filthy and carrying a load of wood for the fire. More figures moved in the shadows and I realized there were more shacks in the trees.

"Are those humans?" I asked. There were several figures moving around up there.

Jack was having a hard time breathing after the climb, so Lily answered.

"Those are kelpies who prefer their human form. It's difficult to shift here, so most keep to one form or the other. The humans serve the horses."

Or they end up being served as dinner, I thought.

"But they keep some pure humans too," Lily said. "Look there." She pointed to a small group of nearly naked humans who were sitting by one of the shacks. They were thin and dirty with the feral look of stray dogs. They ate out of bowls with their hands. While I watched, one stole food from another's bowl and a fight broke out. It didn't last long. They were too weak for more than a few rough shoves.

Mason was looking at the settlement through a small pair of binoculars. After a moment, he handed them to me. The sun was setting, but the binos were one of Mason's alchemical gadgets, and they boosted light as they amplified. The camp went far into the trees. I could see people walking or sitting by the shacks. I took a second to study each face and assure myself that Gunora wasn't among them. Then I turned the binos toward the fire pit where two women worked at adjusting a spit over the coals. The meat attached to it was equine-shaped. The front legs, truncated at the hoof were pulled forward and tied to the spit. The back legs were similarly dressed but pulled backward so it looked like the poor skinned and headless creature was trying to gallop away. It was no bigger than a yearling.

The gorge rose in my throat. How could these monsters eat one of their own? Then my binos dipped, and I spied the body laying in the dirt by the fire.

She was naked and bruised. Her dead eyes stared at the sky even as flies landed on them to suck away the last moisture. Her matted red hair had been trampled into the dirt.

I lowered the binos. Mason caught my eye and nodded. He'd seen her too. Silvia.

I handed the binos to Jack. He squinted through them with his one good eye, then swore in a language I didn't recognize and threw the binos to the ground.

"That's it. You're on your own." He turned to slide back down the hill. I went after him.

"Where are you going? We had a deal."

He stopped and pointed at me. "I got you here, didn't I? If you're stupid enough to go in there, I can't help you. I'm done." He headed back the way we'd come.

Lily grabbed my arm. She bared her sharp fae teeth. "Silvia isn't the first they've taken. If you get a shot at Felix, you kill him." When I didn't respond, she shook my arm. "No hesitations. No remorse. Got it?"

I nodded. "Got it."

Jack and his crew left us in the darkening forest. I'd hoped to convince Jack to join us when we raided the kelpie camp. With Silvia gone that hope died. We were on our own.

Mason leaned against the trunk of a massive pine and watched me pace, kicking up dead needles under my feet. His eyes were dark and hid his thoughts. We'd back-tracked about a half a kilometer so we could talk without being overheard.

"We need a plan," I said. "Gunora must be in one of those shacks." I gripped my sword like I meant to use it.

"She could be anywhere," Mason said. "She could be with those slaves. Or she could be dead."

He countered my agitation with his normal calm. For once, I was glad for the ward that dampened his keening. I needed the old, serene Mason right now. He pushed away from the tree and lowered my hand holding the blade.

"What does your gut tell you?" he asked.

I took a deep breath and let it out. My chest felt tight, and my muscles ached from our long walk. "My gut tells me that she's alive."

He nodded. "Why?"

I flapped a hand at him. "Because she's behind the twins' kidnapping. I don't know how. But she is."

"I agree. And that means she's not a slave."

"Yes!" I jumped at the chance to knock one possibility off our list.

"Jack called her a witch," Mason said. "If the kelpies think so too, they might have kept her alive just for that."

"Right. She'd be taken care of." Gunora's MMC would force her to shift even with the island's dampened magic. The kelpies would see that as strong innate magic. They would treat her with respect, maybe even a little fear.

"That brings us back to the huts," I said. "We should start looking there." Every muscle in my body bristled. I was ready to storm the camp right then.

"Hey, look at me." Mason rubbed his thumb across my chin, forcing my eyes up to meet his. And he smiled. Damn him. I couldn't hold back the Tears that seemed so close to the surface these days, and they fell down my cheeks onto his hand.

I cried for Silvia. And for Raven who would never again see his mother. I cried for the foal on the spit. And for Princess who was hurt and for Tums and Tad, waiting for someone to come rescue them. I let out a few solid sobs, then I wiped my eyes on my sleeve and stood back.

"I'm done."

"Good." He wiped a stray tear from my cheek with his thumb. "Because if we're going to find a way into that camp, I need you in control."

"In control." I nodded and let out a sigh. "I swear, when this is done, I'm becoming a home body. No more adventures."

"You are my adventure." He kissed the end of my drippy nose. That's when you know your man really loves you, when snot doesn't faze him. That and when he helps you sneak into a cannibal's lair.

IN THE END, we didn't have to search very hard. Three kelpies found us while we were crouched on the rise, looking for a way across the river without being seen. The gills on their necks confirmed they weren't human slaves. They were strong and well-fed. Two young males and an older female. One had an arrow nocked in his bow before I could scramble to my feet. My sword was useless in its sheath across my back.

"What do you want?" asked the female. I recognized her. She was the one who shot Cletus and Princess. Tall and brass-haired, her features looked like they'd been hewn from a block of wood. Petra, Cletus had called her.

The males were as alike as Tweedledum and Tweedledee. They were short, scrawny and mean-looking. The one with the bow aimed his arrow at Mason's chest, rightly thinking that he was the bigger threat. The other held a knife like he knew how to use it.

"We just want to talk," I said. "We're looking for my cousin. She's a fairly new arrival."

The kelpies glared at us, unmoved.

I dared a tiny step forward, my hands held open in submission. "We heard there was a witch in your camp. A new one. We'd like to talk to her."

"Should I shoot her," said Tweedledum. Petra was clearly in charge. She slapped him hard across the face.

"Are you stupid or just stupid? The witch said to bring any strangers to her."

"Aw, Ma!" Tweedledum let go of the bowstring to rub his cheek. The arrow shot forward on a wobbly trajectory and pierced the ground at Mason's feet.

His brother menaced us with his knife. "I don't answer to the hag." His grin showed teeth sharpened to spikes. He was bare-chested and the gills on his neck puffed open and closed.

His mother swatted him too. "Keep talking like that and you'll both be dead by morning. Now go tie up their hands."

Tweedledee motioned for me to drop my sword. I caught Mason's eye and he nodded. The kelpies had confirmed the presence of a witch. We needed a way into that camp, and this was it. I shrugged out of the sheath harness and let it drop to the ground. The kelpie grabbed me and put his blade to my throat while his brother frisked Mason. They weren't as dumb as they looked. Mason would never risk harm to me, and so long as one brother had me by the throat, he didn't resist. But his eyes never left mine as they tied his hands behind him.

Dum unsheathed my sword and hefted it, testing its weight. He had a good form, like he was no stranger to a blade. He grinned because my sword was awesome, even if it looked like a medieval hunk of junk. Anyone with any experience could appreciate its balance and heft.

Silently, I cursed myself for not glamoring it. Even with the dampened magic, I could have drawn from my own well, but that might have left me dry, and I didn't want to face the kelpies without resources.

Dee's hands roved over me, looking for more weapons. He grinned as his fingers slid up the inseam of my jeans, and his hands lingered overlong on my butt. I could see Mason's face turning red as he watched, but I shook my head.

The kelpie took only my hunting knife, leaving the rest of my kit alone. When they felt we were secure, Dum pushed Mason forward. Dee grabbed my elbow and tugged me along too. The light was fading fast, but I could see Mason working at the ropes on his wrists.

Petra led the way. I stumbled as Dee shoved me along the dark path beside the creek.

A soft whicker came from ahead, and a horse stepped out of the shadows to challenge us.

"Just us," Dee said to the guard who stood in front of the only ford across the river. She was easily sixteen hands tall. Her withers came up to my eye, and she stood in a challenging pose, with one forefoot slightly extended as if ready to paw the ground. Her deep bay coloring shone red in the last of the day's light. She should have been beautiful, majestic and the dream of any little girl who once wanted her own pony.

She wasn't. Kelpies might look like horses, but they were just a little off. Human eyes—hazel with a round pupil—stared at me from the equine face. Her lip curled in a disdainful sneer that you would never see on an animal, and it revealed oversized pointed teeth. No grain eater ever needed teeth like those. When she let out a low whinny the gills on her neck flared.

"We're bringing these two for the hag," Dee said.

The guard whinnied again and stamped her foot, but Dee pushed past her. "Felix's orders. Take it up with 'im."

Our captors shoved us into the clearing that might have once been grassy, but was now bare dirt, packed hard by hooves. The herd lounged in the pool or by the fire. They were of every size and color—bays, paints, grays and palominos. A few were in their human form, and they sat in camp chairs by the fire with the river at their backs. Heads turned our way and ears were pricked, but no one paid us much attention.

The fire pit with its macabre barbecue was straight ahead. Silvia's body was gone, but I didn't have high hopes that the kelpies had buried her decently.

Half hidden behind a scrawny bush, a stallion was busy mounting a mare. Thankfully, night had fallen like a curtain, and I could only glimpse the coupling in the shadows.

"Zeke, bring the sword," Petra snapped. Dum, who I now realized was "Zeke" shoved me toward his brother.

"Hold her."

He followed his mother up the rise toward the wooden shelters, taking my sword with him.

Mason's shoulders twitched. He was still working to free his hands. One of the human-kelpies sauntered over to examine us. To examine Mason, anyway. She barely spared me a glance. Instead, she ran a hand across Mason's shoulder and over his back.

"Mmmm. Yum. Where'd you get this one, Wally?"

"Hands off, Deidre," Dee said. "Ma says they're for the witch."

"Mmm…okay. But when she's done, I get dibs." Deidre reached between his legs and grabbed his balls.

Mason kept his head down and didn't give her the satisfaction of reacting, but I lunged forward, ready to bite her, since I had no other weapon. Dee—or Wally to his friends—yanked on the rope tying my hands, and I fell to my knees. Deirdre laughed and licked Mason's face.

The stallion rutting behind the bush finally screamed out his sexual culmination, then blundered out of the shadows into the light of the fire.

Deirdre took one look at him and let go of Mason. She quickly returned to a chair by the fire with a half dozen other females. The other kelpies—human and equine—moved back to give the stallion room.

He was a massive draft horse with the musculature of a rhino. The object of his recent affections was a small mare, whose eyes showed white all around as she galloped away to get lost again in the shadows at the far end of camp. She clearly hadn't been a willing partner. My stomach churned as I watched her frantic escape.

We weren't in Kansas anymore. Anything could happen in the next few minutes.

The stallion circled, puffing air out of his big nostrils. This had to be Felix. Unlike the kelpies, the nuckelavee had no gills. His sweat-slicked coat was slate gray, not a usual horse color. Two pointed teeth jutted like tusks from a prominent lower jaw, and powerful jaws flexed as he took in our scents. Red eyes bulged from under an oddly sloping brow.

He trotted behind us and sniffed up my pant leg to my neck. I felt the heat of his breath and heard his teeth grind as his muzzle came within inches of my throat. He circled around to face me and his bulky form shifted.

In another place, with normal levels of magic his shift might have happened in an instant. Here, it felt like an eternity. He didn't scream, but only let out a low moan as his bones cracked and muscles contorted. My own muscles clenched in response. The long snout shrank to a fat nose. Legs shortened and hooves split into fingers. And suddenly, a naked man stood before us.

He was the size of an orc and less pretty. The tusks remained. The rest of his face looked like someone had beaten him with a frying pan. Repeatedly. Wide cheek bones were patchy and red. A bulbous nose was mashed sideways. Neanderthal brows hung over black, bruised eyes. His shoulders were so massive, they seemed deformed. And as my eyes drifted lower—I felt sorry for the little mare that had run off into the woods. The man was hung like a... well, bulls would be jealous. I can appreciate the male form as much as the next girl, but this creature was too alien, in all the wrong ways.

"You like what you see, girlie?"

"I've seen better," I said through clenched teeth.

Felix's eyes rolled toward Mason, who was being held back by two strong kelpies in human form. His eyes blazed with black fire.

If Felix touched me, Mason would kill him, or at least try to. And then we'd never find Gunora because we'd both be dead.

I stepped back.

"We're here to speak to the witch."

Felix snorted. "What do you want with my hag?"

"She's my cousin. I just want to talk."

"Are you a witch too?" He ran a yellow, clawed finger up my cheek. His hands were rough and blunt like badly chopped kindling, and I'd seen cleaner fingernails on trolls.

"Do I look like a hag?" I said through clenched teeth. I didn't like that term "hag." It seemed a little harsh, but I needed to speak this guy's language and use small, easy words.

He laughed and "You're pretty, but not that bright, are you? Think you can come into my home and take what's mine? Here's a bit of news for you." He leaned in even closer. His breath reeked of rotting meat. "You're mine now too." He pinched my nipple, hard. I forced myself not to wince, though the pain brought tears to my eyes.

Mason thrashed in the kelpies' hold and one of them punched him in the gut. He doubled over with an "oof!" as breath rushed from his lungs. Felix ignored the outburst and continued to circle me like a bull in heat.

"And why should I let you near my witch?" His thorny fingers ran up my back, lifted a braid, and scraped across the vulnerable skin at my nape.

My insides went to water. I could barely breathe. We'd been wrong to come here, so wrong. Felix was mad in the worst possible way. His madness was fueled by megalomania. He would never let us go. I had a fleeting moment of rage directed at Jack. He'd known what he was leading us into. Then I directed the anger inward where it belonged. This had been a fool's errand from the beginning. I only hoped that Oscar and Berto had better luck finding the twins because we were going to die on this island.

A stooped figure stepped out of a shack and slowly descended the hill. When she reached the clearing, she stopped. No one spoke, and all eyes were on her.

Despite the heat, Gunora was dressed in a black robe, tattered at the hem and with the cowl thrown back. Her face was so lined with wrinkles that her eyes disappeared in the folds. Ragged-edged lips spread in a grin as she raised a sword.

My sword.

"Leave them be, Felix," she croaked.

The nuckelavee stalked over to her.

"You don't tell me what to do, hag!" He raised a hand to strike her, but before he could, she began to glow.

Felix checked his punch.

An errant wind stirred the dirt, whipping a dust devil between them. Gunora's robe fell open, revealing a thin, wasted body in a white shift. Fluttering wisps of hair glowed white and haloed her face.

Several kelpies dropped to their knees, heads bowed to the dust.

She pointed the sword tip at the stars and threw back her head, letting out a hideous shriek—half pain, half delight. The glow increased until I had to shield my eyes. I felt more than heard a sonic *pop*, and suddenly the night was too quiet and too dark.

My eyes burned with the afterglow of magic, and it took a moment for them to adjust.

Standing where she'd been was beautiful, young, maiden Gunora. Blond hair hung in thick waves to her waist. High forehead, wide cheeks, lips full and pink. Eyes icy blue. Viking eyes.

"Hello, cousin." She smiled. This was the Gunora who led a pack of Valkyrie novices, always at the top of her game. Popular, beautiful and deadly.

"There's my girl." Felix's voice rumbled with undisguised lust. His orcish hands reached out and cupped the breast under her thin shift.

She smiled, then stepped back and swung the sword to backhand him across the face with the hilt. It was a good hit, but Felix was as solid as a butcher block and only stumbled back a step.

"Later, my love." Gunora smiled sweetly. "I must speak with our guests first."

Blood dripped from the corner of Felix's mouth. He scraped it up with one finger and licked it, his eyes never leaving her face. The erection that had sprouted when young Gunora appeared hadn't been deterred by her violence. His shoulders bunched with tension as he looked ready to spring at her.

Then Gunora shifted. Light flared around her and in a moment the matron stood in the maid's place.

Felix wasn't put off by Gunora's new appearance. He reached for her now generous bosom, but was jerked back as a violent seizure shook her, and the matron turned to crone.

She stared at Felix defiantly. He grunted with displeasure.

"You can have that one to play with." She pointed at Mason. "Bring the other one." My two captors, Wally and Zeke, grabbed my arms and shoved me after her. Behind me, I heard Felix's bellow, "Bring meat!" I strained to turn and find Mason, but he'd already been hauled away.

Petra ran over to help Gunora back up the hill.

"I brought you food. You should eat," she said as she let us into the shack.

Gunora nodded. "Thank you, Petra. Please leave us now."

"Tell them not to hurt Mason!" I said, shaking off the kelpies's hands.

Gunora stopped at the door and turned. She considered me, then nodded at Petra. "See to it. Let them have their fun, but don't kill him. Yet."

Petra left with a frown fixed to her face. She didn't seem to have any other expressions.

Inside, the shack was lit by one feeble gleam floating near the ceiling.

Standing in the open doorway, Gunora looked frail enough for the evening wind to topple her. She leaned heavily on my sword, using it like a walking stick.

I gripped her arm before she fell.

She smiled tiredly. "Thank you, cousin. Please help me to my bed."

Together we shuffled to the pallet of blankets and pillows in the corner of the room. The hut's only other furnishings were a small picnic table made of wood with a cement base. On it sat a mug and a bowl filled with some kind of stew. Horse stew, I thought.

Gunora staggered to the bed and lay down. The light flared around her, and she changed again. The crone was gone, replaced by the young maid. She hugged my sword to her chest and sighed.

It never bothered me when a human or even a fae picked up my sword. In their hands it was inert. When the former prince of the fae, Alvar, had kidnapped me, his alchemists tried for hours to unlock the secret of the Valkyrie blade. Eventually, he'd guessed that it took a Valkyrie to wield the magic. In his fat hands the sword was just a hunk of metal or at best, a clunky weapon.

But seeing the rapture on Gunora's face as she clung to my sword made me squirm. Even with my dulled keening, I could sense the blade's unease.

At the training grounds in Asgard, we novices often left our swords leaning against the stone wall that surrounded the field while we warmed up before mock battles. No one ever picked up a sister's blade. It was an unspoken but understood rule. Our blades were an extension of our bodies and our souls.

Watching Gunora stroke my blade, I itched to reach for it. She was clearly taking comfort from the connection, and perhaps energy. With so many shifts one after another, she needed it. That was the Valkyrie blade's true calling—to bring relief. But she didn't deserve it.

She gazed through the open door at the glow from the bonfire, her eyes on a distant place. Then she focused on me. Her bloodless lips opened and she croaked, "You came." A smile pulled at her wrinkled cheeks.

"You took the twins didn't you?" I wanted to strangle her.

She didn't answer but just stared at me with that pale whisper of a smile. I wanted to shake the answers out of her, but she looked ancient and frail. I couldn't bring myself to attack an old woman, but I had no qualms about throwing her over my shoulder and carrying her all the way to Hedge to make our ransom appointment.

"Why did you bring me here? You don't think I'll ever let you enact that bloody ritual? Your plans were all for nothing." I growled the words at her. "I won't be your blood sacrifice. And I won't let you hurt anyone else." My fingers dug into her thin shoulders. I could snap her frail bones with one flick of my wrist.

Her mouth opened again. She made a stuttering "gah, gah, gah," sound and her eyes rolled to white.

And the seizures took her again. The changes came so fast, they were breathtaking. Light burst from her and filled the small room. Her three faces mutated from one to the other, too fast to make them out. Her mouth was fixed, open and wide, and she cried out in a high thin wail. Her muscles grew and shrank, unrelenting in their painful shifts. Magic streamed from her as her soul was being torn apart.

Her screams brought the kelpies running to the shack. A dozen of them pressed inside the small room, and I could hear more murmuring and shuffling outside. None of them would come closer than the doorway until Petra pushed through with an air of authority. She stood over the bed. A frown etched a deep line between her brows.

The light went out. The wind died. Maid Gunora lay on her sweat-soaked sheets, her cheeks flushed pink. She looked like a princess just waiting for a kiss to wake her.

"Is she dead?"

"I don't know." Without my keening, I really didn't. Gunora's breath was so shallow, her chest didn't move. Her hand was flung over the edge of the bed. I reached for it and pressed two fingers to her wrist. A faint pulse thrummed under my touch.

"She's alive." I cut off the "just barely" part of that sentence. No need to tell the kelpies their god-figure was dying.

But she was. It wouldn't be long now.

"Take her away," Petra said. At first I thought she meant Gunora. Then two kelpies came at me. I grabbed my sword from Gunora's frail grasp and swung it like a bat. No time for fancy. My swing caught one of the kelpies in the gut, but the other came at me like a linebacker. We crashed against the table. I dropped the sword and while I scrambled to reach it, the kelpies grabbed my arms and dragged me away.

Outside, human kelpies were dancing and shouting around the fire. The rest of the herd clustered on the edge of the firelight. Someone threw a log into the pit. Smoke and sparks filled the air.

Then I saw it. The kelpies weren't dancing. They were kicking something—a figure that lay on the ground. Mason! A kelpie whooped and kicked him again. He didn't move. Another kelpie lay on its side nearby, one leg obviously broken and pointing awkwardly toward the sky.

Good. At least Mason had gone down fighting. I would too.

I yanked my arm away from my captor and backhanded him across the face. He was small for a kelpie, shorter than me. He shrieked when I hit him. I lashed out at the other stunned guard, stamping my boot on his foot, then kneeing him in the crotch. He doubled over with a muted cry. The first guard had recovered and came at me with hands reaching like claws. I kicked him in the gut. I was off balance and my kick barely grazed him. I ran.

He tackled me and his hands caught my ankles. I landed with a heavy crash. My head rang and I sucked in dust. A foot kicked me in the side. I couldn't breathe. Couldn't move. My lungs screamed for air, but I choked on dirt. Black spots swam before my eyes.

"Bitch!" The kelpie snarled. He yanked me upward by the arm. I was boneless and stood like a rag doll on flimsy legs. I coughed and sucked in a ragged breath.

The kelpie stuck his face in mine. "You'll pay for that." He was bleeding from the nose. I worked my mouth to spit on him, but it was gluey with dirt and all I managed was a wheeze of air.

He didn't like that.

I didn't even see the fist coming, but I felt its impact. I crumpled to the dirt. After that, all I could do was curl in a ball to protect my face and wait for oblivion.

CHAPTER

32

motor whined in my ear. I ignored it. I was too hot and tired to move. The sound waned and grew louder again, like a small plane circling an air field looking to land. That thought brought me out of my sloth state. There hadn't been planes on Terra in years. The whining buzz clipped past my ear again and sticky feet landed on my cheek. I swatted the mosquito without thinking. Pain lanced through me. I jerked upright, and...ow! More injuries made themselves known—a bruise on my lower back, sore wrist, headache... and where in the hells was I? Memory blossomed with the pain.

I was in the kelpie camp. Captive. Morning light leaked through the open door of the shack. I'd been unconscious for hours.

The memories kept coming. Last night, I'd realized that getting Gunora home alive and in time to save the twins was impossible. I'd grabbed my sword and tried to fight my way out of the shack. But they'd made me pay for that. I remember being tackled and I'd blacked out.

Judging from my other injuries, they hadn't stopped after that.

Someone had dumped me on the floor of the hut. Already, the air was muggy. It had to be near noon. I wiped damp hair from my eyes.

Noon! We had only hours to get back to Hedge. Panic flared in me then died.

Gunora had orchestrated all this to get me here. She had no intention of releasing the twins. For all I knew, the could already be dead. She'd gotten what she wanted—my blood to cleanse her curse.

I wouldn't let her have it.

I rose on my hands and knees. The room tilted sideways. I panted as I struggled to stand.

My sword was gone. The kelpies wouldn't trust me with it again.

Gunora slept on her sleeping pallet with a tattered sheet twisted around her bare legs and face buried in a pillow. I could only see a mess of hair, but it was white. She was in crone mode.

I should kill her now. While she's weak.

That crone's neck would snap like chicken bones under my fists.

But then the faces of Tums and Tad would haunt me for the rest of my life. If there was even the slightest chance of saving them, I had to find a way to get out of here and take Gunora with me.

I waved away more ambitious mosquitoes and took stock of my injuries. I could move the wrist, so it was probably only sprained. The pain in my back was worse, but I thought it would loosen if I could find the energy to move. My head throbbed and I gingerly touched my cheek. The skin was hot and swollen. I probably had a black eye. My hand automatically went to my belt pouch, where I kept a small first aid kit and a bit of Gita's willow bark remedy for all things painful.

My belt was gone. Then I saw it lying by the door. Someone had gone through its contents. My bandanna lay in the dirt. The pouches of herbs were torn open and strewn about. Bastards. They were too stupid to know the value of the herbs.

I scraped up the bits of scattered willow bark and swallowed them whole. No one was going to bring me hot water for tea. The pouch of horse nettle I'd brought as a precaution had been torn open. There was no saving that. Before we left on this adventure, I'd had a vague idea of poisoning the kelpies' water trough, but now I knew that was a futile dream.

Then another thought shook me. I felt for the weight of Oscar's locket around my neck. Thankfully the kelpies had overlooked it. I tucked it into my pocket. No point in tempting fate.

I rose and made a few tentative stretches. The muscles in my back protested. I gave up and struggled to wrap my wrist with the dirty bandanna.

I thought of Mason, and how he would force me to look at the problem logically. I would get my sword back. I'd find him and we'd both get away. If Gunora was still alive by then, we'd take her too. But to do all that, I needed a weapon.

I moved toward the door, placing my feet carefully so my boots didn't grate on the dirt floor. I didn't want to alert anyone outside that I was awake. The crack in the door was just wide enough for me to peer into the yard.

A man sat beside the door. He leaned into my view as he reached to swat a fly. It was Wally, one of my original captors. I tried to peer at the other side of the door. I had to assume his brother was on guard duty too. The heat made everyone drowsy and doubling the guards would keep them accountable.

I studied the clearing. Down the slope, the bonfire still smoked. Kelpies lazed in the sun. Tails swatted at flies, but little else moved.

Was Mason being held somewhere? I shifted, trying to see him, but my field of vision was limited. I needed to get out of here and look around.

"Get back inside," Wally snarled. He'd seen my movement.

I ignored him. My throat was dry to the point of painfulness, and my bladder was making itself known. I shoved the door open. It slammed against Wally's chair and he fell over with a curse. He caught up to me when I was halfway to the river that ran around the edge of camp.

"What're you doing?" He grabbed my arm.

"I'm thirsty and I have to pee." I yanked my arm away and kept walking. Zeke watched us from the comfort of the shaded porch. They would either beat me up again—it which case, my bladder would take care of itself—or they would let me go.

They let me go.

I slowed my gait and Wally shoved me. Exaggerating a stumble, I fell to one knee so I could take time to look around. I still couldn't see Mason. Or Felix.

Wally dragged me upright, and I limped toward the river. At this point, it was barely deep enough to cover the soles of my boots. I stumbled over rocks, cursing the kelpies for nine generations back, until I found a spot deep enough to dip my cupped hands and drink.

The water was cool and tasted like dirt. I drank until my stomach felt full, then splashed my face, chest and arms. Wally watched me from the tall grass that grew along the shore. He was naked from the waist up, skinny and sunburned. His chest was pockmarked with mosquito bites.

I moved about five meters down the creek bed. The bank was steeper here. I could be out of the creek and into the woods before Wally scrambled down it. But the herd of kelpies were not far, lounging in the deeper water of the pool. A horse would overtake me in minutes, especially with my injuries.

"A little privacy," I called out. Wally scratched the red welts on his chest.

"Just do it. You aren't going anywhere."

"At least turn your back."

"Not going to happen." His grin exposed crooked brown teeth.

I stomped through the shallow water to where a bend in the river gave me some shielding behind a spray of tall grasses. The water was deeper here, up to my knees. A few more steps and the river would deepen even more. The current picked up too. I could dive in and let it wash me away…

The hump of a sea creature rolled by, long and muscled and deadly.

Draika.

The reedy lowlands here were perfect breeding grounds for the water dragon. I had some experience with draikas, and I tossed out my idea of jumping into the river. It was a juvenile, only about three meters long and probably her first spawning. But I would never get in the water with a dragon again if I could help it.

The kelpies either didn't know the dangers of draikas or didn't care. They ignored the serpent as it lazily undulated up the waterway and through their resting pool.

I undid my jeans and squatted.

"You about done over there?" Wally called down.

"I'm not a race horse," I yelled back.

He could still see my head but not the rest of me. I turned away, pretending shyness, and while my bladder released, my hands scrabbled in the stream bed looking for a weapon. It had to be small enough to conceal, but sturdy enough to do some damage.

Why weren't there any good stones in this damned river? A blunt round stone came loose from the river bed. I hefted it in my hand. Maybe I could rig some kind of slingshot. Then my fingers closed over a thick piece of shale.

I rose, dripping water, and tucked the stones in my pocket as I pretended to struggle with the fly on my jeans.

Wally was getting impatient. He stomped into the water, grabbed me by the arm, and hauled me back up the hill to the shack.

"Where's Mason?" I asked, but he ignored the question and shoved me back inside the hut. I heard his chair scrape as he moved it to cover the door.

Inside seemed much darker after the bright afternoon. I let my eyes adjust until I could see that Gunora had shifted again. Her frizzy white hair was gone. Golden tresses framed a plump rosy face. The matron was back. By the One-eyed Father, so many shifts should have killed her by now.

I had to make my move soon.

I sat on the floor beside the cement base of the table and fished the stone from my pocket. The shale was flat and jagged-edge and about as long as my palm.

I pressed it against the cement and began to sharpen its edge.

The heat inside the shack was oppressive. A fight was coming. I could feel it in my bones. But who would I be fighting? Felix or Gunora? I crouched against the opposite wall, watching Gunora sleep and counting the minutes that Tums and Tad had left.

I slept as much as possible to conserve my energy. The light faded. I shook the gleam to activate it and set it to float near the ceiling. The small room filled with pale yellow light. Outside, the party was reviving as the sun went down. I heard shouts, but couldn't tell if they were raised in anger or sport.

Petra returned to straighten the bed clothes and wiped damp hair from Gunora's face. She brought my sword and pressed it into Gunora's hand. Nothing happened. Did she expect it to flare with fire and wake the sleeping witch?

"Where's Mason? What are you going to do with us?" My voice rasped.

Petra gave me a blank look. "Felix wants you."

My guts turned to water thinking about what Felix might want. I still didn't know where Petra's loyalties lay. Would she protect me from Felix for Gunora's sake?

"What for?" I said.

"I didn't ask." She yanked me up. I stood on legs filled with lead and half asleep from crouching. My sword was too far for me to grab, but oh, so tantalizingly close. The kelpie saw my eyes flick to it and she tightened her grip on my arm until it hurt.

"Gunora brought me here. You know that, right?" It was a long grasp at a supposed straw. I'd seen the way some kelpies revered Gunora. Her power seemed divine, and these people, living in fear and squalor were probably desperate for a god—any god—to intervene on their behalf. I was betting that Petra just needed a nudge to win her over completely, to make her oppose Felix for Gunora's sake.

I nudged. "She went through a lot of trouble to get me here and won't be happy if you let Felix hurt me."

Petra paused, her lips pressed tight, but my coaxing wasn't enough. She dragged me outside.

A crowd had gathered by the fire pit. Felix lounged on an old couch, watching two young stallions fight in the dust. The kelpies were active in the cooler evening air. Equines stood near or in the river. Tails flicked in the constant and unending battle against flies. Human kelpies—all female— sat in the tattered camp chairs around the fire. This was Felix's harem. Not particularly pretty, they were hard women worn down by hard lives, and they watched me with open hostility on their faces.

The bonfire had been stoked with damp wood and smoke billowed from it in lazy clouds. Something large roasted on a spit over the flames. It could have been a deer, but I had the sick feeling it was one of their own, maybe even the one killed in the fight with Mason.

Where *was* he?

The smell of roasting flesh made my treacherous and empty stomach ache.

One of the fighting stallions reared and hoofed the other. The harem cheered. The fighters were bleeding from bite marks on their flanks. Their lips were flecked with spit. Nostrils and gills flared as they whuffed out breath. They were both exhausted. And although, they were probably being forced to fight for Felix's entertainment, I couldn't bring myself to feel sorry for them.

The nuckelavee's attention was on the fight. I pulled away from Petra's grip. She let me go. I had nowhere to run. I turned in a circle, looking for any sign of Mason.

There! On the far side of the camp, a post had been driven into the ground. Mason sat, leaning against it, legs splayed and hands tied behind it. His head lolled to one side. My heart leapt to see him alive. Then I saw the bruises discoloring his face. He was naked from the waist up and black marks dotted his chest like someone had poked him with a burning stick.

Rage burned up from my stomach, battered against my ribs, and heated my eyes. My fists clenched and unclenched as I worked energy into my muscles. We'd gone past saving the twins and punishing Gunora. By the All-father, I would make these evil creatures pay.

I took a deep invigorating breath. First, I would get Mason away, somewhere safe. Then I would come back and erase this scourge from the land.

Petra shoved me forward until I stood only a few feet from Felix. The fire burned at my back, drying the sweat on my skin. He lounged on his shabby throne. Dirty, tattered blankets were piled on it and he shifted his great bulk among them.

When he saw me, he put his fat fingers in his mouth and whistled. The stallions stopped in mid-fight. Both were heaving and dripping blood.

"Enough!" Felix roared. "Get out of my sight." He waved his hand and the stallions found the energy to gallop away. I wondered how long it would be before they were on a spit over the fire.

He flicked a wrist and a young woman came running up to him with a cup and a jug. She poured a dark liquid. Felix downed it in one gulp and held out the cup for more. The girl poured and waited for him to drink it down again. The jug was bigger than her head and her muscles strained to hold it still.

"Leave it." Felix flicked a finger again. She put the jug on the ground and scurried away like a mouse caught in the kitchen.

Throughout this exchange, Felix's eyes never left my face. Seated, the top of his head reached my shoulder. He was still naked and he thrust his hips forward suggestively.

I kept my eyes lifted, ignoring this obvious attempt to unsettle me. He probably thought he was intimidating—his size, his nakedness, the muscles that bulged on his arms just from gripping the small cup. But I'd faced a rock troll, a water dragon and vampires. One arrogant nuckelavee didn't even make my top ten list of big bads.

So I watched him back, letting the silence stretch between us. Silence is a powerful weapon. It creeps past a person's armor and begs to be noticed. Only one who is truly self-confident can ignore its lure.

Felix spoke first.

"What do you want with the witch?"

I shrugged. "We're cousins. She borrowed my sweater and I wanted it back."

Someone behind me stifled a laugh. Felix frowned.

I took that moment to sneak a glance at Mason. His head still lolled at a painful angle.

Wake up, wake up! I shouted the thought in my head as if the sheer force of my desire might rouse him.

Felix moved so fast, I didn't see it. Suddenly he was there, right in my face.

"Don't ever mock me" His hand raked down my chest. Jagged yellow claws tore away my shirt and ripped into my flesh. I choked on a scream and jumped backward, right into the fire. Flames licked at my heels. A spark crackled and landed on my head. I grabbed the ragged ends of my shirt in one hand and swatted the burning ember with the other. The reek of charred hair burned my nose.

Then pain blossomed in my chest.

I clapped my hands to the wounds, smearing soot with sweat and blood.

Felix loomed over me. His eyes were black and soulless.

"Wait." My breath came in stutters. "I came here to bargain for the witch. But you can have her. Just let us go." I fumbled with my jeans, pulled out the locket and dangled it in front of his nose. "Let us go and you can have this too. It's pure magic."

Felix's eyes narrowed as he inspected the locket, then his lip curled up in a sneer. "Stupid bitch. Magic doesn't work here. This is the only real power." He backhanded me.

Blood spurted from my nose as I tumbled backward and landed hard on my knee only inches from the fire. Kelpies were laughing and whinnying. The show had started and they were pleased with first blood. I swayed on all fours, gasping to overcome the white hot pain. Blood dripped from my nose and sizzled on the hot stones.

The locket jabbed my hand where I was crushing it into the dirt. I cracked it open and palmed the pill. Then I pretended to fall weakly onto my side. The heat of the fire washed over my face. I wiped blood that leaked over my lips and popped the pill into my mouth.

No one noticed. The kelpies were cheering. Felix adored the attention. He strutted around the space before his throne.

I bit into the pill.

Once, when I was working an infestation of hellfire beetles, one flew into my mouth. I swallowed it before realizing, and the beetle let off a noxious vapor in my throat, its last defense against being eaten by predators. The acrid taste of that defense had stayed with me for days.

Oscar's pill of magic tasted like that. A sharp, hot spiciness filled my mouth and throat. It wasn't liquid and not quite gas. It saturated my sinuses. My broken nose healed in an instant. Magic burned down my throat and grabbed my heart in its savage grip. Fire coursed along my veins, seizing control of my muscles. I choked and coughed until the feeling eased.

Then I smiled down at the blood-speckled dirt. Grabbing a burning brand from the fire, I rose to my feet in one swift move.

Felix's women cheered, happy to let someone else take the abuse.

"I gave you a chance." I didn't raise my voice. Felix heard me. His eyes narrowed. The moment stretched. The harem fell quiet. The only sound came from the crackling fire.

I stepped forward, pointing the burning stick at Felix. "Now I'm going to kill you."

I felt light. And strong.

My chest filled with life-giving breath. My feet rooted to the ground and released magic deep into the earth, calling to Terra and the green, growing things she gave us in abundance. This was old magic, older than the flimsy ward erected around the prison. It poured out of me and saturated the magic-starved ground.

Felix took my stance for arrogance. He laughed and beckoned me forward with two fat fingers.

Bring it on, said the smirk on his face. His knees bent slightly and he rocked forward on his toes. For all his bulk, he was quick. I'd seen that. And he moved like a fighter, sure of his own body and strength.

I waved the glowing stick in my left hand—a diversion while my right snuck around and pulled the stone blade from my back pocket. I only needed to get close enough to use it without having my head crushed by one of Felix's right hooks.

I circled left. His eyes tracked me. The kelpies, sensing a fight had moved back. I keened each one of their life flames, flickering in the dark. The magic surging through me was a deep breath after almost drowning under the dampener.

I lunged, swinging the branch like a club, and struck Felix in the face with a shower of sparks. It was like poking a mountain with a toothpick. He didn't scream. He didn't even blink. He yanked the stick. I came with it and slammed against his chest. He stank of urine, sweat and dirt.

He grabbed my braid. My head jerked back, mouth fell open, neck screamed in pain. His hot breath furled around me like smog and he licked the blood drying on my face.

"I'm going to use you up." His voice was a bearish growl. "Use you, until I split you in two. Then I'll give you to my boys. If you're lucky, they'll kill you." He smiled. His jagged brown-streaked teeth were only inches from my face. "But not like this." He let me go and it took every bit of strength I had not to stumble backward.

Felix's shoulders hunched. His skin bubbled. Muscle and sinew blossomed along his throat. His chest seemed to turn inside out. Skin melted away exposing red, ripe ribs.

A kelpie screamed in the darkness, the sound of a horse in fear for its life. Others shied away. They were shifting shadows on the edge of my vision. My whole attention was fixed on the nuckelavee.

For an instant, pain or fear made him bend into a ball, then his back arched at an unnatural angle. A guttural scream thundered from his throat. He roared once more and completed the shift.

Felix was no longer man or horse, but some ghoulish centaur with ragged black wings. The horse half was a draft stallion, black as charred meat. His humanoid head was bulbous with yellow glowing eyes. His evil grin revealed a maw full of serrated teeth with those tusks jutting up from the bottom jaw. Two mucusy black holes filed the space where his nose had been. Muscles bulged on a torso that was as skinless as a flayed man—red and wet like viscera.

I blinked. Holy shit. Jack had been right. Nuckelavee's were butt ugly.

He said nothing, but glared as if expecting something from me. Perhaps he thought I would crumple in despair. Or bow down in homage. Or run.

I did none of these. To the watching kelpies, I probably looked dumb with fear. But I was working—calling and cajoling the trees and vines to come do my bidding.

Felix puffed out his already engorged chest. His face was beet red and shot through with veins of ocher. He loomed over me and eclipsed the stars.

A green shoot unfurled from the dirt at his feet. I couldn't see it, but I knew it was there. The tiny vine wound around his hoof, followed by another. And another.

I saw the moment he felt them twine around his hocks. His fat, skinless lips pouted and he looked down. The vines wrapped around his knees. He stamped a foot, but it was already too late to escape. More vines strangled his back legs. The swish of his tail did nothing to dislodge them.

I raised my arms, and the vines exploded from the earth, trapping his arms, waist and back. He struggled, but they held him fast. Only his wings were still free. He puffed out a noxious breath as he flexed them, straining to rise against the earth that was holding him down.

"Your breath stinks." I leaned in and swiped my stone blade across his throat.

His eyes widened, showing white all around. The tusks jittered as he tried to produce a scream. I jammed the blade in his eye.

He wheezed and writhed, but he couldn't even clap his hands to his neck to keep the life-blood from spurting out.

The vines reacted to the blood and swallowed him. They churned around his neck in a choking embrace. Leaves rammed down his throat and sprouted back through his nostrils. One eye bulged. The other was a bloody wreck under my blade. Cheeks puffed until the loss of blood and oxygen finally took its toll.

I jumped back, spitting out the taste of nuckelavee blood.

In seconds, Felix was lost under a mass of leafy foliage. Tiny crimson flowers popped open all over the bush.

The night was silent as dirt.

Then the fire crackled and spat sparks into the sky.

My legs trembled under me, and I fell to one knee. I had used all of Oscar's magic boost and drank deeply from my own well. But I had done it. I'd killed the nuckelavee.

I forced myself to stand. Mason was still out. The herd was quiet. None would go near the pile of foliage to check on their master. The harem turned angry eyes on me. One of them hissed.

How stupid, to fear the dead nuckelavee more than the thing that killed him.

But they weren't afraid of me, as if sensing that I was a one-trick pony and had nothing left to fight with. I had no weapons left but bare hands slick with blood and sweat. I wiped them on my pants, my eyes never leaving the harem of mares who'd risen from their chairs.

What was left of my shirt stuck to the blood drying on my chest. Adrenaline kept that wound from hurting for now, but I was already weak and any loss of blood was too much.

One of the harem kelpies pointed at me. It was Deirdre, the one who'd taken a shine to Mason.

"Kill her," the kelpie said. The other females rose at her back and bared their meat-tearing teeth.

On the other side of the fire, Mason groaned and his head fell back against the post.

Wake up! Wake up!

The mares prowled forward.

"Stop!" A voice rang out.

All eyes turned toward the huts at the top of the hill.

"Leave her alone," Petra shouted. Gunora leaned on her arm. She was once again in maid form and seemed to glow with an inner light. A fae wind kissed her blond hair so it rose in ghostly arms around her flawless face. She stepped away from Petra and raised my sword above her head. Firelight burnished it in red.

"She is here by my devices." Gunora's voice was strong, sweet and pure as an angel's. "I called her to me. I filled her with the magic needed to defeat the nuckelavee!"

The lying bitch. She'd stolen my sword and now she would steal my victory too.

There was murmuring and whuffles from the kelpie herd, whether in astonishment or disagreement, I couldn't tell.

Gunora wasn't done. "Only I have that power!" she said. "I released you from his tormenting rule. And now you serve me!" My sword glowed in her hand. She had to be filling it with her own magic, and I wondered how long she could keep up the show. "Now prepare the prisoner for sacrifice, and I will show you the true meaning of magic."

Felix's harem didn't look pleased, but Wally and Zeke menaced them with clubs and they stepped back. Wally rushed at me and I punched him. He grunted but fell back. A second kelpie in horse form bumped me from behind. I whirled to strike, but it bit down on my forearm. I screamed.

"Kyra!" I heard Mason's hoarse yell. My head whipped around to find him.

A fist found my eye instead and the world faded to black.

felt like I was only out for minutes, but it could have been hours. I woke when my arms were jerked wide. Sweat and smoke stung my eyes. I tipped my head to the right as I struggled to take in my surroundings. Someone was tying a rough rope around my wrist. Then came the pounding of a mallet on wood as the same someone drove a stake into the ground. My arm was tugged violently, and the rope sawed at my wrist as they tied it to the stake.

I might have blacked out again. I next became aware of water spattering my face and stinging the wounds on my chest. Grogginess misted away, replaced by terror. My arms were both attached to stakes now, and someone was working on my feet.

Kelpies splashed in the river where it widened into a pool. They were only meters from me, some in human form, others as horses. I twisted, trying to spy Mason on the other side of the yard. I was spread-eagled, and the rock beneath forced my back to arch painfully. Only the tatters of my thin shirt covered me.

I felt exposed. Vulnerable.

I smelled the river's organic tang. Its faint sighing as it flowed around rocks came from the right and I craned my neck to see it. Then I swiveled my head the other way. The fire sparked in that direction. A huge…something was silhouetted against the glow of the flames. I blinked a few times and recognized Felix's vine-covered grave. His one sightless eye seemed to stare at me accusingly. My knife was still embedded in the other. I couldn't see his bloody throat through the vines. They were wrapped around his neck and sprouting from his mouth and nose. He looked liked some overstuffed god of fertility, and I choked on a laugh.

I was losing my grasp on reality. Weeks of sleepless nights, the constant adrenaline rush of the past days, little food and water. The total depletion of my magic. The beatings. They were all taking their toll.

My tongue stuck to the roof of my mouth. My eyes were hot and scratchy in their sockets.

I rasped out another laugh. Maybe I'd die of dehydration and spoil Gunora's plans. Then all hysteria left me. I'd been a fool. I let her into my life. I'd worried when she was convicted. Part of me actually believed she didn't do it. That part of me also hoped she wasn't behind the kidnapping and we'd break her free and save Tums and Tad together.

I'd wanted to believe. Because I'd wanted to believe I wasn't the only Valkyrie on Terra, that I had a familial tie of blood that couldn't be broken. But I should have known the truth. Family is a choice, not an obligation.

"Kyra!"

I realized I'd been listening to a voice calling for a while. It was hoarse and barely audible over the crackle of the flames and the noise of the kelpies.

"Mason?" My voice was even more raw, barely above a rasp. I turned my head, trying to find him, but saw only bare legs and hooves.

"He can't help you now." Gunora leaned over me. Her face was upside down and I crossed my eyes, trying to bring her into focus. Long blond hair fell down to tickle my cheek.

"Now just sit tight. This will be over in a minute, but I need to make a bit of a show of it. These kelpies are a superstitious lot."

She was going to do it. She had orchestrated everything for this moment when she would take my blood and cleanse the curse from her own. But it wouldn't be a true cleansing. The curse couldn't be broken. It would only pass to me.

I thrashed against my bonds, not caring that the ropes tore at my skin or that the stone abraded by my back.

Gunora raised the sword—my sword—above her head and said in a clear voice, "Hear me!" The kelpies settled down. Gunora lowered her voice, certain of their attention now. "I invoke the gods to witness my sacrifice and find me worthy of their light!"

There was utter silence. Even the fire stopped crackling as if in homage to Gunora's lunacy.

"Just get on with it," I snarled. "You know as well as I do, the gods don't take requests."

"Gag her," Gunora said. Wally's face came into view. He leered down at me and tore away the front of my shirt and my last bit of modesty. He wadded the filthy cloth and stuffed it into my mouth.

I gagged and puffed out my cheeks. Instinct begged me to claw at my throat, but my fingers could only scrabble at the stone beneath me. Black spots clouded my eyes. I closed them and willed myself to be calm.

Breathe. Breathe. Breathe.

My mother's centering ritual came back to me automatically. I sucked air in through my nose. My eyeballs felt ready to pop from my head, but I wasn't going to suffocate. Slowly, my lungs filled with oxygen and I calmed.

My head scraped against the rock as I turned to find Gunora.

She held a second blade, smaller than my sword.

"It wouldn't do to blood you on your own blade," she said with a smile. "Don't know what kind of magic that might conjure. But this will do." The smaller blade flashed in the moonlight. She sliced across the top of my chest. I screamed and writhed against my bonds. This was it. The next slice would be across my throat.

A strange calm came over me. I couldn't fight her. I had nothing left. No magic, no sword, no critter in my back pocket whose slime could dissolve rope and set me free. Even Mason was lost to me. I closed my eyes and waited for the last strike.

It didn't come. I heard splashing instead and swiveled my head around to see Gunora. She stood in the river. The water parted around her and tugged on her white robe. She raised both hands above her head and shouted in a language I didn't recognize. One hand held the bloody knife, the other my glowing sword. Its magic rimmed Gunora in light. The kelpies saw it too. The ones in human form sunk to their knees. Everyone stared in silent awe at the glowing figure poised in the river like an avenging goddess.

She was still drawing magic from my sword. Soaked in so much blood—human, fae, vampire, and divine—it had a lot to give.

The mumbo jumbo of her words started to make sense. I couldn't understand them all, but one or two stuck out from my lessons in Asgard. They were words of power, uttered by the Titan gods when they made the world. Could Gunora really invoke them?

Yes. Even without my keening, I could sense the pressure in the atmosphere, the building of energy, like the wind sucking in its breath before a storm.

My sword burst into dazzling light, and a new fear spiked in me.

Could a sword's power be sucked dry, just like a person's? Would that kill the blade? Was a blade even killable?

I closed my eyes and begged the All-father's favor. When I opened them, a shadow crossed in front of the moon. It was gone in a flash, leaving me only with an impression of great wings spread wide.

The bird—if it was a bird—swooped low over the pool. It was as big as a small jet, the kind Mom and I used to watch land at the private airport on Montreal's south shore when I was a kid.

The shadow swooped again, and a horse screamed as great talons plucked it from the water.

Another scream and more distant shouts.

Someone was attacking the camp!

"Stand your ground!" Gunora's voice was angry but it had an edge of fear. Kelpies ran in every direction. A mare leaped over me, her hoof grazing my ribs.

The bird returned and seemed to hang over the clearing for a moment. I spotted the golden head of an eagle. He had one good eye that glowed with an inner light and a black hole where his other eye should have been. His wings pumped and a crack of thunder reverberated through the night, so loud, I felt it shake the stone beneath me.

Thunderbird!

Before I could wrap my mind around that bit of lore, Wally gurgled a scream and fell across me. An arrow protruded from the back of his neck. Hot blood washed over my shoulder. I jerked sideways and he rolled to the ground with a thump.

Everyone was screaming now. I strained to see what was happening.

Thunderbird screeched by again. The roar of an angry mob drowned out all other noises.

A bluecap ran by me, axe raised and face contorted in rage. One of Felix's harem girls stumbled into my view with a blade in her chest and hair on fire. The war was on. Years of living in the shadow of the nuckelavee's brutality had finally come to a head. Jack had decided enough was enough, and he'd recruited the bluecaps to the fight.

I strained against my bonds. I needed to get free before a stray arrow hit me. They were whizzing across the clearing like giant winged insects.

Something tugged at my wrist. My head swiveled, and I saw a fluffy pony chewing on the rope that bound me with his sharp kelpie teeth.

The rope snapped and I sat up. Princess bounded up and covered my face with wet kisses. Her teeth snagged the cloth gag and I spat it out.

"Enough!" I pushed her off, then hugged her smelly, furry self, so glad to see her. Raven was already working on the rope binding my other hand. It too snapped and I rubbed my raw wrists.

Chaos raged around me. Bluecaps fought human-kelpies hand-to-hand. Equine-kelpies used back hoofs to smash in heads. One was tearing into a corpse with his sharp teeth and tossing strips of flesh onto the fire where they popped and sizzled.

A wolf leaped over me to tackle a stampeding kelpie. Jack's crew was here too. Another mare charged by, nearly trampling Raven who was still trying to unbind my feet. The little horse screamed and ran. Princess growled and took off after him.

"Raven!" My shout was lost in the noise of battle. The tiny, brave kelpie was gone.

I scrambled to untie my feet. My fingers were stiff and clumsy and the ropes were wet. My eyes couldn't focus on the task, but kept goggling at the carnage around me. The vines wrapping Felix bristled as if some creature blossomed under them.

I scrambled to break my foot away, tearing at the last rope. Fingernails broke. Sobs erupted from me in ragged gasps.

Damn the gods! It was no good. I screamed and kicked. The rope scored deeply into my ankle but held.

The vines binding Felix rustled again. An arm—purple and sinewy—burst through the trappings. Felix rose clumsily on hoofed feet with leaves and vines dripping off him.

How is he still alive?

The nuckelavee lurched. Leaves fell from his mouth. But he didn't suck in air.

He wasn't alive. He was animated.

I forgot about my foot, bleeding freely in its binding now, and whipped my head around to find Felix's puppet master. One of the kelpies or dwarves or even Jack's crew had to be the sorcerer responsible for this necromancy. But they were all caught up in the battle.

Then I spotted him.

Mason.

He stood in the middle of the clearing, swaying. At some point, blood had flowed down his face from a wound on his head. Now it was crusted with dirt. He looked savage and powerful. The kelpies shied from him as if avoiding the dark aura around him.

I called out, but his eyes were focused on the dead nuckelavee—eyes that glowed with a faint yellow light. Wind tossed the bonfire flames my way and with them came the faint sulfuric scent of brimstone.

Mason was the necromancer. He'd found his aspect of the demon.

He raised his hands and the nuckelavee rose. Clumsy hoofs skidded on the hard-packed earth. Dead Felix looked much the same as live Felix. The flayed-man torso flexed his reanimated musculature. He reached for a kelpie running by. His massive hands grasped the horse around its throat. He snapped its neck with one deft shake, then used the carcass to bludgeon another mare that was stamping on a bluecap's chest.

But the kelpies weren't stupid. They saw who wielded the dark magic animating the corpse and lunged for Mason. Two kelpies fell with arrows in the neck and eyes before they could reach him. Then the dwarves and and several men from Jack's camp surrounded Mason, protecting him as he wielded his giant undead wrecking ball.

"Looks like your man has a taste of demon power." Gunora's voice came hot in my ear. "It won't help you."

Somewhere in the fighting, she'd lost my blade, but she gripped the smaller one in a dirty, battered fist. She sliced across her hand and shoved me flat on my back with her bloody palm against my chest.

Her blood met mine. She screamed a single word from the gods. It slammed into my mind like a fist made of cut glass, tearing into my memories until something broke in me. I felt it, like a hot yolk bursting through a cracked shell.

Pain—savage and searing and also exquisite—shattered me into a million shards.

And when the pieces were put together again, I found myself standing on a rocky ledge. The wind swept across a vast plain. Hundreds of women massed on the plain, silent and staring. Perhaps thousands. They were tall and short, young and old. Of every color and shape. Maids, mothers and crones. They stood like unearthly sentinels. All eyes fixed on me.

At their head, one woman stood out from the others. She was hunched but not with age. Her shoulders rounded and knees bent as if she were ready to spring at prey. Her naked body was painted in stripes and whorls that defied the eye to study them. Black braids hung around her face, hiding her expression but not her piercing eyes. She circled me. Assessing. Measuring.

"I know you," I said. The memory of her face was hidden behind a gauzy curtain. Her name was on the tip of my—

I was ripped away before I could speak it, whisked back to the pain of my scored body. The hard stone at my back. The shrieks of kelpies dying under bluecap arrows.

Gunora's laughing face above me.

"What have you done?" My voice was barely a croak. My hand went to my chest and came away covered in blood. I felt sick in the well of my magic, disoriented and strangely numb.

"I gave you the gift that keeps on giving, cousin. The gift of Maid, Mother and Crone." Gunora kissed me on the mouth. "And now I am finally free!"

She raised both hands in the air. Arrows whizzed by her, but she didn't care. She was beautiful—neither young, nor old. Not maid, mother or crone. Just Gunora.

She winked at me.

The nuckelavee's fist connected with her jaw. I saw it in slo-mo. Her face shattered. Spittle spewed from her lips. She toppled backward and her skull bounced off stone. The revenant gripped her throat in its jaws and dragged her into the water. The massive equine body crushed her to the bottom of the rocky river. Eventually her feet stopped kicking and the two corpses lay still.

I searched for Mason in the smoke and confusion. He staggered. One hand grabbed the post that he'd been bound too. The light left his eyes and he fell.

35

The fighting tapered off as the remaining kelpies fled into the night. A light rain fell, sizzling and snapping in the embers of the bonfire, but there was no wind to dispel the smog of smoke. Several huts were in flames. Bodies lay everywhere, broken, bloody and burning.

I sat up on the stone that had almost been the altar of my death. I hurt in every joint and muscle. My hair hurt. I probed a bruise on my scalp above one ear. I hadn't even noticed that wound as it happened.

My left foot was still attached to the stake. I leaned down to untie it and panted as I fought down panic. My fingers were raw, and I couldn't budge the knot. In the end, I rose and yanked out the stake with the rope still tied to it.

I took a step and the world spun around me. My knees buckled, but before I fell, my hands caught in a furry ruff. Princess leaned against my leg, supporting me.

"Thank you." I scratched her muzzle. She whined and licked my fingers.

Most of the kelpies had run off—those that weren't lying dead around the camp. Dazed and battered bluecaps were checking on their fallen comrades. Jack's crew helped.

I ignored them all. My thoughts were only for Mason.

He lay crumpled in the dirt, but his back rose and fell with reassuring regularity. With Princess as my crutch, I stumbled over to him and pressed my hand to his shoulder. I shook him. Nothing. I leaned in to whisper in his ear. He smelled of smoke and brimstone. What would he be when he woke? Would the darkness from the demon's blessing have taken over?

"Mason?" I shook him harder. He groaned and rolled.

"Kyra?" He blinked. His eyes weren't yellow or glowing. That was a good sign. How I wished for my keening, so I could taste his magic. But my well was dangerously dry.

"I'm here." The words came out with a sob I hadn't even realized I was holding in. I'd been so afraid. Not of Gunora. Not of Felix. But of losing this man. He'd changed my life and I couldn't go back to being alone.

"I guess you got your aspect of the demon." My tears flowed freely now. Their saltiness burned the cuts on my face. I helped Mason sit. He didn't look much better. Dirt and soot coated his face, not quite hiding the brilliant bruise blooming around one eye.

"Aspect of the demon?" He looked confused. Then memories came back to him and his expression tightened. He turned toward the twice-baked corpse of the nuckelavee lying face-down in the water. "I did that."

"You did. Do you, uh…feel different."

He frowned. A deep line creased his brow.

"I feel empty. Used up."

"It's just this place." I waved a hand at the invisible ward. "The magic dampeners, remember?" I hoped that was true.

"Then how?" He waved a hand vaguely in the direction of Felix. "How did I make that happen?"

"Demons and gods. Their magic can't ever be dampened. Your magic." I poked him for emphasis. He might have some demon in him now, but he was still human. Mostly. Kester had mastered his demon blood and so would Mason. And I'd be right by his side when he did.

I rested my head on his shoulder. He leaned against me like he needed the comfort of another warm body and my arm snaked around him.

"Are you okay?" Mason asked. "That blood yours?"

"Some of it." I clutched the rags of my shirt against my chest.

I didn't know if Gunora's spell had worked. She'd meant to transfer her disease to me. I didn't feel any different, but the memory of those women standing on the hill watching me…Welcoming me? Warning me? They would haunt me for many nights to come.

"But Gunora's dead," I said. "We have nothing to bargain with. Tums and Tad…"

"I won't apologize for killing her. This was never about Tums and Tad." Mason's expression was grim. "She brought you here for that spell. For your blood. She was never going to let the kids go. She was never going to let *you* go."

I nodded. I knew he was right.

"I had to stop her." His voice choked. I looked up and saw tears streaking through the blood and dirt on his face. "I couldn't let her curse you. I couldn't lose you." His hands found mine and he gripped them hard. I fell against him and he wrapped his arms around me in a cocoon of his warmth and strength.

"Did I get her in time?" His voice was raw against my ear. "Did she do it?"

I knew what he was asking. He wanted to know if Gunora had completed her spell, if I would one day spontaneously turn into a crone.

"I don't think so. I think…" I paused and pushed away to look him in the eye. "This is going to sound crazy, but I think Terra intervened." I couldn't stop thinking about that hill with those women standing vigil.

"Terra?" Mason quirked his eyebrow in that way he did when I was totally off the mark.

"Crazy, right? But someone stepped in on my behalf. Gunora's spell didn't work."

"You sure?"

I felt only a flutter of uncertainty before I answered, "Of course."

The shadow of great wings blanketed us. The colossal eagle landed in the clearing. As soon as his feet touched ground, he shifted into the form of a man, fully dressed and unbloodied by the night's violence.

"Jack!" I jumped up and hugged him. He patted my back for a moment, before awkwardly pulling away.

"Thank you," I said.

He nodded once. "We had a deal."

"We did."

If it was possible, Jack looked even older than yesterday. His one eye was shrunken in his skull, and his skin seemed pulled too tightly across his features.

He scowled. "You'll take him with you?"

I scanned the clearing, looking for Raven. He was helping with the cleanup. His sharp teeth grabbed the shirt collar of a dead kelpie and hauled the body toward the smoking pyre. His tiny hooves dug deep into the dirt and his fluffy wings flapped as he tugged. My heart squeezed. He was too little to have such experience on his résumé.

In a year, maybe two, he'd hit puberty. Would this cute, sweet pony turn into that monstrous nuckelavee? Or would his wingspan become as big as a god's? Only time would tell.

I squeezed Mason's hand and he winked at me.

"We'll take him," I said.

Lily came around with water for everyone. I was glad to see she'd made it through the battle. She took one look at my bloody, naked state and hurried away. She came back with a t-shirt. It was stained and too big and probably came off a dead man, but naked, wounded Valkyries can't be choosers.

She hooked a thumb at Felix's corpse. "Did you do that?"

"It was a joint effort," I said.

"Well, good job."

She limped off to help with the other wounded.

I drank from the canteen Lily provided and wandered over to the river. Felix and Gunora's bodies lay half submerged. No one had wanted to claim them for the pyre.

Felix's equine legs were bent at odd angles under the weight of his body. His humanoid torso and head were still partially covered in vines. I didn't remove them, didn't need to see that repulsive fleshless face again.

Gunora's face was half submerged in the river. The current surged past her nose and open eyes, and I kept expecting her to blink the water away. But of course, she wouldn't.

I kneeled in the water beside her and lifted her head to rest on a stone. I brushed her wet hair from her eyes and closed them.

"I'm sorry cousin." She had tried to kill me, or at least to infect me with some mystical virus, but I was still sorry that she'd felt desperate enough to take those steps. If I hadn't burned the bridge to Asgard, she could have gone home long ago and lived out a long life with the Golden Apples.

I rose and splashed back to shore. We should just leave them be, I thought. Let time and water do their work. Let the draikas and the snails have them.

But there was one thing I wouldn't leave behind. My sword. I found it caught against rocks like driftwood. I raised it up and let water slough off it. The blade was dull gray. I felt no spark of life in it. I hoped that was only an effect of the ward and it would come back to me once we left this cursed place. I tore the shirt off a corpse and dried the blade.

Cletus came huffing down the slope from the huts. He was red-faced and puffing, but seemed unharmed by the fight.

He handed me a leather-bound book. "We found this. Thought you might want it."

I recognized the book immediately. I had a similar one tucked away in a box at home. The cover was thick and worn to suppleness. It was embossed with a pair of wings. I flipped it open and ran my fingers over the distinct, rough texture of real paper. It was Gunora's Valkyrie journal. Every novice was given one to record her daily thoughts and goals. Tears burned my eyes, making the perfect flourishes of Gunora's handwriting blur. I closed the book. There would be time to read it later.

I held my hand out to Cletus.

"Thank you for coming to our aid."

He looked at my outstretched hand, then squinted up at me. Finally, he wiped his filthy hand on his even filthier pants and shook mine.

"You did us a favor," he said. "I won't have any more of my people taken by these damned ponies."

I looked around the camp. The kelpies were no doubt regrouping somewhere else on the island. But for now, they'd be rudderless and disorganized.

"Well, if you ever make it back to Montreal, look us up," I said. Who knew, maybe in another fifty-one years, I'd still be around. I liked to take the wait-and-see approach to mortality.

BEFORE THE PRISON guards decided to investigate the turmoil in the kelpie camp, we left for Jack's place. I was anxious to leave the island now. We had only hours left before we were supposed to meet the kidnappers in Hedge. Without Gunora, we had no bargaining power. But like Mason, I thought the ransom note and demands were all a ruse.

Gunora had always taken what ever she wanted. This time she'd wanted my blood and she'd died for it. My only hope now lay with Oscar and the Guardians. They had to find the twins or I would never be able to face Arriz and his family again.

It was a two-hour walk with wounded people and a limping hound, and we arrived after midnight.

Jack offered us the back room in his own house to rest. As soon as he lay down, Mason fell into a deep sleep. Being a demon really took it out of him. I wanted to let him rest until daybreak, but we had to leave now. Apart from the twins, I worried for Cricket. How long could he hold up his camouflage? We needed to be off the island before sunrise. But I could give him a few winks while I cleaned myself up and tended to the cuts on my chest.

The claw marks from Felix weren't deep, but the gods only knew what festered under those nails. Jack had a decent supply of first aid materials (dropped once a month from the Grandill Prison Society), and I cleaned it as best I could.

The wound from Gunora's knife still seeped blood, but I didn't want to take time to stitch it.

Mason woke as I was trying to close the cut with butterfly tape.

"Let me do that." He took the tape and gently secured the edges of the wound. "That looks bad. You should let me stitch it." His fingers were strong and deft, but I still winced under his touch.

"I'll be fine. You can stitch it when we get home."

He traced the line of bandage on my chest. "I'm just glad you're okay."

"I feel like this was all for nothing."

Mason grunted. "Not for nothing. You were worried about Gunora. Admit it. Despite everything, leaving her on the island was eating at you. Now you know. She would have killed you to save herself. And I…" He paused for a long moment. "And if I had to suddenly access my necromantic powers, I'm glad I did it in front of a bunch of convicts. Who will believe them anyway?"

I loved his half-full glass.

He rubbed a hand through his matted hair. I leaned in and kissed his dirty, blood-stained lips. They tasted just like Mason. Then I pulled away and tucked my shirt into my pants.

"We need to get moving. I'll find Jack and see if our little package is ready to go."

I left him to get cleaned up and found Jack in the front room of his house. He was standing by the open front door, holding a knitted blanket with a far off expression.

"You okay?" I asked.

His eyes dropped to the blanket. It was a cross-hatched pattern in an array of colors as if the knitter had used up the ends of yarn balls to make it.

"It's just hard to believe she's really gone."

With everything that had happened in the last few hours, I'd almost forgotten about poor Silvia.

"How's Raven taking it?"

"Better than me. I think he already knew on some level."

He put down the blanket and started tidying the hut, though his motions seemed automatic. I stood awkwardly in the doorway to our room.

"You have something you want to say?" he asked without looking up.

"It's just that you're…a Thunderbird."

"*The* Thunderbird." He cracked a small smile and his one eye seemed to blaze with fire.

By the One-eyed Father! *The* Thunderbird? That was like meeting Odin himself. A deity walking among humans.

"But that would mean you're hundreds, no thousands of years old!"

"Not exactly. It's complicated. This body is as old as it looks. Worn out and ready to rest for good. I'll leave it soon for another. Or maybe not. Maybe I'll take a rest too."

"But Thunderbird!" I could barely wrap my mind around the idea. "You could have left this prison at any time. Why did you stay?"

His gaze strayed to the knitted blanket again, and I knew. He stayed for Silvia. And for Raven.

We stood together in another moment of awkward silence. Then Mason came through the door, holding Oscar's radio in his hand. There was a burst of static over the line and then some indistinct shouts.

"They found the bodies at the kelpie camp," Mason said. "We have to go now while their attention is elsewhere."

I nodded. We needed the cover of darkness to get out of the ward again. And we still had several hours to go before we could rest.

"Have you told Raven? About our deal, I mean."

"Not yet." Jack squinted at me. His face lost that wise eagle look. He was just Jack again. Grubby, ornery Jack.

"I'm not telling him. That wasn't part of the deal." I crossed my arms over my sore chest.

"You won't have to." He went to the door, put two fingers to his mouth and let out a piercing whistle. A few seconds later I heard the distinct clop of tiny hooves on the dry ground. Raven skidded to a stop outside the hut with Princess doing her best to keep up.

"It's time to say goodbye," Jack said.

The pony tossed his head and stamped his feet. Jack, probably used to this display of stubbornness, just waited it out.

The pony shifted to a boy. He held out his hand to me as if to shake it.

"Goodbye. It was very nice to meet you."

I kept my hands wedged in my pockets and glared at Jack.

Jack knelt to be face to face with his son.

"Do you like Princess?" he asked.

"Very much!" Raven said. "She runs as fast as me."

"Would you like to play with her every day?"

Raven's eyes were huge in the dim light. But he wasn't a stupid kid. He knew something wasn't right about his father's tone.

"What do you mean?"

"I mean that Kyra and Mason are going to take you with them. You're going to leave this island and live free like you were meant to."

"But Papa! What about you?"

"I'm tired, son. It's time for me to go back to my kind. But one day I'll return. I'll come find you. I promise."

"No! I won't go! I won't leave you!" Raven flung his arms around his father's neck. It wasn't a hug. It was a desperate attempt to cling to the only life he'd ever known.

Jack put one hand flat on his son's back and said, "Sleep." The air stirred around us like a sudden storm was brewing. Raven's eyes rolled back in his head and he crumpled. Jack caught him.

Mason took the boy in his arms. Raven was a limp rag. Princess snuffled at his trailing hand and whined. Jack smoothed the black mane of hair from Raven's face and touched the white lock.

"He'll be out for a couple of days," he said. "When he wakes, tell him… tell him I love him."

EPILOGUE

The journey home seemed to take forever. Adrenaline kept us going until we found the breach in the ward. Cricket had stayed the course and kept it hidden. I crawled through first, tugging Princess behind me. She panted with pain and exhaustion, but we made it. Mason lifted Raven through and I caught him by the shoulders, dragging him the rest of the way.

Princess danced around Cricket, trying to lick his face.

"Leave off!" I commanded and she sat on her haunches, tail wagging. Cricket was swaying on his feet. His bark-like skin was a sickly gray. I handed him my canteen and he drank deeply.

"We have to run now," I said. "Without your camouflage, they could find that breach any time. Can you fly?"

Cricket shook his head. "Not yet. I run."

We all did.

I gave Mason a break and carried Raven. He was small, but he slowed me down.

At the canal we rested for an anxious minute while Cricket drained my canteen. Faced with the choice of swimming or flying, he chose flight. I watched his wobbly escape over the gap for only a moment before slipping into the icy water.

We had nothing to use as a raft. Raven would be dead weight in the water.

"I'll take him." Mason was swaying with fatigue but he reached for the boy.

"No, you take this." I handed him my pack and the makeshift sheath I'd made for my sword at Jack's place

"I was a lifeguard for a summer. I got this." I took Raven from his arms.

We waded into the water until the canal floor fell away. I had a desperate moment of treading water and trying to keep Raven's head above the surface. Princess paddled around us in circles. Then I flipped onto my back and got a good grip on the boy with my elbow around his collar bone so his head rested on my shoulder. I kicked my feet, thinking of nothing else—not the cold, not the exhaustion, not the imminent arrival of the Grandill guards. Just kick and kick and kick.

And then Mason was pulling Raven from my arms and my feet hit solid ground.

Another ten minutes at a dead run, and we made it back to our boat to find…

Angus.

"Hellfire and roses, it's good to see you two!" The green man hopped out of another boat. His wings fluttered as he landed lightly.

Jacoby jumped out of the boat behind him.

"Kyra-lady!"

Then we were all hugging, laughing and crying. Princess licked every bit of exposed skin she could reach.

"How did you get here?" Mason asked.

"Got home yesterday and found you gone. Oscar went over your plans with me. He said you took that old jalopy of a boat." He pointed to our little rowboat. "I thought you might prefer a faster get-away." He patted the other boat, a sleek, black, metal-bodied craft with a silent alchemical motor attached.

"You didn't sign that out from Perrot island, did you?" Mason frowned.

We didn't want any record of us on or near the water for these past few days.

"Nah." Angus waved a hand. "No worries. I stole it."

I wanted nothing more than to go home and sleep for days, but that wouldn't happen.

I gripped Angus's arm. "What about the boys? Tums and Tad. We've got to get to Hedge."

"Don't fret yourself." Angus patted my hand. "They're home safe, eating ice cream and telling tales about the giant who kidnapped them. Seems like it was quite an adventure."

Something burbled up from my chest, a sound halfway between a sob and a sigh of relief. Only Tums and Tad would think being kidnapped was an adventure.

"Now I don't mean to look a gift horse in the arse, but who's this little fella?" Angus tweaked a lock of Raven's hair.

"This is Raven. He's coming with us," I said.

"I see that. Well, let's be going then."

A burst of shouting from the radio made us pause. Mason put it to his ear. After a moment, he said, "It's okay. They haven't found the breach yet, but they know something's wrong. We go now."

We all piled into the boat and Angus started the engine. I had so many questions for him about where he'd been in the last months, but those could wait.

"Get down," Angus said. "We're heading for open river." We reached the end of the rivulet that let out into the St. Lawrence. We all crowded into the bottom of the boat like a pile of exhausted puppies.

"Hold on to yer lug nuts!" Angus put the motor in gear, and then we were flying.

RAVEN WOKE TWO days later. I'd set him up in the spare bedroom next to ours and checked on him every hour, anxious for him to wake and anxious about what would happen when he did. Princess spent most of her time napping at the foot of Raven's bed. I left her there to recuperate. She needed it.

I was having coffee in the breakfast nook, enjoying the view of the fall colors through the window. The sun was brilliant and brassy in that way of September suns. The goblits were playing soccer in the yard. Their shouts and squeals were like music to my heart.

The twins seemed no worse for wear and had regaled me with stories about the giant who took them on a holiday. Apparently, he brought them to the old abandoned amusement park on Saint Helen's Island. They'd no idea they were in danger. I left that lesson for their father to teach.

Arriz wouldn't talk to me or even look at me. That was okay. I had broad shoulders and could accept the blame. It was well deserved. I just hoped that one day, even if he couldn't forgive me, he would at least bear to be in the same room with me.

He and Dekar were building a new cabin for Cricket. The hidebehind didn't need much since he would hibernate for the winter.

Our property was turning into a little village. Mason was right. All we needed was a sign saying "Kyra's Critter Sanctuary."

Thoughts of Mason made my hand stray to the wounds on my chest that were slowly healing and then lower, to my stomach. As soon as we'd left the dampening field of Grandill's ward, I'd keened the tiny life growing inside me. I would tell Mason today. It wouldn't be easy.

Mason had lived several lives before he met me. He'd outlived three wives and a dozen children. He'd sworn he would never do that again. But things were different now—Mason was different. He was no longer immortal. He could grow old with a grandchild on each knee. That didn't mean he'd welcome the news. He had a strand of demon magic inside him now. We didn't yet understand the full repercussions of that, but it would change everything, .

I rubbed my belly, wondering what kind of surprises this tiny new soul would bring us.

Raven startled me as he sat down at the table. Princess followed behind him and flopped on the floor.

"Where am I?" Raven's voice was raw. I rose and poured him a glass of juice before answering.

"Your in my home. Mason's home too. In Dorion Park just outside Montreal."

He drank down the juice, leaving a wet line on his upper lip. He wore only shorts and his thin body looked fragile. He might almost be a teenager, but he looked younger than the twins. He hugged his arms over his bare chest.

"I want to go home." He looked at me with big, trusting eyes.

"I know. But we'll do our best to make this your home now." I reached over and squeezed his shoulder.

"It's not! You're not my mother, and this isn't my home!" He shrugged me off and ran for the patio doors. Once outside, he shifted, going from gangly boy to galloping pony in an instant. He took off past the startled goblins and into the forest.

"Go after him," I said to Princess. She was already on her feet, wet nose pressed against the window. "Make sure he's safe."

Princess's claws clattered in the patio stones as she ran after him.

I sighed and sipped my tepid coffee. If he didn't come back soon, I'd send the goblits to find him. It would take time and patience, but Raven would be all right.

Mason appeared, freshly showered and dressed in a suit and tie. Oscar already had his week booked with meetings and campaign rallies.

"Where's Raven?" he asked.

I nodded toward the window. "Out there with Princess. He's pretty upset. I'm giving him time to vent."

"He'll come around. I'm sorry I have to leave you to deal with him today." He poured himself a cup of coffee. "I'll try to be home early."

I rose and put my arms around his neck. "Before you go, I thought we could do a little magic training." I laid my cheek against his chest and listened to the slow tolling of his heart.

He kissed the top of my head. "Right now?"

"Humor me." I lifted my gaze and he kissed my lips.

"Always."

I took his hand and placed it flat on my belly.

"Let down your shields, just a bit."

Errol's lessons were ongoing, but this was advanced. Shielding and unshielding was easy. Letting them down just a bit to sense someone's magic signature was complicated.

He scrunched his brows, confused by my request. I poked him.

"Just do it."

I had my own shields wide open, and I keened his tentative probe.

His eyes widened. So did his grin.

"Is that what I think it is?"

I nodded.

He let out a whoop, picked me up and carried me to the couch.

With my arms still around his neck, I looked into his shining eyes.

"You're not upset?"

"Of course not. Babies are the only true miracles in this world."

My hand went to my stomach. "But this little miracle—"

"This miracle will be ours."

I laughed. "And to think I promised you no more adventures."

He grabbed my hand and kissed my fingers. "You don't think I actually believed that, do you?"

Dear Reader,

I hope you've been enjoying Kyra's journey so far. It seems like Kyra and Mason are all snug in their new home. I didn't want to leave you on a cliff-hanger, but I also didn't want you to think that there are no more adventures to come. So please enjoy the sneak peek at Book 5 of the Valkyrie Bestiary Series (as yet, untitled) below.

And you probably know that authors love reviews, but do you know why? Reviews are important because they help other readers know what to expect from the book, they let me know how my books are received by readers, and they help booksellers decide which books to show to new readers.

If you enjoyed this book I would be grateful for your honest review. It can be as short as you like. Even a few positive words will go a long way. And I'll try to make it as painless as possible. Use the links below to find the review site of your choice.

kimmcdougall.com/review-kelpies-dont-fly

WANT TO FIND OUT MORE ABOUT KYRA'S WORLD?

Learn more about the Valkyrie Bestiary series at KimMcDougall.com including deleted scenes and more series fun.

Or join Kim McDougall's reader group to get the latest release updates and a free eBook at KimMcDougall.com.

Poke around at Kyra's blog at ValkyrieBestiary.com.

Other places you can follow Kim McDougall: Amazon, BookBub, Goodreads, Facebook, Twitter, or Instagram.

Before Times

3 Valkyrie Prequels

The Last Door to Underhill: In the last hours of the Flood Wars, a fae princess makes the ultimate sacrifice to save the human world.

The Girl Who Cried Banshee: Kyra Greene is a pest controller, not an exterminator. She has to be clear about that when the pests can be anything from pixies to dragons. But when her fledgling business teeters on the brink of bankruptcy, Kyra takes on a job that blurs those lines.

Three Half Goats Gruff: Kyra Greene, pest controller of fantastic beasts, takes on a rock troll and meets the man who will haunt her dreams for the next three-hundred and twenty-one nights. Come sing around the campfire with satyrs and discover how Kyra found one little lost cephalopod.

Before Times tells the tales of Kyra Green, pest-controller of extraordinary beasts and Leighna Icewolf, Queen of the Fae—two warriors learning to navigate new roads in a world where magic is the only rule of law. Each story takes place 1 to 50 years before the events of Dragons Don't Eat Meat, Book 1 of the Valkyrie Bestiary Series.

With over 2000 five-star reviews, readers say Valkyrie Bestiary is "Very funny," "A sweeping adventure," "A slow burn romance." And more than one has said, "I want to be a supernatural pest controller too!"

About the Author

If Kim McDougall could have one magical superpower, it would be to talk to animals. Or maybe to shift into animal form. Definitely, fantastical critters and magic often feature in her stories. So until she can change into a griffin and fly away, she writes dark paranormal action and romance tales, from her home in Central Ontario. Visit Kim online at www.KimMcDougall.com.